# It's Always Been You

## Been You

## F. Y. Dawn

Dawn2Dawn Publishing

10174 Austin Dr #2917

Spring Valley, Ca 91977

ISBN-13: 978-1-947311-90-9 (sc)

Published by Dawn2Dawn Publishing 03/2019

This book is dedicated to my husband and my sons. Thank you for all the love, laughs, and memories. You are my greatest blessings.

# Prologue

June 2008

"What up, Lamont?" Jason stepped out onto the porch and shut the door behind him. His mom couldn't stand Lamont. Even though he was practically a grown man and heading off to college in a few weeks, he didn't want to hear his mother's mouth about Lamont being a bad influence.

He wrapped Lamont in a bear hug. It had been too long since they'd last seen each other. His six-foot-five stature towered over Lamont. At one time, Jason could've easily lifted him off the ground, but Lamont had bulked up while he was away.

"I can't call it. What up with you, fool? Rumor has it, you got some big-time basketball scholarship and are heading off to college. I told everyone they had to be lying, because my boy would've told me that."

"Sorry, man. I just didn't want to brag, but it's true." He air-dribbled around Lamont and faked a jump shot. "Basketball kept me entertained while you were locked up."

"Yeah, well it's my first night back. We got a lot of time to make up and little time to do it. Get your shoes on and let's hit the streets."

Jason hesitated. Getting caught up with Lamont again could lead to trouble. That was the last thing he needed. He decided, however, a couple of hours couldn't hurt. In a few days, they'd probably never see each other again. Jason ignored his wariness and grabbed his shoes.

"Jay, pull up at the gas station over here. We about to head over to Niecey's house, and I need to get a few things to make sure we have a good time."

Jason chuckled. He knew what type of girl Niecey was and assumed Lamont was going to buy condoms. He didn't hesitate to pull into the gas station. If the night went as planned, he would need a few for himself, as well.

1

*He threw the car in park and took off his seatbelt to get out, but Lamont stopped him. "I got this. I told you tonight's on me. Keep the car running; we'll be out in a minute." He let Dane out of the back seat and the two of them headed into the store.*

*Lamont and Dane reached on top of their head for what looked like plain old beanies. They rolled ski masks down, pulled guns out of their pockets, and walked into the store, their guns leading the way. Jason was so caught up in the night's planned festivities, he hadn't noticed a thing.*

*"Move before I tell you and you'll catch this bullet." Dane raised the gun to the cashier and smiled at the fear that lit his eyes. The cashier glanced down, and Dane already knew what he was planning. "Reach for the gun and I'll light you up before you get your hands on it."*

*Lamont wanted to slap Dane across the back of the head for that corny line he always used. If the cops ever asked the right questions, they'd instantly link him to several other robberies from those words alone. He'd have to talk with his boy. That type of dumb stuff—leaving a trail that led directly back to you—had landed him in a juvenile detention center for two years. Organized crime needed organization, or someone would wind up dead or in jail. Lamont operated by three simple rules. Rule number one: stick to the plan. Lamont stuck to the plan and headed around to the refrigerators. Dane handled the register. Lamont always handled merchandise and any unwanted customers.*

*Rule number two: get what you came for and get out. Don't get greedy. Two cases of beer and a box of condoms was all they needed. Items in hand, Lamont returned to the front, where Dane was collecting the money. Dane looked over to check on him. In a split second, the cashier lost his mind and went for his gun. It was drawn and pointing at Dane before he turned around. Rule number three: don't get distracted.*

*Without thinking, Lamont raised his own gun and pulled the trigger. His bullet hit the cashier in the side of the head. Time seemed to slow as blood splattered everywhere and he slumped to the floor.*

*One mistake—deviation from the rules—changes everything.*

*"What did you do? What did you do?" Dane screamed repeatedly. He chanced a look over the counter and hysteria started to set*

in. *"You changed the plan. No one gets hurt; do you remember that? I'm not down with this."* Panic-stricken Dane paced in circles.

Lamont stood there listening to Dane rant, gun still pointing toward the path its bullet had traveled. Taking a life will do one of two things to a man. It will crumble his heart and make him regret everything that led up to that moment, or his heart will cease to exist. Lamont was the latter. His heart was replaced with a stone coated with malice void of all emotion and remorse. A smirk spread across his face as he slowly turned his gun on Dane. *"Get the money and let's go."*

Dane was scared out of his mind and on the verge of tears. With trembling hands, he reached across the counter and into the register. Something had taken over Lamont. Dane noticed the change in his voice, his walk was different, and the eyes that glared back at him through the ski mask told Dane that now was not the time to challenge Lamont.

A friend from high school had pulled up to get gas. Jason stepped out of the car to talk when gunfire suddenly blared through the quiet night. They hit the ground and both crawled back to their respective cars. Jason slipped in behind the wheel, not the easiest of tasks when trying to remain low. He white-knuckled the steering wheel, debating whether he was going to leave his friends. Seconds later, Lamont came rushing out of the store wearing a ski mask. He practically pushed Dane toward the car, face covered in the same. *"Nigga, why in the hell is the car off? Didn't I tell you to keep it running?"*

Jason fumbled with the key in the ignition, stammering to formulate a thought. *"What are you doing?"*

*"Just shut up and drive."*

Lamont's cold voice made the hair on Jason's neck stand up. He looked at Dane in the back seat and could see the fear in his eyes. He didn't know what went down in that store, but it definitely had Dane bugging out. *"What—"*

Before he could finish his sentence, Lamont rested the gun on his thigh, the barrel pointing directly at Jason. He recognized the action for the threat it was and Lamont's one-word command, *"Drive,"* was followed without hesitation.

3

# 1

*Present day*

    *Sitting in church on a Friday night... Wow, who would've thought?* Candice should've been at Illusions, turning down advances and knocking back free drinks. She almost laughed out loud when she realized the only drink she'd get would be a little sip of communion wine. *My, how the tables have turned.*

    Candice kneeled next to her good friend and new first lady of Zion Pentecostal Church, April Hawkins. It was Candice's first time serving as her pal's adjutant. April's declaration that she didn't trust anyone else had coerced Candice into the position without actually knowing what the job entailed. If she'd known she had to be in the spotlight with April, she would've declined.

    "Hallelujah," April mumbled a little too loud. Candice side-eyed her.

    Was this really her life? Yes, Candice wanted a change, but kneeling in front of an uncomfortable wooden pew while the entire church stood at attention, waiting for April and her husband—the pastor, for crying out loud—to take a seat. Hell, her cell was still blowing up with invitations for the night. There were at least a dozen other places she could be. Yet, there she was at the church's anniversary service on a Friday night. Candice closed her eyes to focus on how much she needed the Lord, hoping that thoughts of Him would drown out the body-beckoning, club-pounding bass that was on repeat in her mind. She could hear it so loud and clear, it nearly made her twerk right in the church pew.

    Candice squeezed her eyes shut a little tighter. Not having the words to speak, she listened to April pray. Thoughts of drinks, bass, and booty shaking disappeared. She might not have been familiar with how to live saved, but she wasn't dumb enough to disrespect the presence of God.

    "Amen," April proclaimed and quickly stood up. In sync as they always seemed to be, Pastor Hawkins was standing as well.

    Candice stood and tried to copy what she saw other people doing. They clapped, she clapped. They raised their hands, she did the same—

that is until she felt foolish and dropped them down. She stood there feeling and looking awkward until the choir started singing. *Yes. Now this I can get with this*, she thought.

For a few brief minutes, the sanctuary was lit and Candice decided she might possibly survive the transition to Christian life after all. The musicians were on fire. The bass was calling her name. She had to remember where she was before she embarrassed herself in church.

"We made it! With all the chaos, we made it. Church members leaving, loved ones going home with the Lord, welcoming a new first lady…" Pastor Hawkins bowed in April's direction.

Candice couldn't help the sappy "Aww," that slipped out of her mouth.

"…And everything the enemy tried to take you through. God brought us through it all and has blessed us with another year of ministry under our belt."

Lillian, the pastor's mother, brought April her giggling little girl, and Candice hated the sting of jealousy plaguing her lately. Partying was fun, but she couldn't help but wonder if what her friend had found was better.

"Go tell three people that we made it." Pastor Hawkins was saying, but Candice didn't move. She watched April snuggle her baby to her chest and walk to the podium to kiss her husband. April had survived what some would consider hell. She deserved that happiness. Candice sighed away her jealous thoughts and the rest of the service came roaring back into focus.

Everyone marched around hugging and singing *We Made It*. Candice made her way to Mother Sable, whose surly demeanor had weaseled its way into Candice's heart. Mother had quickly become her favorite member of the church, probably because she reminded Candice of her own mother.

"Don't come around here hugging me, little girl. It's too hot for all that touching."

Candice's smile broadened across her face and she hugged Mother anyway. No matter how much Mother Sable complained about her being so touchy feely, Candice knew she needed and loved the

5

affection. She kissed the mother's cheek, turned to walk back to her seat, and walked into the most gorgeous wall of muscle she'd ever seen.

"Excuse me." She tried to side step him, but his hand to her elbow stopped her.

"My bad. I should've given you more space." He pulled a slip of paper out his pocket and passed it to her. "But I wanted to make sure I had your attention. That's my number. Give me a call." He flashed his pearly whites and backed away from her.

A small smile tipped the corners of her lips as she went back to her seat. She unfolded the paper; however, before she could read it, April had snatched it out of her hand.

"What are you doing?" Candice reached for the paper, but April moved it out of reach.

"These brothers ought to be ashamed, setting up booty calls in church."

"Booty call. What?" Candice snatched the piece of paper back and put it in her purse. The celebration was starting to settle, so she leaned toward April and mumbled, "Do you really think that's the only reason a man is interested in me?"

April gasped and stepped back, trying to gauge whether Candice was serious or not. "Candy, you know…" before she could get another word out, Candice was marching down the aisle and out of the sanctuary.

She paced around the foyer waiting for April to come after her. The double doors creaked open and she twisted around, expecting to see April, but instead it was the man who'd given her his number. He strolled toward her, the fingertips of one hand tucked in his front pocket and the other casually swaying at his side.

Candice scanned the length of him and nearly purred in appreciation. She smiled with a bat of her long lashes, her irritation with April's comment fueling her flirtation. She met him halfway, and before he could open his mouth, she extended an invitation. "You want to go grab a coffee? There is a twenty-four-hour diner up the street."

"I'll follow you." One corner of his mouth lifted.

The cocky grin should've been a turnoff, but it fell on the cusp of confidence and arrogance. She liked it…liked it very much.

He held the door for her to exit. Candice smiled sweetly and ignored the little voice telling her to behave.

He parked next to her at the diner and rushed over to open her car door. He did the same with the door to the restaurant and even helped her into her chair at the table.

*So far, so good.* She checked her phone that had buzzed on the drive over and shook her head.

*I saw you leave with him. Be careful, Candy. Call me when you get home.*

Candice shook her head at how things had changed and dropped the phone back into her purse. That was the line she'd spoken to April on too many occasions. Who would've ever thought they'd switch roles and April would now be the more cautious one?

"So," Candice gave her attention to the gorgeous man sitting across from her, "I'm Candice." She extended a handshake, and he gently grasped her hand smoothing his thumb along her palm.

"I know who you are. I'm Ben."

His roughened hand against her smooth palm brought up images of those palms roaming elsewhere. *STOP IT!*

She halted those thoughts before they got out of hand. She'd just met the man, and although that had never stopped her before, she was trying to turn over a new leaf. She grudgingly pulled her hand back and grabbed the menu. She scanned it, trying to silence her old self. If she was ever going to find what April had, she'd have to get herself together.

She ordered coffee with a slice of apple pie and waited patiently while Ben rattled off his three-course request to the waitress.

"How long have you been a member at Zion?"

"I'm not actually a member yet. I'm military, been here about three months. I'm trying to make sure Zion is the right fit."

Candice nodded her head. Most of her family was so sure in their salvation, but she was in the same boat as Ben, even more so. The word, the praise, the pastor, everything was on point, but was this life really for her?

"You caught my eye the first Sunday. Each Sunday since, I've been more and more impressed."

"Really?" She smiled, leaning closer to the table.

7

"Absolutely." There went that cocky grin again. Candice nearly swooned. "First it was them curves, and then that hair. Then the way you move and, now that I'm sitting here talking to you, your voice got nigga thinking about getting the check before the meal even gets here."

"Oh, so you think you can just finesse your way into my panties?"

"Not at all, but you strike me as a woman who knows what she wants and doesn't waste time getting it."

"Is that so?" She leaned back, taking the steaming cup of coffee the waitress had inconspicuously placed in front of her with her.

"It is."

*Cocky bastard.* With one brow raised, she considered him over the brim of her coffee cup. Yes, he was cocky, but God help her, she was intrigued. She guzzled a slurp of coffee, careful to not burn her tongue, and then dove into her pie. She was a junk-food junkie to the core. She could have the most hellish of days, and some sweet, rich, moist, flaky goodness would make it a little bit better.

Conversation was sparse, which was fine with Candice. Between sips of her coffee, she watched him and was impressed. Somebody had taught the brother some table manners. She couldn't stand men who ate like pigs. Ben popped the last bite into his mouth, dabbed his lips with the napkin, and laid it across the table

"So, are we splitting this down the middle, going Dutch, or what?" He slid the check across the table.

Candice laughed out loud until she saw the look on his face. *Oh Lord, you have got to be kidding me. Broke or cheap, which one is it?* Candice let her face say it all.

"What? You did ask me out. Isn't that how this whole dating thing works with the new-age independent woman?"

"You are absolutely right. This one," *the last one!* "Is on me." She held up her credit card, letting her eyes bore through him as she waited for the waitress to slide it from her fingers. She took a deep breath and shut her eyes for a moment. It was all she could do to keep them from rolling.

*All that lusciousness wasted on a cheap bastard... At least the pie was good.*

8

She signed the check and hopped to her feet, not bothering to wait for Ben to assist her. He was on her heels as she high stepped to the car.

"So, can I get your number?"

Candice paused, foot already cresting the threshold of her car. She took a moment to scan the length of him and came up with the same conclusion. *What a waste…*

"That remains to be seen." She plopped down in her seat and gently shut the door.

# 2

Jason stepped outside the prison gates and listened to the loud clank of the door locking behind him. If he never heard that sound again, it would be too soon. He lifted his hands toward the sky, allowing his lungs to be filled with the cool morning air. Outside air was the best thing he'd smelled in a long time—crisp, clean, and free from the stench of despair and depravity. The same sun that lit up the yard every day shined a little brighter. He lifted his face to enjoy the rays. Free sun, free air; he was finally free.

Exactly 3,650 days of his life had been taken from him, and not a day went by where he hadn't thought of that night and the so-called friend who had landed him behind bars.

"Hey, Mom." Jason smiled from ear to ear as he squeezed his mother.

Yvonne held her son tight, trying to make up for all the days she'd missed. Each visit, the misery in his voice beckoned her to embrace him, but the watchful eye of the guards forbade it.

Jason felt the tremble of her sobs and all he could do was admonish her gently, "Don't cry, Ma. It's over now."

The ride home was quiet. Jason ignored the tears still trickling down his mother's cheeks and stared out the window. The world had vastly changed. Billboards stood erect, advertising products he'd never heard of. His eyes raced to read them all, mentally noting the ones he'd have to try. He leaned out the window to get a better look and a gust of wind blew in and took his breath away. He chuckled, remembering all the times that very thing happened when he was a child. He constantly got in trouble for hanging out of the window, but would still do it just for that feeling.

Relaxing back in his seat, he allowed the breeze to caress his face. The world was a strong contrast to prison. It was so full of color, life, and hope, whereas prison was dark and dreary, and the only ray of hope came from someone being released. If it wasn't for the church's prison ministry, Jason might have lost his mind. The group of brothers that had visited every week helped him keep a positive outlook. On the days where he couldn't dredge up any positivity, they accepted his collect calls. They even took the time to write him. He was never big on writing letters. In high school, he'd get them all the time from his infatuated classmates, but never wrote back. While incarcerated, letters meant the world to him, and he made sure to reply to every last one.

The last two months, a woman had taken to writing him. Her handwriting perfectly flowed across each page. Each curl of a letter was an artistic creation. It piqued his curiosity to know what woman would take the time and put so much care into writing him. She began the first letter and everyone thereafter as if they were old friends.

*I'm embarrassed to admit it, but I fell down the stairs today LOL. I was heading out for work. Looking fly, like I always do, heels clacking, curves swaying, and I missed a step. Boom…boom…boom…boom, down four steps and right onto my butt. I wanted to jump up and make sure no one saw me, but I was in too much pain to move. I'd hate to see what my legs would've looked like if I'd been wearing a skirt. I was still sitting there when my neighbor came out, and she didn't even offer to help me up.*

*But enough about my mishaps, I'm sure you don't want to hear it. How are you? Do you need anything? I don't know the procedure for sending you things. Or should I just put money on your books? Let me know.*

*Chantel*

He wasn't sure how to respond to such a letter from someone he didn't know and had first thought she'd written the wrong person. It took him almost two days to reply. He figured what harm could come of it. Either she would realize she had written the wrong person and he'd never hear from her again or he would make a new friend.

*I'm touched that you'd want to spend your hard-earned money on me, but I have everything I need. Your conversation and friendship are nice though. Never think that I don't want to hear what's going on in your life. You actually made me laugh out loud… Thanks!*

*How are you feeling? You should go to the doctor and have your butt checked out.*

*As to how I'm doing, I'm good, considering where I am. I have a couple months left. I'm trying to stay positive and focus on the life I want to live when I get out. With people like you on my side, I think I'll be all right.*

Hearing from Chantel became a little piece of heaven inside Jason's hell. The first time she referred to him as *sweetie,* the word ran warm across his skin and he had to force himself not to read too much into it. As his release date approached, he found himself obsessing over whether she'd want to see him intimately or just continue their friendship. Maybe she wouldn't want to see him at all. Maybe she was just one of those jail groupies Paul was telling him about. In his last letter, he gave her his mom's address. He'd just wait and see what she did with it.

Things in his old neighborhood hadn't changed much. There were overgrown lawns, stray dogs roaming the streets, a crowd of thugs in front of the corner liquor store, and dilapidated houses that no one cared enough to fix. Jason's mom pulled into the driveway, and when they saw who was sitting on the front porch, Yvonne grabbed her son by the shoulders. She looked him straight in the eyes. "I don't know why he is here or how he knew you were getting out. From what I hear, he is not a person you want to be involved with again."

Nodding in agreement, Jason stepped out of the car and made his way toward Lamont. A scowl spread across his face as he watched Lamont stand with hands raised and a smile on his face. Before Jason could protest, those arms were slung around him in celebratory hug. With all the strength he had, Jason pushed Lamont off of him. Jason wasn't the same scrawny eighteen-year-old little boy everyone remembered. His shoulders had broadened and every muscle, from shoulder to abs, was rock solid. He left a boy, but had returned as a man who'd learned how to defend himself in prison. The power in his arms sent Lamont stumbling backwards onto the grass.

Standing over Lamont as he lay on the ground, Jason clenched his jaw to bite back the bark in his words. "I don't know what made you think things were good between us. I haven't seen or heard from you since the last day of my trial. I did ten years in jail for something you did. You threatened to kill me and my mother if I told the truth. We'll never be cool again."

"I'm gonna let you putting your hands on me slide since you served that time for me." Lamont stood, chuckling so coldly the hairs on Yvonne's neck rose. He stepped into Jason's face, breath gusting into his nostrils and nearly snarled. "But if you ever put your hands on me again, I'll personally chop them off and feed them to my dog. You might want to think twice about what side you want to be on. A lot has changed in ten years. I run these streets now. My bad side is not a place you want to be."

Yvonne and Jason watched in silence as Lamont walked to his car and drove off. Jason didn't back down, flinch, or show any sign of fear. Prison had taught him that standing your ground deterred some from harassing you, but if you let on you were afraid, they would make your life hell. A man could go crazy when locked up like an animal. A few had tried to violate his manhood, but Jason fought back. Although he was smaller than most, he did what was necessary to let them know he wasn't an easy prey. Eventually, they got tired of fighting him for something some men were giving away freely and left him alone. Knowing that it was just a matter of time before they tried again, Jason started working out and lifting weights pretty hard. Within a few months, he had the muscle tone to match his height, which made everyone think twice before stepping to him.

"Just let it go. He is not worth your time or effort." Yvonne grabbed Jason by the arm and pulled him into the house.

"Surprise!"

Jason stumbled back from the shock, but was even more surprised when he looked around at all the people who had come to celebrate his release. Younger cousins who once looked up to him were just about grown. Aunts and uncles looked a lot older than they used to. There was his high school basketball coach who stood by his side throughout his entire trial, and, last, but certainly not least, a few of the men that had come to visit him the past few months from the church's prison ministry.

Making his way around the room, Jason greeted everyone, reacquainting himself with the relatives and neighborhood friends who stopped by. Not once was he concerned about those who hadn't visited him in jail. The excitement of being out and home was all he could bear.

He was being nice and trying to speak to everyone, but his stomach was crying out for some home cooking. The smell of barbeque had a hold on his nose and wouldn't let go. He made his way to the kitchen, returning with two plates piled high. Ribs, chicken, homemade mac-n-cheese, potato salad, baked beans, and momma's homemade potato rolls. He lost all good sense and ate until he couldn't take another bite. Within minutes, he was leaning over the kitchen sink, praying for his stomach to settle. The smart thing would've been to ease his way into eating soul food again, but the aroma had gotten the best of him. It felt like everything was going to come back up.

"Excuse me," Candice quietly crept into the kitchen. "I was watching you and thought you might need these." She placed two antacid tablets on the counter.

Jason chuckled, but willingly popped the tablets in his mouth. The chalky taste was disgusting, but the instant relief he felt was well worth it. "Thanks."

"Not a problem. Are you feeling better?" Candice tried not to stare, but the man was gorgeous. She wanted to run her fingers down his arms and across his chest to feel every curve of muscle, but that was the last thing he needed.

"Much better, but I do have to be honest about something." Jason licked his lips and smiled. The innocent gesture quickened Candice's pulse. "If you haven't noticed, I've been avoiding you. I look at everyone else here and know exactly who they are. I am embarrassed to say that I don't remember you." Jason cringed as he waited for her response and was surprised when she returned a soft smile and caressed his arm.

His eyes followed her hand and Candice quickly snatched it away, berating herself for even touching him. Nervously, she cleared her throat, "We've never met. Tim and Paul are my brothers. After visiting you, they talked about you so much. I was moved by your story. It takes a strong man to go through what you did and come out standing."

"It's only by the grace of God." He looked up toward the ceiling, mind roaming over everything the grace of God had spared him from.

"So, how does it feel to be free?"

"I don't know." He shrugged his shoulders and stared off into space. "I know this may sound strange, but I have mixed emotions about being out. Is that crazy or what? I am excited to be free, but everything has changed, and all I can think of is how much I've missed. Lamont was

14

here when I pulled up and it seemed like he just expected us to pick up where we left off."

"Who's Lamont?"

"Well..." Jason smoothed his hand across his tightly corn rolled hair. His first step in moving on with life was going to be forgetting about Lamont and the betrayal. If he was going to do that he couldn't keep spilling his guts every time someone asked. "Let's just say he is an old friend who I would gladly replace with a new one."

Candice eyed his extended hand and couldn't help the excitement that came over her. A new friend was always nice, especially one as fine as him. She took his extended hand between hers, opting to squelch the speech she'd prepared to give him.

"Well, it was nice meeting you..."

"You leaving?"

Candice smiled at the disappointment she heard in his voice. "I think I've intruded long enough. I'll let you get back to your loved ones." She stepped away, ignoring the inner-voice telling her she was stupid for departing from that gorgeous work of art. She chanced a look back, hoping he was checking her out. He wasn't. She let disappointment carry her out the door.

# 3

Trying not to let her irritation show, Candice searched through the small vase of faux flowers to see which one was actually a pen. Why they chose to play hide-and-seek with the pens, she didn't know. She loved the facility, so she didn't complain about its one minor flaw. She signed her name on the clipboard and glanced around the hotel-like lobby with its concierge desk, uniformed clerks, and carpeted floors. The potted plants, high-end furniture, and her personal favorite, Java Hut, further diminished the sterile medical facility vibe of most rehab centers.

"Hey, Suzy. How's it going?" Candice placed the pen down, expecting the same friendly banter they'd developed over the years. The deer-in-headlights look she received immediately sent her into defense mode.

"I'm good... Do you have a moment?" Suzy came from behind the counter, motioning for Candice to follow her.

"Sure..." Candice was hesitant to follow, but what other choice did she have? Her mother had been residing at the Senior Recovery Center for almost two years. They were the absolute best in the city and offered programs she wished her own job would implement.

She was led into the director's office and her heart sank as her mind ran wild with worry. Her mother had to be okay. They would've called if she wasn't. She let that run over in her mind, but it did nothing to ease her concern. Her sweaty palms clutched the strap of her purse as she sank into the plush chair in front of the facility director's desk.

"Ms. Matthews, it's nice to see you again."

Candice was so caught up fearing what was going on, she didn't hear the director approach. She offered a polite smile, waiting for her to get situated behind her desk before asking, "Lidia, what's going on?"

"Hey," she rushed to clarify. "Your mother is fine. We haven't had any more setbacks."

Candice exhaled. Diabetic complications after a stroke had turned what should've been a six-month stint into two years and counting.

16

"It's been a long stressful journey. You've been by your mother's side every step of the way. You've made a lot of sacrifices. I'm sure your mom sees how hard this has been on you, which is the only explanation for this."

Candice didn't mean to be rude, but her already rankled nerves had her snatching the paper Lidia offered. Her eyes widened as she read, she took a deep breath and blew out the steam that was percolating. She didn't need to read any further. Her mother had filed a request to have her blocked as a visitor.

"There has to be a misunderstanding. I'll talk to her." She hopped to her feet and Lidia was right with her.

"Candice, you know once this form is turned in, we can't let you see her."

"This is absolutely ridiculous. I make sure all the bills are paid here. She just can't block me."

"Candice, you're a social worker. You know that paying the bills doesn't matter. It's a patient's right." Lidia stepped around her desk and passed Candice a sealed envelope. "I asked her to write you a note to explain. Give her some time. I'm sure this is her way of trying to help you."

Candice clamped her mouth shut, trying to remember Lidia was just doing her job. She'd been in similar situations, advocating for the patient against what the family wanted. She politely took the note and marched off without another word.

Once in her car, she tore through the envelope so fast she nearly ripped the note in half. Her mother, being a woman of few words, had kept the note short and to the point.

*I want grandbabies. Stop spending so much time down here and go make me some.*

Candice couldn't help the chuckle that bubbled out. That was her mother, taking charge of a situation and determining her own outcome. She tossed the note in the passenger seat and dropped her head on the steering wheel. "Okay, Mom. You want grandbabies, then grandbabies are coming up."

Her mom didn't know how much she wanted that, too.

"Step one, find a man." Sadly, there weren't many prospects she'd actually consider procreating with. She needed to stop being picky. Her mind flashed to Ben. He was good looking and seemed pretty cool until the whole check fiasco. Maybe he deserved another shot. Without giving herself a chance to change her mind, she sent him a text.

*This is Candice. We should get together again.*

Regret was instant. She read and reread the text, hoping she didn't come off as desperate and that he didn't read more into it than what she intended. She rolled her eyes at the lengths she'd go through to please her mother.

Her phone buzzed and she closed her eyes, inhaling and exhaling a deep breath before reading the incoming text.

*Nice surprise... Seeing your beautiful face would be the perfect ending to this week. Meet me at Mandy's in the valley at seven.*

Oh God. She hadn't intended to meet up with him right away. She couldn't think of a substantial reason why she should say no. It was Friday. She didn't have plans and the whole point of texting him was to give him another shot.

*See you there.*

She tossed her phone into her purse and pulled away from the curb. She knew Mandy's well and was surprised someone she met at church wanted to meet there. She'd partied there many times. Although it was a nice respectable establishment, it was also a meat market. What man in his right mind invites a date to a place like that? One thing for sure, she was not going to sit around and watch his wandering eyes all night.

She walked through her front door and blasted Queen Bey through her Bluetooth speakers. She needed mood music to get her mind right for the evening. She bounced around to Bey's, *Single Ladies*, doing her best to keep up with the queen's dance moves while making a light snack. She didn't want to eat too much, because she planned on testing Ben's frugality again with the most expensive item on the menu, since he had definitely asked her out.

Candice showered and primped for over two hours, all the while dancing and singing herself into a good mood. She was ready for a fun time. She pulled into the parking lot just after seven. She stepped out of

18

the car and the lone royal blue patent leather, peep-toe pump exiting the vehicle and crushing the asphalt beneath garnered male and female interest from the patrons loitering out front. When her full frame stood erect next to her car, she smiled at the whistles of appreciation.

Her strut was sublime and in need of its own theme music, with a pounding bass that accentuated the lift and sway of her backside. She ignored all summoning looks until a chocolate Adonis exited as she approached the door. His eyes ate up the length of her and she wanted to scream when she remembered she was meeting someone there. He reached for her and "I'm meeting someone," were the hardest words she ever had to speak.

She walked through the front door, eyes searching through the dim light. Did she really know Ben's face well enough to spot him in the crowd? If she couldn't find him, she was going to be pissed she had let a night of fun slip through her fingers.

Gracefully, she moved about the room, dodging around tables and huddles of people seemingly enjoying the night. Men eyed her with hunger, even licking their lips like she was a meal worthy of savoring. She didn't feel the same thrill of being chased that she did the last time she was there. The longer it took to find Ben, the more she wondered how she ever enjoyed this type of place. She kept moving, trying her best not to make eye contact. She started to feel uncomfortable and her confidence slipped a bit.

Someone grabbed her hand and she spun around set and ready to tear into to them. "Keep your hands—" She caught the words on the tip of her tongue before she said something to ruin a night that hadn't even begun. "Ben," she smiled. "I was beginning to think you had stood me up."

"Never." He twisted a lock of her hair around his finger and the heat in his eyes made her a bit apprehensive. "Beautiful as usual."

"Thank you." She wanted to bolt. *What is wrong with me?* She shook her head trying to clear her mind and understand why she'd gone from one hundred to zero so quick? Ben seemed nice enough, but the sight of him lodged a boulder in the pit of her stomach. *I should go.* Why was she even there? Her feet planted for an about face and then it hit her. *Grandbabies...right. Mom wants grandbabies.*

19

Her mother wanted grandbabies, and that alone was the reason she had followed Ben to a table filled with three other men. She introduced herself, because Ben sure didn't make the effort and had to smile at that hungry 'T-Bone steak', 'Neanderthal' look three times.

By the looks of things, they were all three beers in. She looked to Ben, lips wrapped around the frosty, long-necked bottled. Maybe a drink would help her relax and get back into party mode, but instincts reminded her to keep her mind sharp. Ever since what had happened to April, that little voice was something she no longer ignored. She sat there for forty-five minutes, watching the condensation glisten and slide down their beer bottles as they exchanged barbs and rehashed the work-day events. They ordered more drinks, stepping it up from beer to something a little stronger. Not once did Ben ask her if she wanted anything. Yeah, she would've turned it down…maybe would've turned it down, but she would have liked the opportunity to do so. *Cheap bastard.*

Other than the hand she had to keep swatting off her knee, Ben had pretty much ignored her since the moment she sat down. Babies, grandbabies, or not, she'd had enough. "So, um…" She picked up her clutch purse and pointed toward the exit. "I'm gonna go."

"What?"

She had his attention then, but it was too late. She was up and moving through the crowd before he could formulate a sentence. He called after her, but she kept right on stepping.

*Don't follow me, Ben. Don't do it.*

She made it outside and was thankful there were no footsteps behind her. *Sorry Mom, those grandbabies will have to wait.*

# 4

A waterfall of sweat ran down Candice's face. She flopped down on the hard-foam mat, begging God to keep her lungs working. She looked at her workout partner, trying her best to remember how much she loved April. "You know you don't have to lose all the baby fat in one workout." She panted between each word, sounding like she hadn't worked out in years.

"Girl, there are too many women trying to get my husband's attention. I have to get this body back in shape to make sure his eyes stay on me. The competition is real out here."

Candice almost choked. She couldn't believe the nonsense coming out of April's mouth. "You've got to be kidding me. That man's eye isn't straying anywhere. He could have every last one of them, but he chose you. I understand wanting to look good for your man, but let that be the extent of it." She rolled over and struggled to her knees. "Now, stop being silly and get over here and help me get up. I need to shower and get to work."

"Not so fast…"

Candice recognized that tone and her eyes rolled on auto pilot.

"What's up with you?" April was a dog with a bone, so, there was no point in not answering.

A half-truth would make life easier. "Mom had me blocked from visiting." She put up a hand to silence April's gasp. "She wants grandkids, and apparently my visiting her so much is hindering me from making them."

April laughed out loud and Candice wanted to punch her, but her muscles were dead. "Nice…laugh at my expense."

"Sorry, Candy, but your mom is hilarious." She laughed again and Candice couldn't help but join in.

"Ouch, ouch! Don't make me laugh." Candice clutched her stomach, taking slow deep breaths to calm her chuckles. "Every inch of my body hurts. Laughing is too much. Now, get over here and help me up." She sucked her teeth at how easy April hopped up and extended her hand.

"Not so fast. Spill it. What happened when you left the anniversary service?"

Candice rolled her eyes. "Absolutely nothing... He's a cheap bastard who wanted to eat on my dime after he ordered a king's feast. You know I don't do cheap."

"I know that's right."

"I can't believe I called him up for a second date."

"What!"

"Yes, girl. Momma on strike for grandbabies had me thinking crazy."

"Did y'all hook up?"

Candice side eyed her. "Marriage must not be too great if you have to live vicariously through me."

"Girl, please. Marriage is implicit, complicit, and explicit. His control, never spoken but understood; his moves, skillfully intentional; the power of it, force of it, and effect of it should be illegal." April moistened her lips and eyes slipped out of focus.

"Earth to April," Candice snapped her fingers, hiding the twinge of jealousy over the sappy expression on April's face. "Okay, now that we established that your sex life is better than mine and you've officially made me jealous, I'm going home."

"You have another set of squats, but since you look like you're getting ready to die, I'll let it slide."

"You sure that's the reason why? I think your letting it slide because you're about to have a flashback-induced orgasm in the middle of the gym." Candice's mock disgust turned to giggles at her lack of denial. She shook her head at her lovesick friend and limped off to the locker room, not even bothering to say bye.

She made quick work of a shower. The idea of showering in a public place grossed her out, but April, the fitness Nazi, insisted on early morning workouts. The way Candice had been panting and sweating, going to work without showering was out of the question.

Lifting her legs into her pants felt like she had weights strapped around her ankles. She was grateful she had opted for flat shoes instead of her usual heels. If she was already stiff and sore right after her workout, she dreaded what her body would feel like after her muscles had time to settle.

Despite how her body felt, a burst of energy came over her. She slid behind the wheel of her little Hyundai Accent, plugged her iPod in, and searched for the one gospel artist she'd downloaded. Vashawn Mitchell blasted through her speakers. She loved his music, probably because the church choir always sang his songs. Whatever the reason, it was what she wanted to hear.

She pulled up to her job and the music, combined with her morning exercise, sent her energy skyrocketing. The voice that usually growled about how much she hated her job was a mere whisper. She was a case manager working under a senior social worker named Vince Barker. He was content to continue in the same thirty-year routine he'd picked up from his predecessor, even though it was deteriorating employee and client morale.

She was feeling so good she ignored the stiffness in her legs and stopped by Vince's office with a smile and a wave before she made it to her cubicle.

Morningside Senior Center was the city's largest retirement and convalescent facility. Right out of college, Candice interned at a youth center and was hoping for a permanent position. Funding wouldn't allow it, so she accepted the first offer she received. She knew she'd hate it, but was afraid there'd be no other offers. She said yes without even applying for anything else. She was ready to leave and see what else the world had to offer, but with Morningside recently coming under fire for a seemingly healthy patient dying, she couldn't very well abandon them during their time of need.

She had a list of changes and new programs she wanted to implement, but Vince and his *I'm in charge* arrogance wouldn't take suggestions from anyone.

"Good morning, beautiful."

Candice looked up from logging in to her computer, instantly cocking a brow at Vince and his choice of words. He was so full of himself, he didn't notice her annoyance.

"Good morning. How can I help you?"

23

He stepped inside her cubicle, perching his butt next to her keyboard. His voice dipped to a seductive timbre and Candice blinked several times to keep from rolling her eyes. One little smile and the brother had taken it as an invitation to go all Barry White on her. Barry White's deep, soulful voice sang many women into a tizzy; Vince could not.

Even though she'd sensed where he was headed, she couldn't stop the cringe that tensed her body as he uttered the words, "I'd really like to take you out sometime."

His eyes darted around, ensuring no one was listening to him. He knew good and well the company had a strict sexual harassment policy. He could lose his job by simply asking that question.

Her facial expression must've been horrible. He locked eyes with her and instantly started back tracking. "...to discuss some of the ideas you have for the facility." His smile broadened the width of his face. She wasn't fooled for a minute.

Two could play that game. "I'd love that." If he wanted to use work as a ruse to take her out, then she'd definitely make it a business meeting.

"Are you free tonight? We could get an early dinner after work and go from there."

*Go from there...* Candice frowned at that statement and what it implied. She didn't want to lead him on, but she couldn't pass up the opportunity either. "Sounds good. Pick the place and I'll follow you there."

The smile on Vince's face as he backed away made her stomach drop. She'd have to remember to make it clear that it was just business. Aside from him being her boss, Vince was easy on the eyes and knew it. If arrogance wasn't such a turnoff, she'd be happy to date him. He seemed immune to the silly giggling little intern that all other male case managers seemed entranced by. She applauded those two traits—looks and ignoring the bimbo—but that's where her admiration stopped. Everything else about Vince grated her nerves.

Mind set to thwart all Vince's romantic advances, Candice turned toward her desk and spent the majority of her shift tweaking a proposal that had been taking up space on her hard drive for months. By lunch, she was definitely prepared to knock Vince's socks off with her ideas.

"Hey, Candy."

Candice forced a smile at the resident bimbo, hoping to mimic some of her exuberance. That nickname was reserved for family and close friends, Heather was neither. All the case managers were assigned an intern and she didn't know who she'd pissed off to get stuck with Heather. She was a chatterbox who hovered over Candice's shoulder, running her mouth for about a week, until Candice flat out told her to shut up.

Candice made her way to the refrigerator in the staff break room, hoping someone hadn't helped themselves to her lunch. She'd never understand what would possess a grown person to grab a lunch that wasn't theirs and eat it. It happened to her several times, and it never ceased to piss her off. She smiled at finding her tray of Greek salad right where she'd placed it and plopped at the table next to Heather, hoping to enjoy it in peace.

As soon as the first word passed Heather's lips, Candice sighed and cut her a look that said don't get started. Heather ignored it and kept right on talking.

"So, you and Vince looked pretty comfortable this morning. Care to share?"

The crease in Candice's brow deepened letting her annoyance show. "Oh no. We will stop this rumor before it even gets started. Nothing is going on with me and Vince." She gathered up her lunch and marched back to her desk, opting to eat in her cubicle rather than deal with Heather. When it came time to give her recommendation on which interns to hire, Heather wouldn't be on the list.

# 5

Already annoyed, Candice pulled out of the parking lot behind Vince. He'd copped an attitude when she rejected his offer to drive her and then refused to tell her where they were dining. She couldn't stand men with control issues. Why they felt the need to be in charge was beyond her; however, it wasn't a romantic date, so she was over it. She huffed out a breath and relaxed back in her seat. It was a business meeting and nothing more, regardless of what Vince wanted.

Vince blew through a yellow light and she had no choice but to follow. She checked her mirrors for flashing police lights and made a mental note to inform Vince of caravan etiquette. He switched lanes and passed cars like he was driving for NASCAR. Candice did her best to keep up, but the brother had no clue how to drive when someone was following.

They pulled into the parking lot, her irritation level now skyrocketed. The swank Italian restaurant definitely didn't say business meeting. On top of that, he had to pick the one restaurant in the entire city where the chefs were good friends with her brothers. If Marlon or Cole walked out of the kitchen and saw her, she'd have her two nosy brothers sitting on her sofa when she got home. Since Marlon saw her as a little sister, he might take it upon himself to sit at their table and begin the interrogation.

Before she could gather her thoughts, Vince rushed over from his car to open her door, which turned out to be more irritating than impressive. "Maybe we should go someplace else." She stepped out of the car, her frown combating his smiling face. "This restaurant doesn't really say business meeting."

Vince reached inside her car, grabbed her belongings, and shut the door. "We can talk business anywhere. I love the food here." His free hand touched the small of her back and guided her toward the front door. The need to present her ideas bit back the objection perched on her lips. It could possibly be her one chance to make a difference.

26

There never ceased to be a line waiting to get a table at Pavoli's. The way Marlon and Cole could throw down, they'd have to start seating by reservation only. Candice stood outside while Vince went in to speak with the hostess. She took a few deep breaths to exhale her frustration and roll the tension out of her neck.

"Hey, Candy."

"Hey, girl."

Those voices made her shoulders tighten back up. Without even turning around, she knew exactly who they were. Being seen by their wives was almost as bad as being seen by Marlon and Cole themselves. Of all the nights, why this night?

"Hey Meme, Latrice." She gave them halfhearted hugs and tried to rush inside before Vince came out. She wasn't that lucky. His hand slid around her waist and she wanted to punch him in the face for violating her personal space.

"It'll be about forty-five minutes before we can get a table."

"That's nonsense. You'll sit with us." Latrice moved toward the door. Candice was not about to let that happen.

"That's okay. We're actually here on a business meeting. I don't want our discussion to interrupt your meal."

"A business meeting?" Meme glanced down at Vince's hand still around Candice's waist and smiled. "Sure, we'll let you dine alone then."

They walked away and Candice was already preparing her mind for the backlash. Paul and Tim would want his name, birthday, social security number, and a blood sample if she could get it. She was in her twenties before she even knew she had brothers, and they seemed determined to make up for lost time. Honestly, she loved every minute of it. Their good-for-nothing father had never shown much interest. The only good thing he ever did for her was help her track down her brothers. It felt good to have male figures looking out for her.

She often wondered if her daddy issues correlated to her man issues. She was picky and wanted good looks and money in a man just like every other woman. Deep down, she just wanted a man who treat her right and not abandon her.

"There's a spot inside if you'd like to sit while we wait."

She scanned Vince's face, discovering a slight dimple in his left cheek. She never took the time to notice before. Would he treat her right if she gave him the chance? He had to have a good heart. It was hard to work in the human services field without it. She locked eyes with his, hoping for a spark, glimmer of chemistry, or the love at first sight her entire family swore by. With her luck, she wouldn't get the chemistry, but something similar to the disaster that was her father, a *hit it until responsibility arises then disappear* type of man.

"Vince!"

He turned around to see who'd called him.

Candice took the time to shake silly fantasies from her head.

"Your table is ready."

"That was quick." He guided Candice in front of him to fall in step behind the hostess.

"Well, it seems you have friends in high places."

Candice rolled her eyes, took the seat Vince held out for her, and tried to ignore Latrice and Meme sitting across the restaurant watching her. As soon as Vince took his seat, she sifted through the documents in her manila folder and got down to business. She didn't want her friends across the way to get any ideas in their mind and go running back to her brothers.

"Morningside Senior Center offers extraordinary quality care, but it can be so much more than a sanitary living environment with a caring nursing staff."

"Candice." Vince placed his menu on the table, shaking his head in frustration. "You have until our entrees arrive and then I want to enjoy my meal and your company." He reached across the table and gripped her hand. "I hope you want to do the same." The look in his eyes left no room for doubt. He was no longer hiding behind the ruse of a business meeting. He wanted her.

She slipped her hand from his to pass him a few papers. She looked across the restaurant to see if Meme and Latrice where watching and of course they were.

*Great… So much for them not getting the wrong idea.*

"Our clients are retired senior citizens. They are not dead. Morningside has mastered quality of care, but what about quality of life?

As long as our clients have blood running through their veins, they can enjoy life. The dayroom is being used as a TV room, which is a waste. If you turn to page two, you'll see my proposal."

For thirty minutes—pausing only to place her order—Candice outlined her ideas. She tried to hide her excitement at Vince's appraising words, but couldn't help the warm flush his words brought. She was so high off her passion for improving Morningside that when their meal arrived, she had no problem relaxing to enjoy it.

"I never got around to thanking you for doing such an amazing job planning the New Year's celebration." Candice beamed at his praise, even though it was a couple of months too late. "Although there were a few mishaps, I think the clients really enjoyed themselves."

Candice laughed out loud, not caring if people stared. "Mishaps? You mean Ms. Wilson's teeth falling into the punch and her diving in to get them like she was bobbing for apples." Her laugh became even more robust as she thought over that night. "Maybe you meant Ms. Winters and Ms. Kelly hitting each other with their canes because they both wanted to dance with Mr. Parks. Or are you referring to Mr. Life-of-the-Party Johnson nearly dancing himself into cardiac arrest." She hated to laugh at the client's expense, but sometimes she had to.

Vince joined in the laughter. Thinking about Mr. Parks sitting back cheesing like the man of the hour while two women fought over him had his side hurting he was laughing so hard.

"I'm glad Mr. Johnson is okay, but the brother was out there dropping it like it was hot." Candice patted the tears leaking out the corner of her eyes, trying to get her laughter under control.

"Yes, he was. I thought he was gonna break a hip, thrusting like he was really getting some."

They talked and joked around well past the end of their meal. Vince suggested they head on out and Candice was shocked at the disappointment she felt. She gulped the last of her wine, hoping he hadn't noticed. He took care of the check without hesitation and she couldn't help but compare this to her date with Ben.

The walk to her car was quiet and reflective. Vince really wasn't the uptight arrogant jerk she'd pegged him to be. He actually had a lighter side. She stopped on the side of her car, turned to thank him for dinner,

29

and he closed in on her so smoothly, he took her breath away. His lips descended on hers, demanding her submission. Her resistance caved before it really had a chance to build up. His kiss trailed along her jawline, down her neck, and she stood in stunned silence helpless to halt his pursuit.

"I have your number. Is it all right if I use it personally?"

She was so shocked, her head nodded on its own accord. The brother could kiss, and his confidence to just go for it knocked her off balance.

"I'll call you later to make sure you made it home safely. Make sure you save my number." Vince smiled at her lack of response, kissed her again, and then took the keys from her hand to open her car door.

*What just happened?* Candice climbed into her car, trying to get her brain to start back up. She drove home in a fog, but by the time she arrived, the shock had worn off. She was left to face the reality that she'd inadvertently agreed to something personal with her boss.

She plopped down on her sofa, groaning into the pillow, "What happened to 'just a business dinner'?"

As if answering her question, her cell rang. She sent the unknown number to voicemail, and went to drown her sorrows in a hot bath.

# 6

Sunday morning was a struggle. The alarm on her phone went off and Candice nearly chucked it across the room. Vince and Ben had been tag teaming her nerves for days. Between the two, she had eleven missed calls and nearly double that in text messages. Not one call or text was returned. At least Vince had been decent enough not to confront her at work. There were a few times where his eyes said he was about to show out, but he reeled it in. Nothing stopped him or Ben from blowing up her phone at night, though. Their persistence was going to make her snap.

Along with all that, she still hadn't heard from her mother. She needed to see her. It had been just the two of them for so long, fighting for and with each other, she didn't know how to cope. She was going through mommy withdrawals.

*Grandbabies,* she laid there for over an hour—ignoring texts from April asking where she was—mind roaming over her mother's wishes. Was she really ready to be a mother? She definitely wanted a man, someone stable in her life, but a child... Maybe she should put that thought on the back burner. Sooner or later, her mother would start to miss her and realize how unreasonable she was being. Candice wanted a man, a husband, before she'd even consider having a baby. She loved her mom, but she didn't want to walk in her shoes. Single parenting wasn't for her. Yes, she had prospects, but of the two men interested in her, neither captured her attention. The man who did probably hadn't thought about her since the day they met.

She shut down thoughts of him and quickly jumped out of bed. He was dangerous. His effect on her was more potent than a volcano preparing to erupt. The possibility of running into him at church put a little pep in her step. She made quick work of a shower, opted to go make-up-free, and let her curly mane drape along her shoulders. She loved the mixed-chick hair moisturizer. It made her curls shine and pop like they were soaking wet. She had absolutely no idea what she was mixed with since her father was pretty much an orphan with no knowledge of his ancestry. At least, that's what he'd told her... She'd learned the hard way that his word wasn't much to go on. He always manipulated the truth for his needs. Maybe he knew more and didn't want to share. Either way, she didn't care. She just loved her hair.

She finally arrived at church and could've kicked herself for getting there so late. She may have had a reserved seat, but not a parking space. The parking lot was almost full, and she had to park in the back. At the sound of the music seeping through the walls, her exasperation quickly subsided. Despite all her worries, she was able to smile at the friendly faces greeting her.

She smiled until she headed toward the sanctuary door and saw Ben was standing there, waiting to get in. Her steps slowed and her eyes darted around for some place to hide. Sure, it was ridiculous and she probably looked absurd, but the alternative wasn't happening. She preferred to avoid Ben. The adult thing to do would've been to greet him, shake his hand, and say, "by the way I'm not interested." Instead, she found a spot behind one of the floor to ceiling pillars in the foyer and hid there until he went inside. She released the breath she was holding, only to have the wind knocked out of her when Jason stepped into Ben's place. She continued to stand behind the pillar, admiring him. Hopefully, her mouth wasn't hanging open and she wasn't drooling, but that was certainly the reaction he elicited from her.

Zion Pentecostal church was on fire. Jason could feel the heat oozing through the doors and into foyer. He'd grabbed the door handle several times to go in and join in the excitement, but couldn't do it. There were so many people in there. What if they knew he was fresh out of prison and didn't want him there? There were still so many things he didn't know about the world, so much he'd yet to experience. How could he compete or fit in with any of them?

"You know, they won't bite."

Jason spun around to the face that continued to pop into his mind at the most random times. He allowed his eyes a brief scan. She was more beautiful than he remembered. Way out of his league, but a man could dream, couldn't he? "Yeah, I'm just trying to decide if I'm ready to do this."

"I hear you. It's like a whole other world in there. I don't know if you remember, but I'm Candice." She extended her hand in greeting and couldn't explain the sensation that shot up her arm when he clasped his hand to hers. It felt so spectacular, she didn't want to turn him loose.

"I remember." He smiled and shook his head at the rest of what he wanted to say.

"What?" The smile in her voice was just as bright as the one on her face.

"You are not forgettable."

Her smile faded as his eyes scanned the length of her. The moment his eyes met hers, *something* sizzled between them. It was so hot, there had to be steam surrounding them. Dumbstruck, awestruck, paralyzed, or whatever you called it, she couldn't move. She stood there, slack-jawed, until someone squeezed by her to get into the sanctuary.

"Um, so…" She cleared her throat. She'd never been so nervous. "We could sit together, if it'll make going in easier."

"Sounds like a plan." He sucked in a deep breath to bolster his courage, but she saw past the front he put up.

"Good, let's do it." Candice walked into the sanctuary with her heart in her throat. Why he made her so nervous, she didn't know.

She looked back to make sure he was following and the apprehension on his face touched her. She reached back and grabbed his hands, assuring him she was there for him. He squeezed her fingers and pulled her closer. She stumbled at the sudden movement, but quickly recovered. She cupped her other hand to the back of his, sandwiching his hand between hers as her eyes implored his wellbeing. He sucked in a deep breath and expelled it with a slight nod to let her know he was okay. Candice admired his strength.

Being the first lady's best friend afforded a few perks and her usual seat, right behind April, was still open. She sat down, grateful for the empty seat next to hers. She waited until Jason was comfortable and then leaned over to whisper in his ear, "I'm proud of you for taking this step." The smile he gave her was a gift like no other. She stared, mesmerized by the small curve of his lips and returned a timid smile of her own.

She forced her eyes away, her heart pounding in her chest. This had to be it—the undeniable crackle of chemistry, which had caused her brothers to abandon bachelorhood and marry after only months of dating. That same fire had made her best friend embrace domesticity over the party life.

Candice sat next to Jason, barely breathing, but more aware of him than she'd ever been of any man. Praise was going on all around her. The only thing she noticed was him, his praise, his tears, and his essence. By the time service was over, she was giddy with awareness and was already plotting to stay in his presence. She let a few people clear out before grabbing her things. She didn't want anyone to overhear her shamelessly asking him out. She stood to her feet and the face standing before her stole the words off her lips.

"Ben…" He cut her off before she could greet him.

"Who's your boy?" His head motioned toward Jason.

The look on his face let her know where Ben's mind was, and she had to pause to keep her mouth in check in the house of God. Two dates didn't sanction inquiries into her personal life. Before she could tell him off, Jason leaned around extending his hand in greeting.

"Just a friend. I'm not encroaching on your territory."

They gripped hands in silent understanding and Jason walked away.

*Just friends…* His words and departure left Candice deflated. *Right, just friends…* She'd do well to remember that. She turned to Ben and the look on her face knocked the smile off his. "Let's get this straight. Two dates…both unsuccessful, does not give you the right to question me. I would think my not calling you was notice enough that I'm not interested." She tried to stomp off, but he grabbed her arm and pulled her back.

"Who do you think you're talking to?"

Before she could respond three men—she didn't know was watching—surrounded him, looking angrier than she'd ever seen them. Paul, Tim, and Cole were breathing down his neck. Her hands shot out to Paul and Tim's chest, halting them, but where was Meme when she needed her. Cole gripped the back of Ben's neck with so much force, he nearly collapsed on Candice. She hopped out of the way and Cole used

34

his neck like a joystick steering him around the pews, out of the sanctuary, and into the parking lot. Meme noticed the commotion and chased behind them.

"What happened?"

Candice's shoulders slumped at Paul's no-nonsense voice. She wasn't ready for that conversation. "You should go make sure your boy doesn't catch a case."

"It would be well earned. Now, what happened?"

She turned to Tim, the younger and less volatile of the two, and he looked just as upset as Paul. "We went on two—semi, kind of sort of—dates. I guess he was feeling some type of way about me sitting with Jason."

"Candice, what are you doing? Dating that jerk, then all hugged up with some man at Pavoli's, and today you walk up in here holding hands with Jason."

*Meme and Latrice did snitch.* She'd cautiously stepped into her apartment that night and was shocked to find it empty.

"You know you're not my father, and—"

"Maybe if I was, you wouldn't have daddy issues and be running through men faster than you—"

"Whoa!" Tim cut him a look to let him know he was going too far. He should've jumped in sooner.

"You are just like him." Candice tried masking her hurt with anger, but the tremble in her voice gave it away. She locked eyes with Paul. His eyes sparked with anger. She should've been ashamed of the joy she felt, knowing her words had cut him the way his had cut her.

"He was never around long enough for either of us to know that." He glanced away, chuckling to curb his anger and shaking his head, trying to shake away what he really wanted to say. He'd worked his butt off to be exactly the opposite of what his father was. How dare she equate him to the man the three of them spent most of their lives despising. He collected himself and stepped a little closer to finish his thought without eavesdropping ears overhearing. "All I'm trying to say is that you deserve better, something constant and unwavering, a man who sees your value and won't do anything to devalue you. But if you don't want that for yourself, please don't let Jason get caught in your web."

35

Candice watched him walk off, hating that he thought the worst of her, but even more so hating that she'd compared him to their deadbeat father.

"Both of you are hitting below the belt today."

"He started it."

"What are we? Five?"

She rolled her eyes and tried to stomp off, but Tim stopped her.

"You okay?" The concern on his face was a welcomed change. Without hesitation, she went into his embrace.

She nodded against his chest and he squeezed a little tighter.

"Paul means well."

"Don't make excuses for him," she chuckled, her laugh devoid of humor. "Let him know his precious Jason is safe from big bad Candice."

"Jason has been through a lot, but it's nothing the love of a good woman can't help him overcome."

"Tim, it's not like that." Even if she wanted their assumptions to be true, the reality was she'd been friend-zoned. "He was having a hard time coming in, so I held his hand just to comfort him."

"It felt good, didn't it?"

Candice rolled her eyes, but he continued.

"When I first met Camilla, the attraction was instant. We wound up at Sunset Cliffs that night and it was freezing. I jumped at the opportunity to put my arms around her to warm her up. It was the absolute best feeling in the world."

Candice smiled at the way her brother's face lit up when he talked about the love of his life. "Not everyone is as sappy as you." *And yes, it felt amazing.* She kept the last bit to herself. Tim really didn't need to know.

He ignored her teasing smile and handed her a bit of truth. "Okay, whatever you say. Just know that I watched you walk in, and I watched you throughout the service. Nothing on your face said friendship…yours or his." He walked away, leaving Candice stammering for a rebuttal.

Commotion drew Jason's attention to the entrance of the church. He couldn't help the smile that spread across his face at seeing Cole roughing up Ben. Cole mumbled something, Ben pointed, and Cole jerked him in that direction. He slammed Ben against the car and paced like a caged animal until Ben hopped inside and drove off.

The small thrill was short lived. Jason got in his car and looked at his reflection in the rearview mirror. If Ben was the type of man Candice was attracted to, there was no shot for him. Tall, lean, clean-cut brother suited up in the best money could buy, or a prison-ripped thug sporting jeans and a polo shirt with cornrows down to his shoulders; the choice seemed simple. So, instead of getting worked up only to be let down, he resolved to just keep it moving.

There were other women out there, like Chantel. He hoped she'd contact him. Maybe letting her decide whether their relationship continued wasn't such a good idea. He should've made it clear he wanted to see her. He just hoped that Paul and the rest of the brothers hadn't been right about her. There was no way a woman as thoughtful as Chantel was a prison groupie. That's what he'd told them and what he continued to tell himself. The longer it took her to contact him, the harder it was to believe.

The beat-up car he'd borrowed from his mother revved to life and putted across the parking lot just as Candice exited the front door. She made the pencil skirt she was wearing come to life. And her high heels made the definition of her calf pop with each step. He followed the line from the tip of her heel, up those calves, around those thick thighs, to a backside that had his tongue sticking to the roof of his mouth. He'd always had a thing for girls so thin he could snap them in two. They were the cheerleaders, the most popular, and the ones everyone wanted to be. Of course, he had to have the best, but Candice was making him appreciate curves and everything they had to offer.

He pulled up in front of his house and Candice was still walking in slow motion across his mind. He was so focused on her assets that it took him a minute to realize someone was calling his name as he walked across the grass to the front door. His mind honed in on the sound and he froze. *Lamont!*

"Why are you even here?" Jason spun around so fast, he caught Lamont off guard.

"Chill, damn. Just came by to see what's good with you." He held up a bag, chuckling without a care in the world. It could've been a bag of

37

poop the way Jason looked at it. "Bet you ain't had nothing like this since you got out. You used to tear these burritos up."

Jason grabbed the offending bag, nearly squeezing the contents out of it. The muscle in his jaw ticked as he tried to contain the fury rolling through him. "Why are you here?"

"You know, I gotta catch up with my boy. It's been too damn long."

"Your boy?" Jason chuckled, the tension coiling throughout his body contradicting the sound. "My mom always said you were crazy." Jason tossed the burrito as far as he could. "We aren't friends!"

Lamont's eyes followed the path of the burrito. His ice-cold, expressionless face slowly turned back to Jason. If there was ever any doubt before, it was put to rest right there in that moment. Lamont was a sociopath—he had no true emotion or ability to feel anything genuine. "There are only two types of people in this world: friends and enemies."

"We aren't friends. You stole ten years of my life…" Jason's voice rose with each word and he paused biting his lip, fist clenched at his side, trying to fight off everything he wanted to do to Lamont. He deserved every homicidal thought, but Jason was better than that. Vengeance was the Lord's. At least that's what he kept telling himself. "Leave before I have you arrested for trespassing."

"So, what you're saying is you want to be enemies? All right then, but I guarantee you'll wish you'd eaten the damn burrito."

Jason met Lamont's wicked grin with an ice-cold glare of his own and held it until Lamont backed away.

# 7

Jason's eyes popped open and were immediately drawn to the red numbers glaring from the alarm clock on the nightstand. He'd hoped to see the morning sun, but the room was still dark. He had just fallen asleep a few hours before, but was wide awake and anxious for the day like he'd slept all night. Saying he was excited was an understatement. The same anticipation that made it difficult to fall asleep was still surging through him.

Opting to kill a little time before he got out of bed, his hand sought the letters on his nightstand. Other than his Bible, they were his most prized. Think him soft if you wanted to, but those letters gave him life every day. Even on the outside, they meant so much to him that he grabbed one of his momma's old tins that never contained the cookies advertised on the outside, discarded her things, and filled it with his letters. He grabbed the one on top. It was by far his favorite. The worn folds had been manipulated by his hands many times. Delicately, he unfolded it, hoping it didn't rip. It was a short letter, but it never ceased to encourage and give him hope.

*When the days are dark and your nights are cold... When you're alone and your heart is heavy... When you feel like giving up and all hope is lost... When you're at your lowest and weakest point... Remember there is life after this. Just a few more days to go, YOU GOT THIS! I'll be waiting.*

It was the last three words that had him anxious for his last days to tick by. It was also those last three words which made Chantel's silence confusing. Why say it at all if you didn't mean it? Maybe she was just a prison groupie.

Carefully, he tucked the note back into the tin and rolled out of bed and onto his knees. The first thing he said in prayer every morning was, "Lord, thank You for my freedom." There were so many things he could complain about, but he opted for gratefulness. "Lord, I thank You for the fresh air and the ability to breathe on my own. I thank You for being able to come and go as I please. I thank You for being able to relax in Your peace, without the fear of being jumped on. I love You and know that all things are working together for my good. Please be my strength as I stand for You. This felony and my past will not hinder me from being successful. I will prosper in the Name of Jesus."

He paused for a moment. Prayer was so much more than speaking. It was also listening. Did the Lord have something He needed to say? Was there some direction or clarity He wanted to impart? So, instead of just hopping up, Jason took time to listen. He definitely wanted to hear from the Lord. Living saved while locked up was hard, but being on the outside gave him the freedom to indulge in certain pleasures that weren't available on the inside. And he was a man with needs who hadn't had those needs met in ten years.

He crept out into the stillness of the morning. The house was quiet, and he stilted his movements, hoping not to wake his mother. He cringed at the slight creak of the front door opening and slowly eased through the crack. Standing on the porch, the neighborhood was even quieter. He sat down on the top step to enjoy the cool breeze of the morning. An occasional dog bark roused him out of his musings, but he let his mind wander. There were so many opportunities brimming in that day, he couldn't wait for the sun to rise. He was meeting with Paul and Tim to finalize a deal that guaranteed he wouldn't be a part of the recidivism of the prison system. Contracts were pretty much signed and sealed, but he still wanted to put his best foot forward and not take anything for granted. He wanted them to trust him and believe he could get the job done.

The sun finally dawned upon the day. He took a moment to enjoy the beauty of it. The newspaper man rolled by, tossing out deliveries. Jason waved and he waved back. Sluggishly the neighborhood started to wake up. Before long, he heard the creaking of the screen door behind him and couldn't help but smile at the sound of his mother's feet shuffling behind him.

"You okay, baby?"

"Yeah, I'm just out here absorbing all I can, trying to make up for lost time."

"I hear you. I do it myself. Time can just get away from you if you're not careful." She shook her head, staring off into the distance, envisioning the years they'd lost.

In that moment, Jason saw it all. Yes, he had suffered, but his mother had as well. There was only one thing he could do to help her redeem the time she'd lost because of him. "I'm going to move out soon."

"Why?" She didn't attempt to mask the shock and hurt. "I've been alone for ten years. I love having you here."

"That's exactly what I'm talking about." He reached up to grab her hand and guided her onto the step next to him. "You put your life on hold for me. I may have been locked up, but you served time, too. I want you to live, Mama—meet a man and invite him over without worrying if I'm here."

"Boy, please." She swatted at his shoulder and covered her blush with the other hand. "I ain't bringing a man home."

"Why not? You're a beautiful woman who deserves to be loved by a good man."

"My time has come and gone. Your daddy was all the good man I needed. My selfish decisions put him in an early grave. No man can replace him."

"You've atoned for that stuff a long time ago. Everyone deserves to be loved."

She turned her head blinking away tears. He didn't know she carried guilt and still grieved his father's death. He tossed his arm around her shoulders and she leaned into his embrace.

"What you should really be worried about is finding a nice young lady and giving me some grandbabies."

Jason dropped his arm and shook his head. *So, it begins.* He walked in the house laughing, leaving Yvonne sitting on the steps.

After a quick workout and breakfast with his mom that took longer than he'd expected, he only had a few minutes left to shower and get dressed. If his mom hadn't had noticed time was getting away from them, he probably would've let her talk all day.

The suit he'd purchased fit him perfectly. In high school, he hated that the varsity basketball team had to wear slacks with a dress shirt and tie on game day, but this suit was different. It put a power in his stride,

41

made him feel like he was on equal footing with the rest of the world. He stepped out of the house feeling good, strutting like Blaxploitation star Shaft, with theme music and all.

It was the first day of his new life. He was a business man in control of his own destiny. He ignored the sting of having his mother drop him off—it would soon be rectified—and shifted his mind into business mode.

He tried not to let Paul's posh conference room—with an expansive table boasting of power meetings full of people who'd look down their nose at him—intimidate him. He took a deep breath and pushed through the door.

"Good morning, everyone." He stepped up to the table, grateful he'd opted for the suit instead of his normal attire. The greeting he received bolstered his confidence. He shook hands and shoulder hugged the men who'd treated him like family since the first day they visited him in prison. "Hope I haven't missed much."

Paul and Tim were already at the table reviewing blueprints with the contractor. Excitement over seeing his dream come to reality surged through Jason.

"Not at all. Paul is just impatient and nosy."

Jason laughed and instantly relaxed. Their backed-handed snips at each other were just a fragment of the brotherly camaraderie they'd welcomed him into.

Paul shook his head and settled back over the blueprints. "Well, he said he made changes without our approval. I needed to see it."

Jason's eyes shot over to the contractor he'd yet to meet. He introduced himself and immediately asked for an explanation.

"Like I was telling Paul, yes, it's more expensive, but it's in your best interest. This is a youth center. You want the kids to be safe and you want the parents to be comfortable with sending their kids. We are not building in the best of neighborhoods, which, I know you understand, because you've opted for a top-of-the-line security system. I'm simply suggesting the one-way windows as an added measure of security. Also, this door back here is asking for trouble."

Jason tuned the guy out. Whatever decision needed to be made, Paul and Tim would make it. It was their money, after all. His eyes

42

roamed across the papers in front of him. He couldn't believe it was actually happening. He'd shot the idea down when they had first mentioned it, thinking there was no way a criminal could be around kids, but here he was now looking over blueprints. He was actually going to be able to turn his experience into something positive.

"There is nothing on the back side of the property to deter criminals from breaking in."

That statement snapped Jason back to the conversation and the contractor had his undivided attention.

"You have your most valued possessions right next to the door, the computer room. I just switched the offices with the computer room."

"I hear you, but doing that moves the supervision out of the area."

The room fell silent and Jason couldn't help but think they both had a point. Leaving the computer room in the back made a 'grab and dash' too easy. On the other hand, a room full of unsupervised hormonal mischievous teenagers was asking for trouble. Jason didn't know anything about architecture or measurements, but he did have common sense.

"This room here is just an open area, right?" Their nods encouraged his thought. "If we cut it down just a bit we could make a small office. It can run the length of the computer room. With the walls' half-windows on each side, staff can monitor both rooms. Staff will be required to walk the floors, but if they need to be in the office at all, it will be this one. The office in the back will be for me and the social worker we hire." Jason held his breath as he awaited the contractor's reply. He watched him scanning the blueprints and couldn't help but smile when he finally answered.

"That's doable."

Jason stepped back and let the contractor and Paul discuss his suggestion. He kept quiet about how the previous design, even before the changes, failed to provide space for adequate observation of the kids. He scanned the drawings to see if there were any other changes needed. Satisfied there weren't, he grabbed a notebook to jot down more ideas while Paul and Tim negotiated price. He was so caught up in planning that he hadn't noticed the meeting was over until Tim patted him on the shoulder.

"The wives didn't get a chance to meet you on Sunday. So, they made us promise to bring you over. Since I'm giving you a ride home, I'm not even going to ask if you want to come over for dinner."

Jason shook his head as Paul walked away. He'd definitely have to get used to being part of the family: a very large, in-your-face, and in-your-business type of family.

His jaw nearly hit the floor when they pulled up to Paul's house. He knew the brother was paid, but never would've guessed how much.

"Head on up and press the bell. Someone will let you in. I need to take this call real quick."

He watched Paul pull his ringing cell phone out of his pocket and wanted to tell him he'd just wait, but he was a grown man. He had to get used to meeting new people. He jogged along the walk way to the front door and held his breath as he waited for someone to answer his knock.

"Hey." He smiled at the face smiling back at him through the crack in the door. Once again, her beautiful face had come to the rescue and calmed him.

"Hey, it's good to see you."

"It's good to see you, too. Paul's in the car taking a call. He said for me to come on in."

"Okay." Candice's mind was cluttered with so many things she wanted to say, so many questions she wanted to ask. If only the sight of him in a suit hadn't short-circuited her brain. The suit and the cornrows were a lethal combination. Her fingers itched to reach out and peel the coat from his broad shoulders.

Jason smiled and playfully asked, "Can I come in?"

"Oh, I am sorry. Please, come in." Candice nervously laughed. "My sisters-in-law are so excited to meet you. They would slap me silly if they knew I had you standing out here this long."

Jason stepped inside whistling in awe of the inside of Paul's house. "This is nice." The foyer rivaled that of cathedrals with its high ceilings, arched entryways, hand-carved banisters, and furniture suitable for royalty.

"Yes, it is nice. Would you like a tour? I can give you one, or Paul and Sheena can."

"I'd like to wait, if that's all right with you."

"Of course, it is." She cleared her throat to hide her disappointment.

"But..." He stepped as close as he could without touching her. "I'd like for you to do it."

"Follow me." Was that really her voice, all wispy and everything? She cleared her throat, but didn't fare any better. "I'll introduce you to everyone." Candice led him into the backyard, wondering what had happened to the quick-witted, smart-mouthed woman she was known to be. She looked back over her shoulder and smirked. She had definitely met her match.

Paul and Tim's wives walked up to greet Jason, and he had to hide his shock. He glanced at Tim, letting his facial expression say what his mouth couldn't.

"Watch it, bruh." Tim chuckled and introduced his wife, Camilla.

"Pleased to meet you." Jason shook her hand and couldn't help but take a dig a Tim. "This explains so much about you. I was concerned for a minute, but now I understand why you talk about her so much."

"I'm Sheena." She stepped forward extending her hand. "Paul's wife, who I thought was arriving with you."

"I'm right here, babe." Paul cut through the small crowd and kissed her cheek.

"Y'all are some blessed brothers."

"You will be, too." Tim glanced at Candice, and she rolled her eyes and walked away.

Jason was deceived by the stereotype all successful black men married white women, and assumed Paul and Tim fell into that category. When he received his scholarship to play college ball, it was an ongoing joke that he'd be in the NBA with a white woman on his arm, but Jason was adamant that he would never sell out. He loved black women.

"Hey, Jason. It is so good to finally meet you." Marlon's wife, Latrice, stepped forward with Marlon glued to her side. The worst of the bunch was Cole. He was the biggest and seemed like the toughest of the group, but seeing him around his wife removed all the hard edges and made him more approachable.

By the time Jason had been introduced to everyone, he was a bit overwhelmed by all the people who he didn't know that knew him and had already made a place for him in their hearts.

Once all the introductions were made, Jason gravitated back to Candice. Something about her intrigued him and made him want to be near her, even if it was just standing there. When she'd opened the front door, her smile beamed at him like a ray of sun on a peaceful summer's day at the beach. He couldn't help but return it.

"Hey," she blushed.

He didn't know what he did to make it happen, but he wanted to do it again. The way her cheeks changed colors and she dipped her head to avoid his gaze was the most adorable thing he'd ever seen. One of the many curls toppling from her head tussled in the wind. Like he'd been trained to do so, his hand sought the curl, tucked it behind her ear, and then slid his finger along her jaw to tilt her chin back toward him. The moment their eyes meet again, there was no denying the jolt that zapped between them. Nervous, her tongue darted out to moisten her parched lips. Jason was dumbfounded. He stood there gaping in awe.

He opened his mouth to say something, but was interrupted by an overly excited mob of children. They surrounded him and drug him off to join in their game.

"Whoa." Jason tried to steady himself against the rush of the mob. There was no use; it was either go with the flow or be trampled to the ground.

"Good luck." Candice's smirk had him worried.

Candice watched Jason being led away and was finally able to take a deep breath. *What in the world was that?* The moment she opened the front door, her oxygen was compromised. The sight of him in a suit was too much for her heart to handle. *My God!* Her tongue stuck to the roof of her mouth while she allowed her mind to roam back over the image of him standing in front of her, body to die for bulging behind that crisp white dress shirt. And then those corn rows. *Oh God!*

Her chin still tingled from where his finger had touched her. This had to be it—the moment Sheena had experienced in her office when Paul came to talk about one of her students. The moment Camilla experienced when she showed up for Thanksgiving dinner and Tim had been invited. The moment April experienced when Richard came to the hospital to pray for her. The moment when they all had absolutely and utterly lost their heart. At first sight, in an instance, without warning, they surrendered to love. Candice tried to shake it off and attribute it to the fact that she'd been mesmerized by him for months, but when she looked up and her heart thumped a little harder at the sight of him chasing after her nieces and nephews, there was no denying it. *What am I going to do?*

Jason growled and chased after screaming children. He grabbed them as they ran by, picked them up, and tickled them until they cried for mercy. He was having as much fun as they were.

He noticed Candice's trance-like fixation on him. The look on her face stopped him mid-tickle. Again, he had an innate urge to be near her. He would've been there in an instant if the child in his arms hadn't wiggled free and joined the others in tackling him to the ground. He lost his footing, toppled to the ground, and all the kids piled on top of him.

The sight of Jason and all his muscle being overtaken by a crowd of five-year olds was enough to knock Candice out of the spell he had cast. She laughed so hard it hurt. She had definitely been there before. Her nieces and nephews could be lethal when they finally got the upper-hand. Jogging over to his rescue, Candice growled and all the kids scattered screaming, "Auntie Candice is going to get us."

"Are you okay?" Candice tried to hold back her laughter.

Jason rolled over and looked up at her. The sun glowing behind her made her look angelic. The wind slightly blew her sun dress and her hair danced lazily in the breeze. Her hair was incredible. That one little touch wasn't enough. He wanted to run his fingers through it, feel it beneath his chin when he wrapped his arms around her, see it sprawled across his chest as they lay in bed together... He let that last thought die before he got carried away.

Even through his suit jacket, Candice noticed his muscled arms bulging and flexing as he lifted himself from the ground. She forced her eyes away before her mind got her in trouble. He rose from the ground in front of her, lighting a fire within that threatened to burn out of control. For several tense seconds, she stood there silently wondering if he felt the energy flowing between them.

She sensed her now-or-never moment and desperately wracked her brain for the right words to express her thoughts. Why couldn't she just accept the friendship he was offering? Then again, she knew things he didn't and it was high time she told him.

"So, how's Ben?" Jason stepped toward her, hoping she'd say they were over, that Ben was never a factor, or anything along those lines.

His words nearly slowed her heart to a stop. *Right...Ben.* Why hadn't she chased after him that Sunday and set him straight about her connection to Ben.

"Look, Jason…"

"No need to explain." The look on her face hit him in the gut, and he immediately channeled his disappointment into anger. He silenced her with a palm in front of her face. Being in prison all of his adult life, he was no match for women his age. High school girls had played games, but they were childish antics he'd probably see coming a mile away; Candice was on a whole different level. "I understand grown women nowadays believe faithfulness is tied up in a diamond ring. I have a lot to learn, thanks for lesson number one."

She watched him walk away, her mouth stuttering for a comeback. How dare he make such an assumption about her character? Finally finding her words, she stormed off after him. Her short legs were nothing for his long strides and she had to run to catch up. "How dare you talk to me like that? You are a guest here, and if that's how you're going treat me, maybe I should tell my brothers not to invite you over here." The sudden tears that burned her eyes took Candice by surprise. This was not how the conversation was supposed to go, but she couldn't stop the words from flowing out of her mouth. "Maybe you should get to know a person before questioning their integrity."

"Candice…" He reached to touch her shoulder, but she knocked his hand away before he made contact, and marched off. His head sagged between his shoulders. Maybe he should've chosen his words more carefully. Now he'd gone and offended her, possibly ruining all the friendships he had made. He looked up and every eye in the yard was on him. Tim moved toward him and he steeled himself for the confrontation.

"You good, bro?"

He shrugged his shoulders and Tim laughed.

"Welcome to the world of women. Now come over here and taste these ribs. Candice can throw down on the grill. Some people think grilling is a man's job, but my little sister does it better than anyone I know."

"Maybe I should go."

"Look man," Tim slapped a hand on Jason's shoulder and guided him toward the food. "I have no idea what that was about. It looked pretty intense, but it's for you and Candice to work out."

Jason let Tim lead him to the food. He was going to enjoy the fellowship while it lasted. Surely, when they found out how he'd spoken to Candice, it would be over.

Tears swelled in Candice's eyes as she walked away. She was so furious she didn't hear April sneak up behind her.

"Hey, I was watching you guys. What's up?"

"Nothing." She kept right on marching, giving April a workout for a change.

"Do you have feelings for him?

"No!" That got her to stop marching like she was going to war. She spun around so fast she nearly knocked April over.

"Well, if you don't feel anything for him, why are you so upset?"

"Don't start. I barely know him."

"Okay, calm down and realize who you're talking to. Save the, *I barely know him,* bull for someone who'll believe it. If you don't have feelings for him, why is he having this effect on you?" April wrapped her arms around Candice's shoulder pulling her close to whisper in her ear. "I'm the last person to give relationship advice, but I watched the whole interaction between the two of you, even before the argument." April laughed when Candice dropped her head in shame. "You're not fooling anyone. I've seen you with guys that you felt nothing for. You wouldn't give them the energy of a fight. Jason has you all twisted up and confused. Ask yourself why. You may not know how you can feel something for someone so soon, but if I were you, I wouldn't turn my back on it just because I don't understand it."

Candice looked at April then at Jason, who had been stopped across the yard by Tim and felt like a fool. Maybe she'd over reacted. Gradually making her way toward him, Candice considered what she was going to say. Half way to him, he saw her coming. Stopping his conversation, he stared at her, wondering what her next move was going to be. The look on his face stole her nerve and she turned toward the house instead.

She'd never felt so foolish in all her life and didn't want to face anyone. *Find your purse and go.* She heard the backdoor slide open and shut. She kept right on looking for her purse, set to ignore whatever April had to say. When she turned and saw Paul's big looming figure, she nearly passed out.

"Let's talk." He issued the command without as much as a look in her direction.

In the short time they'd known each other, she'd come to recognize the 'this is not up for discussion' tone of his voice and plopped down on the nearest sofa, getting comfortable for what would surely be a long lecture. Sometimes, she was glad she'd finally met her father and forced him to introduce her to her brothers. Other times, she wasn't so glad.

"What's up with you?"

"Nothing." She rolled her eyes, obviously annoyed.

"You, of all people, know how much time and effort Tim and I put into building a relationship with Jason, so that when he got out of jail he would have a bond with us. In less than an hour, you've gone from pleasant host to almost cursing him out. So, please don't belittle my intelligence by saying nothing is up. Obviously, something is going on. Now speak."

"You're just going to take his side." Candice jumped up pointing her finger in Paul's face. "He was rude and obnoxious. He insulted me and you're going to back him instead of me." She marched across the room—where her purse had magically appeared—picked it up and marched toward the door.

Paul was up on his feet following behind her. "Can you be an adult for one second?"

She spun on him, jabbing a finger to his chest. "I am so sick and tired of you always bossing me around." She poked his chest with each word, finally giving in to the hurt his judgment always caused. "Maybe you should call up our deadbeat father and force him to be a part of my life, so you don't have to be bothered." Her chest heaved as she gave way to the tears. "What you need to work on is being my brother, because clearly you haven't read the job description. Every other one I know would be up in whatever man's face who dared to disrespect his sister. Here you are coming down on me. I know Jason means a lot to you, but damn, can I get some sympathy?" She stormed out of the house, slamming the door so hard the house shook.

The walk to her car was a torrential downpour of emotions. She wanted to curl up in a corner and die of embarrassment. She was two for two in the overreacting category. She sat in her car—head resting on the steering wheel—taking slow deep breaths to rein in her raging emotions. She'd never felt so out of control in all her life.

Growing up without a father and barely having two nickels to rub together were things she couldn't control, but her feelings and how she let people affect her, she could handle. *Never let them see you sweat* was her mother's motto, and it was drummed into Candice's head at a young age. From being bullied to being teased to feeling left out on Father's Day, *never let them see you sweat* was her mother's answer to everything. Adopting the phrase for herself, Candice mastered the art of being emotionally detached. Jason had come along, and all her practice was for naught. If there was ever a day she needed her mother, that day was it.

# 8

It was cold that morning, but Candice didn't let that stop her. Her friend had called, and she showed up. April had been more loyal to her than her own flesh and blood, so when April called, Candice answered. She wiggled her hands into her leather gloves, tugged her coat tighter, and exited the warmth of her car. Cars were scattered around the parking lot, but she didn't pay them any mind. She was too concerned about why April had summoned her to the church so early.

The lights were low and music hummed softly throughout the sanctuary. Candice had never seen it in such an intimate setting. She tiptoed to the front, as if her steps would distract those in prayer. She deposited her coat, gloves, and purse at her usual seat and then stood next to April, who was kneeling at the altar. The soft light illuminated her presence and made her feel like God had shined a spot light on her. She fidgeted. She'd been to the altar dozens of times, but something felt different this time. It was almost frightening. She motioned to tap April on the shoulder, but she seemed to be in some kind of trance, staring up into the lights like she was seeing something no else could. Candice opted to kneel next to her and wait.

With her head thrown back, gazing at the ceiling, she contemplated. What could she say to God? Didn't He already know everything? Could she confess her truths? That she was still hurting from the rejection of her father and now her mother's actions were reigniting that pain. Or, that she always felt like an outsider and worried that her brothers wished she'd never found them. Most of all, she was tired of being alone, in her apartment alone, eating her meals alone, and feeling alone. No, she couldn't talk to Him about that. The pain of those topics was too excruciating to deal with. Instead, she allowed the tears collecting in her eyes to trickle out the corners.

Finally, April turned to her. "That's what it's all about." She reached down and intertwined their fingers. "Letting Him touch you and you touching Him; it's called relationship. In relationships, you don't have to be tough. You can cry and let Him know that you hurt."

Candice's head snapped to April in shock. Had she just read her mind? Yes, she hurt, but that was for her and her alone to know.

"In relationship, you have to be honest with each other. Now, tell Him what's wrong. Yes, He's all-knowing and all-seeing, but for you to open your mouth and tell Him your sorrows shows Him that you believe in Him and you put your trust in Him. He's listening."

The gut-wrenching sobs that ensued cracked the still atmosphere of the sanctuary. No matter how off-putting the sound, her sobs seemed right in place. She leaned forward, resting her face on the plush carpet, and gave in. Her tears spoke the words her mouth had been taught to never utter. Apparently, God spoke that language.

Candice sucked in a deep breath and held it, trying to stave off her tears, so she could talk to God. The more she thought about what she wanted to say, the more the tears fell. It was pointless. She opened her mouth to speak and the shaky rasp of her voice sounded pathetic even to her. April slid her arm around Candice's waist, becoming the strength she needed.

"God, please forgive me for my sins. I've done a lot of foul things, embarrassing things, but if You could find it in Your heart to forgive me, I'd appreciate it."

"I hate to interrupt, but He doesn't want the same old rehearsed prayer you say every day before you go to bed. He wants to hear your heart."

Candice turned to April and the tears swelled in her eyes even thicker.

"That thought right there, the one that hurts you so much I can see it on your face. That's what He wants you to give to Him."

Candice tried to pull away, solely because running away was what she was used to doing. April's arm cemented around her waist gave her the excuse she needed to stay.

"Tell Him." The soft-spoken command was the key to open her mouth.

"God, You say that You love me and that You're always there, but why do I feel so alone?" Her voice cracked, and April tightened her grip. "I know I have family and friends who love me, but how do I let that be enough? The one person that should be here, that I need more than anything, abandoned me. How can a father do that? How can you allow Him to do that?"

Her tears silently flowed. The only sounds were April's soft-spoken pleas to Jesus.

"Because of him, I always feel unworthy, unloved, and I'm constantly waiting for the next person to leave me. I'm no one's main priority. Even my own mother found it easy to set me aside. What is it about me that is so unlovable? Is it my attitude, the way I talk, the way I look, my clothes, my hair, personality? Whatever it is, can You help me change it?" She didn't think she could cry any harder, but she proved herself wrong.

April collected Candice into her arms. "That's where you are wrong. It is all of those things that make you lovable. There is nothing I can do or say to make you see all the love surrounding you. I hate your father for causing you this kind of pain. I would say you should forget about him and never utter his name again, but maybe you should go see him. You've never said these things to me, so I know you've never said them to him. You may not get answers, but you can get some things off your chest. Or, at least cuss him out real good. I'd be happy to help."

Candice chuckled in spite of herself. April was always quick to cuss someone out. She rested her head on April's shoulder, and April kissed the top of it.

"You know I love you, right? You are a priority for me. I'd move heaven and earth for you, just like I would for my husband and daughter. I know, without a doubt, you have two brothers that would do the same."

Candice took a moment to enjoy the comforting presence of her only friend. This April was a lot more concerned about others than the April she used to be. Candice was still amazed at how she'd changed.

"I'm sorry. I didn't expect that," Candice said, finally pulling away and dabbing the moisture on her cheeks.

"No need to apologize."

"So, what's up? What did you need me to help you with?"

The look on April's face said it all.

"Got it…this is why you called me down here."

"Don't you feel better?"

"My nose is stuffy, head is throbbing, and eyes puffy, but yes I feel better. Thank you."

April sighed and shook her head. "Don't thank me yet. Let's go to my office and figure out how you can make things right with Jason."

"You know what?" Candice hurried to her feet.

Once April got her in the office, there would be no holding back. This new April had a way of getting people to open up and share their deepest secrets.

Candice couldn't have that. "I think all it's going to take is a sincere apology and I'll be forgiven."

"Well, is forgiveness all you want, or do you want the man?"

Candice couldn't help the giggle that bubbled out. She grabbed a few tissues from the box under the first pew and changed the subject. "Let me get out of here. Mother Sable asked me to pick her up this morning." Candice smiled at April's responding glare and walked away.

"Make sure you apologize to Paul, too."

*Yeah, when hell freezes over.*

She walked out of the sanctuary and was standing face to face with Ben. She was surprised he had the nerve to show his face after he tried to manhandle her. She took a deep breath, steeling herself for the confrontation and tried to step around him. He blocked her path. She shuffled to the other side and he did it again. She glared up at him, hoping her face hid the terror pounding through her. There was no one there to protect her, and the look on his face said he wanted retribution for Cole embarrassing him.

He stepped closer and her head snapped back to maintain eye contact. She placed a hand on his muscled chest to halt his forward movement. His eyes dropped to her hand and slowly returned to hers with such vehemence she nearly choked on the fear that swelled in her throat.

"Careful, a simple touch can get you escorted from the church and slammed against a car." His menacing snarl stole her nerve and her eyes dropped to ground. He shouldered past her, knocking her off balance, but she didn't dare say anything.

The soft thump of the door closing helped her lungs to relax. He was gone, and she could breathe freely. She rushed out to her car, clutching a shaky hand to her erratic-beating heart. The look on his face and the acid in his voice had her fumbling with her keys; she was so terrified. Finally unlocking the door, she hopped inside the protection of her car and instantly locked herself in. Feeling a modicum of safety, she calmed down and steered her mind back to picking up Mother Sable.

Mother Sable lived in a neighborhood that had seen better days. The more Candice looked around, she realized Mother Sable didn't live too far from Jason. Just that one visit to his mother's house when he first got out and now the path to him was etched in her brain. She gripped the steering wheel a little tighter to keep from making a detour to see him. By the time she arrived at Mother Sable's, her fingertips were tingling from the pressure.

She crept up the walkway—eyes searching for the pesky cat that always jumped out to scare her—and pressed the doorbell.

"Good morning, how can I help you?" The deep baritone answering the door was a surprise, but what was even more shocking was the perusal his eyes took along the length of her and the blatant licking of his lips.

"Y-yes," Candice stammered, trying to regain her composure. "I'm here to pick up Mother Sable for church."

"Really?" His head cocked to the side, pondering something, and as if he'd figured it out a smile spread across his face. "Please come in."

She hesitated, not really knowing who this man was or what he was capable of. It was her turn to cock her head to the side and peruse him. Her momma didn't raise a fool. She was just about to decline his offer when Mother Sable called out to her from somewhere in the house.

"Candice, get on in here and get something to eat." Since she'd skipped out on the barbeque and was too consumed with thoughts of Jason to eat, her stomach took over and moved her feet forward. Mystery man shut the door and followed behind her.

The kitchen table was covered with entirely too much food for the three of them. Candice looked around to see if there was anyone else in the house. Mystery man stepped around her and pulled out her chair.

"I'm sorry about this."

"About what exactly," she asked with a raised brow.

"I'm Dewayne." He extended his hand in greeting. "If I know my grandmother, I'm pretty sure she's mentioned me."

56

Candice's eyes widened as she realized who he was. She shook his extended hand. "It's nice to finally meet the man who is man enough to remind me of what a woman's role is supposed to be and fix it to where I don't have to be so smart all the time." She waved off his apologetic smile and took a seat.

"Well, it's nice to meet the woman with good childbearing hips who knows how to treat a man and can *tame* my wild ways."

"Aww," Candice clutched her hands to her chest. "That's nicest thing she's ever said about me." They shared a laugh until he suddenly sobered.

"Seriously though, I want to apologize." He waved his hand toward the stove.

Candice looked around, noticing Mother Sable was nowhere to be seen.

"It looks as if meddling Ma Dear—is what we call her—has orchestrated our first date."

"Well," Candice grabbed an empty plate and started scooping grits onto it. "Since she's gone through the trouble, let's not waste all this food."

"I like the way you think."

They ate, talked, and laughed so much Candice hadn't noticed the time. It wasn't until Mother Sable suddenly appeared in the doorway, clutching her handbag, that Candice checked the clock. They'd missed Sunday school and morning worship was due to start in ten minutes.

"I'm sorry." Candice stood and motioned toward Mother Sable. "But, I have to go." He stood and clasped her hand. She knew what was coming before the words left his mouth.

"I'd really like to see you again."

The conversation was good. He was good looking. Seeing him again would definitely be worth her time. She hated that her mother's declaration had her examining whether he'd be suitable as a father. *Desperate much?*

Her mind flashed to Ben and Vince. Her life was definitely complicated enough without adding another man to the mix. Her eyes dropped to their joined hands and she searched for even a fraction of the zing she'd felt when Jason touched her.

57

Dewayne touched a finger to her chin to lift her eyes to his just as Jason had done the night before. She couldn't help the comparison.

"If I'd known how perfect you were, I would've let her set us up a long time ago."

"Dewayne…" His words were a bit overwhelming for a first meeting. She didn't quite know how to accept them. "I'm sorry, but at this point in my life, friendship is the best I can offer."

"Ouch, friend-zoned on the first date." He clucked and she apologized. "I'll take it. Put your number in my phone and maybe we can hang out this weekend."

Candice hesitated. *There's nothing wrong with a new friend.* She grabbed his extended phone and entered her number.

# 9

It seemed like she was just living from Sunday to Sunday, avoiding Vince through the week, hoping to see Jason on Sunday, and repeat. Saturday was her only day of peace, and thoughts of Jason had tried to steal that, too. The midweek struggle was definitely a hump to get over, especially since Jason had now taken to invading her dreams. She'd already determined that Friday was going to be a mental health day. She pledged to burn eight hours of the sick leave she'd been stockpiling. The plan was to pamper herself, hair, nails, massage, and then nap until Sunday. First, she had to get through Wednesday and the emergency meeting Vince had just called her to.

The caress of Vince's eyes touched Candice from her toes to her lips. The smile turning up the corners of his mouth revealed his true motive for the meeting. She returned a smile, hoping it was cordial and not reflecting the interest that was in his.

*He's not a bad consolation prize.... Consolation...ugh!* That certainly redirected the corners of her lips. She deserved better than settling. The question was, how could she obtain better? She brushed past Vince into his office, trying to maintain an impassive expression.

Vince had kept a professional distance at work since their *business meeting*, but a night hadn't passed where he wasn't ringing her cell phone. He inhaled her scent as she walked past, and she spun back around, disbelieving his nerve. The male hunger that greeted her made her heart sink into her stomach. The soft click of the door closing could've been heard on the moon; the world had gone that silent. Predator to prey, he stalked toward her and without request or invitation, pulled her into his arms.

"Vince, we're at work," was all she managed to utter before his hand slipped behind her head, locking her lips to his.

"Mmm," Vince moaned through the lingering pecks of her lips. "Sorry, but you can't give a brother a sample and then cut him off." He released her and stepped behind his desk. "Are you done ignoring me, or are we going to keep playing this game?"

59

"Vince, you're my boss…"

"And if you quit ignoring my phone calls, this doesn't have to happen at work."

"It shouldn't be happening at all."

"Look." He leaned forward, eyes boring into her with such intensity that she had no choice but to quietly listen. "I've been feeling you for a while, and dinner the other night just confirmed what I've always suspected. We're good together. So, please answer when I call tonight."

He smiled at her barely perceptible nod and she shakily descended into one of the chairs in front of his desk.

"Now, Ms. Matthews, if you care to pick up the files you dropped by the door, we could start our meeting."

Candice jumped to her feet and rushed toward her discarded papers. Her cheeks warmed with embarrassment. It was obvious he assumed she dropped the files because she was flustered. He'd simply caught her off guard. There wasn't a noticeable spark of chemistry. He didn't give her butterflies or make her heart skip beats. She did like the way he kissed though.

*Sex…or the lack thereof.* That had to be the only explanation for liking and allowing his kiss. She'd gone from a healthy—overly so—sex life to abstinence. Yes, that had to be what it was. She was going through withdrawals.

"Just as we discussed at dinner the other night," Candice cleared her throat, hoping the awkwardness would flee with the phlegm. "As long as there is oxygen in your lungs, there is life in your body. Our clients should be able to enjoy that life to the fullest." She passed a folder to Vince. "That being said, I've decided to focus on only one of the programs. I don't want to overwhelm the board."

"Smart move." He flipped open the folder and drug his eyes from Candice's lips and back to business.

"Life for our clients can be so much more than TV, knitting circles, and naps. They have decades of knowledge and experience that's wasting away within the four walls of Morning Side. I propose that, instead of waiting for volunteers to come here, let our clients become volunteers. They can host reading time at daycares and libraries. High schools teach about U.S. History, why not a visit from someone who lived through it? We don't have a garden. Let them volunteer at a nursery." Candice spent an hour expounding on her proposal. She laid out operating expenses and logistics that couldn't be refuted. At the end, Vince nodded his head in approval, but Candice knew what she was up against. Vince was the roadblock that everyone blamed for keeping Morning Side in a rut, but the board of directors called the shots behind the scenes— operating on a meager budget and still trying to line their pockets.

"Like I said, I can't promise anything. But, I'm impressed. There is a board meeting in the morning. I'm allotted thirty minutes to address facility needs. I'll give you ten. Hit your key points and hit them fast."

"Will do." She smiled at the possibility of actually making a difference. Many had tried, and Vince had shot down their hopes without a second thought. So what, she had used his attraction to her to get that far. Women had used far worse, and she wasn't going to feel guilty.

She stood, packing up her belongings, and felt Vince glide up beside her. She backed away from him shaking her head. "I said I'd answer your call. Now, let me get back to work."

She turned on her heels and exited his office. She scolded herself for the extra sway in her hips, but couldn't help it. His interest reminded her that she was still a sexy woman, a sexy woman who hadn't had the attention or affection of a man in a long time.

She stepped out of Vince's office and was greeted by Heather, smiling like she had a secret. "How was your meeting?"

"Productive." Candice stood up a bit taller and let her facial expression warn Heather to cancel her train of thought before her mouth got her into something she wasn't ready for.

"I'm sure it was." Her knowing smirk was like nails scraping on a chalkboard. Candice should've walked away before the irritation got to her, but it was easier said than done.

"What is that supposed to mean?" Candice sucked air through her teeth. The hood girl in her was scratching to get out. If Heather wasn't careful with her implications, she'd get a taste of the way Candice was brought up.

"Nothing. I'm just saying it must be nice to have private meetings with the boss."

61

"Unlike those after hour meetings you've had with every man up in here except for the boss, this was a business meeting." Candice stepped into Heather's face, her sweet smile opposing the words coming out of her mouth. "I have the wrong reproductive organ to turn a blind eye to the woman you really are. Come for me again with the nice-nasty nonsense and you'll regret it."

Heat flared into Heather's cheeks, but Candice couldn't care less. She walked off with a little extra bounce in her step. She was comfortable in her cubicle before she considered the repercussions of having an altercation with Heather. It was time to tread lightly.

As mad as Candice was, Heather had actually done her a favor. Her comments gave Candice the excuse she needed to convince Vince that an office romance was too risky. Neither of them needed the rumors, but to be on the safe side, she'd wait until after her meeting with the board. *Until then, absolutely no more kissing.* She shut down her conscience and picked up her buzzing cell phone. She looked at the text message and rolled her eyes

*Dewayne: dinner tonight? Just friends…*

She chortled at the ridiculousness of her situation. Three men that any other woman would probably fall head over heels for and she didn't want any of them.

*Tonight's not good…honestly don't know if any night will be.*

She tossed her cell into her purse and allowed her mind a reprimand-free moment of Jason. Her mind conjured up his long thick cornrows, looking like he hadn't had a haircut in the ten years he'd been locked up. Usually, the look was too thuggish for her taste, but combined with the body of fantasies, she couldn't resist. Just the thought of him had her reaching for the water bottle on her desk. She had to have him. Work be damned, she would have him and there was no time like the present to figure out how. Grabbing a note pad and pen, she set her mind on coming up with a plan to get his attention. Forty-five minutes later, all she'd come up with was, *apologize.*

Candice dropped her pen and picked up her glass of wine as she eyed her ringing cell phone. She'd been sitting at the kitchen table for the

last hour and a half obsessing over her brief presentation to the board. A distraction was welcomed, but one from Vince she could've done without. As promised, she answered.

"Hey." She followed that one word up with a gulp of wine and waited for him to say what was on his mind.

"Damn," he groaned. "If I'd never seen you, I'd want you just off the sound of your voice."

Amused, her lips twitched to keep from engaging him. The last thing he needed was encouragement.

"When can I take you out again?"

"Hmm…"

"Don't act like you didn't enjoy yourself. You can't fake that type of laughter."

"You're not used to having to work this hard, are you?"

"When two people share a sexual attraction, it shouldn't be hard."

"Sexual attraction?" She guffawed, "So, that's what you're about, trying to get the panties?"

"Well, yeah…"

Candice spewed out her wine and covered the phone to muffle her coughing.

"Isn't that the goal of any relationship, to connect on a physical level?"

"A goal? No. Connecting on a physical level is not something you put on your to-do list to achieve. It's a reaction. It's the basic law of cause and effect. Simplistically, you've done something, and it is the effect of what you've done. Physical connection is the result of being there for her, loving her, rubbing her feet after a long day, putting her pleasure before your own. I bet you know nothing about that."

The line was silent.

She sipped her wine and guffawed. "You men and your damned trying to get the draws…"

"Give me a chance and I'll show you how much I know about that."

"Good night, Vince." She smiled at his responding groan.

"Good night, Candy."

63

Candice hung up the phone. Her own words were ringing back at her. She couldn't make a plan to get Jason. She had to follow her own advice, be there for him, and things would happen naturally. She grabbed her purse and keys and was out the door before she could change her mind.

# 10

It was a little after nine in the evening and Candice stood on the porch wondering what had possessed her to get up and drive to his house. It had been weeks since she'd told April she would apologize. She just kept losing her nerve. She was so amped and motivated at home, but standing on his porch, she'd chickened out again. He didn't live in the best of neighborhoods. Standing out there alone probably wasn't the safest of options, but she couldn't bring herself to knock on the door.

*I should just go.* She took three steps toward her car and stopped. If she left, she'd never come back. Just as she turned back around the front door creaked open.

Yvonne stood in the doorway wearing a hair scarf, bath robe, and a look on her face that made Candice regret coming so late. "What's wrong with you out here pacing on my porch? You got my neighbors calling me all hysterical and ready to call the cops."

"I'm sorry for stopping by so late." Candice paused to calm her stammering voice and summon the courage she had before hopping in the car. "But, is Jason home?"

"You're Paul and Tim's sister?"

"Yes. I was here for the barbeque when Jason came home."

Not saying another word, Yvonne stepped aside, allowing Candice to enter. Escorting her to Jason's room, Yvonne couldn't help but remember similar occurrences when Jason was in high school. He'd be in his room sound asleep and some young girl from the neighborhood would come knocking on her door. Her reaction was a little different. Back then she'd ask them, *"Do your parents know you're out this late?"* Then warn them, *"If you don't take your little fast tail home and go to sleep, I'm going to call your momma."* Her son was always the lady's man, and it looked like it hadn't changed.

"He's been locked in this room for days. I can barely get him to come out and eat. If he doesn't answer, just go in. The company will do him some good."

She waited until Yvonne walked away and then knocked. The slight rap on the door garnered no response. Just walking in was going to take nerve she wasn't sure she had. He could still be mad at her. She could be the last person he wanted to see, but the thought of him hiding in his room day after day made her grip the knob. Little by little, she turned the door knob, pushed the door open, and peeked inside.

The sight of him motionless on the bed stole her breath. His smooth, chocolate bare back caught her eye and set her feet in motion. Candice kneeled on the side of the bed, trying to decide whether she should shake him or call his name to wake him. She lifted her hand to tap his back, but dropped it. *I should go.*

The words ran through her mind, but as nervous as she was she couldn't get her feet to move. She'd come too far to turn back. "Jason," she whispered, tapping him in the middle of his back. If her voice didn't wake him, the butterflies migrating in her stomach surely would.

Recognizing the voice, Jason held his breath and his pulse quickened. He'd been wide awake and assumed it was his mother knocking…again, to ask more questions…again, about why he'd been in a foul mood the past few weeks. He lay real still, hoping she'd think he was sleep and leave him alone.

He rolled over in a state of disbelief. The wall he'd erected over his emotions threatened to crumble at the sight of her smile. He gave one of his own and, on its own accord, his hand reached out and caressed her cheek.

The sheets slipped down his bare chest. Candice closed her eyes and took a deep breath to ward off the thoughts that assailed her. *Flawless! Simply perfection!* She balled her fist to keep from touching him. From day one, she'd imagined what he looked like without a shirt. The reality was better than anything her imagination came up with. *Say what you came to say.*

She had to give herself a pep talk. Her hands burned with the need to feel all that chocolate-covered muscle against her palms. That wouldn't end well for either of them. *Well, it would probably end fabulously, but…* She blushed at her train of thought and rushed herself to get to the point of her visit.

"Jason." Her voice wavered as she spoke and she paused to gain more confidence. "I overreacted, and I'm sorry."

"No, I'm sorry. I said some harsh things. Who am I to judge anyone?" Jason laughed. "You've been really nice. Not once have you treated me like an ex-con. I appreciate that."

"You don't need to apologize…" Her eyes trailed down his gleaming torso and she caught herself before they traveled too far. She jumped to her feet, fumbling with the strap of her purse. "So, um…" She looked around his room at any and everything just to keep her eyes off of him. "I guess I better get going. It was good seeing you again."

Jason leaned forward and gripped her arm before she could leave. Her eyes dropped to their connected skin and then roamed to the scrap of blanket barely covering his lap.

"Don't leave." His smile had her inching toward the bed, cheesing in return. "It would be nice to have conversation with someone other than my mom."

"So, you weren't sleep?

He laughed and scooted over to make room for her in his bed. "Nah, I thought you were my mom. Don't get me wrong, I love her, but I have to get my own place soon."

"I have a spare room. You could move in with me." *Girl, what are you doing? You can't live with this man.*

She sat tensely on the edge of the bed, waiting for his response. Any minute, he'd laugh at her outburst or kick her out of his house. She was sure of it. She sucked in a deep breath, releasing it slowly, preparing to take her words back until his hand stroked her arm. *Oh my God!*

The voice screaming for her to get off that bed, retract her statement, and retreat back to her apartment was getting softer by the second. Just a simple touch of his hand had her entire arm tingling. Him being under her roof, feet from her bed, would try what little faith she had. The fact that his naked torso had her glued to a spot her conscience told her to flee should've been warning enough.

"You'd let me live with you, even after I was so rude the other day?"

"Of course." *No, no! No, you won't!*

"You're not afraid to live with someone like me." His head bowed in shame. Candice didn't hesitate to touch the tips of her fingers to his chin and lift his head.

"You're the most harmless person I know."

"How can you be so sure?"

"Because I know you." She let her eyes say the words she'd been holding in far too long.

"Thank you for saying that." He smiled, trying to brighten the mood, but Candice could see the pain in his eyes. "I'd insist on paying rent. I'm not looking for a free ride." He scooted to the back of the bed and leaned against the wall. Candice unclasped her shoes and followed his lead. "Why is it so easy to talk to you? Feels like I've known you my entire life."

Their eyes connected and there it was again, the undeniable crackle of chemistry, searing and solidifying her desire to have him in her life. Candice nervously threw off thoughts of naked bodies between tousled sheets and tried to get comfortable as possible without touching him. She took a deep breath and focused on casual conversation.

"Have you had any luck finding a job? I don't mind footing the bill until you find something. I can only imagine it has to be hard."

"It would be hard if I didn't have your brothers backing me. I mentioned to them when they first joined the prison ministry that I wanted to do something to help young people stay out of the hellhole I was in. They never let me lose sight of that. They encouraged me to make a business plan and focus on the type of services I wanted to offer. They even set some things in motion to get me started. They wrote a few grants and got my salary and all expenses paid for six years. They even got funding for me to hire two youth leaders and a social worker. Then, after the six years, the investors will visit and assess whether the center is worth keeping around."

"Wow!" Impressed was an understatement. "When do you get started?"

"A few months, maybe... I could've used the building they selected as is and opened right away, but there are certain amenities that I want the kids to have. I want this to be a safe place for them to relax after school, which means we have to install an alarm system and cameras.

68

There has to be a study hall with reference books for school work. An entertainment room is a must, as well as a kitchen. Then, I still have to hire the social worker and I want them to have enough time to set up a program that will minister and provide resources for economic advancement. I met with a few a couple days ago. When I asked what their motivation was for working in this field they said, *"I feel sorry for these kids and I want to help."* I don't want somebody to feel sorry for them. The kids don't need it. What they need is someone who can say, *your current situation doesn't have to hold you back. I've been where you are and I made it out. Let me show you how you can, too.* Does that sound crazy?"

"Not at all. Social services are full of people feeling sorry and is severely lacking in people making a difference. So, how does someone go about getting an interview?" Candice was impressed with his enthusiasm for giving back to his community. His kindness mingled with his passion and ruggedness further ignited her desire for him. It took all her willpower to hide it.

"I have been searching through one of those online job databases, but if you know someone who is looking for a job, let me know."

"I am." *Are you…really?* She continued to shock herself with the words coming out of her mouth "You are under no obligation, because I'm your business partners' sister, but I would love to work with you. I don't know if my brothers told you, but I'm a social worker. I interned at a place that sounds similar to yours and I loved it. Their funding wouldn't allow them to hire me, so I took a job at a convalescent home and I hate it."

Jason chuckled to himself. Suddenly the grant Paul and Tim wrote for the social worker's salary made sense. He had questioned them as to why the pay was so high. They claimed that the higher the pay, the more qualified the applicants would be, but now he was sure it was because of Candice. "So, you'd just up and quit?"

*No and especially not now.* "What you're planning sounds like something I want to be a part of."

Jokingly, he asked, "Do you think you could handle working with me?"

69

"You sure you won't get tired of me, living with me and working with me?"

"I should be asking you that question." His voice dropped and his eyes dipped.

"I'm absolutely positive." Candice allowed herself to hope he was checking her out.

"Good." His eyes slowly rose to hers, and by the time they did, she was on fire. "You have a few months to think about it. If you change your mind, there's no hard feelings."

They laughed and talked for hours, discovering they had a lot in common. They'd grown up in similar neighborhoods and both liked Italian food. Their favorite ice cream was plain ole vanilla and they both loved jogging.

Jason was so caught up in telling one of his stories, he didn't realize Candice had nodded off to sleep. He took a moment to admire her beauty. All that hair tumbling around her mesmerizing face was going to be the death of him. Now that her eyes and voice weren't bewitching him, he couldn't believe he'd agreed to move in with her. He didn't need the drama from her man. If she were his woman, he would, without a doubt, have a problem with some man renting a room from her, so there was no question that Ben would. Looking at her resting, calm, at peace, almost angelic, he knew there was no way he'd pass up the opportunity to be near her every day. He fought the urge to lean in and brush his lips across hers. *She's not mine...* He had to keep repeating it. Her lying in his bed wasn't doing anything for his attraction to her. He needed to find his own woman to restrain his craving for the one he couldn't have. Maybe it was time he broke his promise and looked up Chantel.

The next morning, Candice jumped up out of the bed, nearly knocking Jason to the floor. "Oh my God. I knew I should've gone home last night. I'm going to be late for work. I have a meeting this morning. The one time I'm given the opportunity to make some changes, and I screw it up." Frantically, she raced around the room collecting her belongings.

"Relax, it is only seven." Jason stretched and yawned, fighting off the grogginess. "What time is your meeting?"

"It's at eight thirty."

"That's plenty of time. Tell me how to get to your house. I will get you a change of clothes while you shower. Is there something in particular you want to wear?" He was the peace she needed to calm her frazzled mind. The calmness in his voice soothed her nerves.

"I have to wear business attire and all my outfits are put together, so grab anything. Make sure the shoes match. Also, there is an accordion file and briefcase by the door. Can you bring those please?"

She jotted down directions to her apartment while Jason dressed. Then, he rushed out the door. He cut a thirty-minute round-trip drive into twenty, grabbed everything she needed, and rushed back. He even had time to buy a couple dozen doughnuts for her meeting.

"Candice, hurry up it does not take that long to put on some clothes." Jason stood across the room, staring at the bathroom door, waiting for her to come out.

"Jason, I'm moving as fast as I can. Stop rushing me." The bathroom door popped open and Jason nearly passed out. Candice strutted across the room wearing a button-down white shirt that stopped right above the hips, black, satin-lace panties and red heels. She didn't even notice him staring, but he watched her every move. The sway of her hips and the muscles flexing in her thighs virtually sent him into cardiac arrest. He held his breath as she sauntered across the room, picked up her purse, and returned to the bathroom. On auto-pilot, he floated to the bathroom door. His hand gripped the door knob, mind battling with his loins. He wanted to bust down the door and give her the ten years of sexual tension surging through him. Where would that leave them? He didn't know where he got the clarity of mind, but he let go of the door knob and backed down.

When she stepped out the bathroom again, she was fully clothed, but in his mind, she was as naked as the day she was born.

"You better go," Jason groaned from his seat on the bed. He didn't dare move a muscle or he'd lose it.

"I know." Candice skipped over to him and planted her lips on his cheek. "You are a life saver. I will call you later."

Jason balled his fist in the blanket. Her scent wafted up his nose and he clenched his jaw to keep his lips from finding out if she tasted as good as she smelled. Strawberry vanilla was going to be with him all day. She was in such a rush, she hadn't even noticed how she'd affected him.

Jason carried her bags to the car so entranced by the sway of her hips that he didn't notice the car idling across the street. He sat her bags on the passenger seat and barely got out a good bye. It wasn't until she'd driven away that he looked up and met the eyes of Satan himself.

Lamont smiled.

Jason stepped forward, determined to end the nonsense once and for all. The tip of a gun sticking out the window halted his steps.

"You're going to shoot me?" Jason's nostrils flared. After all Lamont had put him through, he was going to take the coward's way out. "Put the gun down and step to me like a man. Let's settle this once and for all. You run these streets? Then put me down and I'll run them with you." His pulse kicked up as Lamont exited the car. He tossed his weapon and coat on the seat and walked across the street. The sag in his pants was so low his stride was hindered.

"When I lay you out, you better leave me alone and stop riding my block." Jason stepped forward clenching his fist.

Without warning, Lamont rammed his fist into Jason's gut. Jason stumbled back, evading the right hook coming for his jaw. Lamont kicked his legs out from under him. "Let me show you how we do it in these streets."

He raised his foot to stomp Jason into the ground. He rolled out of the way and hopped to his feet, but Lamont was quick with it and landed a jab to his ribs. It hurt. God, it hurt, but he'd felt worse. Prison life wasn't nice, and neither were the fights he'd endured. He channeled those experiences and rose up with a jab right to Lamont's nose. It ruptured instantly, giving Jason the upper-hand. He had the physical power to put Lamont down while he was stunned, but he had ten years of payback to issue. He lowered his fist and went to work on Lamont's torso. Two, three, five more shots to the ribs. He wanted to break them; wanted Lamont in so much pain he'd feel how he felt for ten years.

"Jason!"

He heard the voice, but kept right at it. Lamont had to pay.

"Jason, stop it! You are going to kill him."

It would serve him right. He had stolen ten years of Jason's life. It was only fair for Jason to take years from his life. He gripped Lamont by the collar to hold him steady and pulled his power into one final punch to put out the lights.

"Jason!"

Water sprayed his face, shocking him back to himself before his fist could connect. Lamont crumpled to the ground as Jason stumbled back, gasping for air.

"Go in the house."

Jason looked up, finally acknowledging his mother. He looked at Lamont laid out on the grass and shook his head. He tried to be remorseful, but couldn't. Lamont got what he deserved, and Jason was happy to have been the one to give it to him. Without a word, he walked in the house and laughed at his mom spraying Lamont with the hose and yelling for him to get out of her yard.

Candice made it to work on time and knocked her presentation out of the park. The board members loved her ideas and wanted to implement the changes as early as next week. Her first thought was to call Jason, but they hadn't exchanged numbers. She thought about calling her brothers to get it, but didn't want all the questions. She called Tim to share the good news about her job and before she could even get it out she heard Jason in the background. "Is that Jason?" She tried to keep the smile out of her voice.

"It is, and I wish you'd apologize for being so rude. He was a guest in your brother's home and you—"

"Tim, give it a rest and put him on the phone."

"Look, Candy, something went down today and he doesn't need any more drama."

Her heart dropped in her stomach. She shut her eyes to the scenarios that instantly assailed her. "Can I talk to him?"

"Candy…"

The censure in his voice pissed her off. "Tim, just put him on the phone."

73

"Okay, but be nice." She smacked her lips and he quickly passed the phone to Jason before she cursed him out.

"Hello."

"Are you okay?"

"Yeah."

"What happened?"

"I really don't want to talk about it."

"Okay." She masked her hurt and moved on to the real reason for her call. "Guess what?" His somber mood dimmed her excitement. "The board loved my proposal."

"Congrats."

"I wanted to call you, but I didn't get your cell number."

Jason laughed, "I don't have one."

"Oh my goodness," Candice exclaimed. "Who doesn't have a cell phone?"

"The guy who just got out of prison and hasn't quite caught up with technology."

Candice cringed at his statement. She had to remember that there was going to be a lot of things he wasn't up to speed on. "Please forgive me. It was inconsiderate of me to say something like that. Can you give me your home number?"

He mumbled off the numbers, but wasn't sure why. He would be moving soon. He looked out the corner of his eye to see if Tim was listening, but couldn't tell. He was going to have to explain why Candice wanted his number. Was he ready to tell Tim he was considering moving in with his sister?

"Well, I should be home by 4:30, if you want to start moving your things in."

"Candice, I..." He paused, trying to find the words to discreetly relay his uneasiness. "This is—"

"A friend helping a friend..." She let that word *friend* hang out there and she hated it more by the minute.

"Yeah, but people talk."

"Let them...if I can do something to help you feel more like the incredible man you are, I'll do it. Other people's opinions be damned."

"Candice, I can't let you—"

74

"Jason, please."

The soft pout of her voice did him in. He ended the call thinking ten years in prison was going to be a cake walk compared to living under the same roof with a woman he craved with every breath in his body but couldn't have.

The rest of the day flew by. Candice busied herself making more concrete plans for the changes that were going to take place at Morning Side over the next few weeks. She was given the green light to speak with the departments that would be affected the most. By the time she finished talking to everyone, it was three in the afternoon. She packed up her things to head out a little early to stop by the mall on her way home. Before she could sneak out, Vince was standing in her cubicle, watching her with an intensity that had her fidgeting to get away.

"Hey." She smiled, trying to side step him, but he held his ground.

"Let me take you out to celebrate."

"I can't." She averted her eyes, feeling guilty for rushing off to celebrate with another man. Without Vince, she'd have no reason to celebrate.

"If not tonight, then sometime this week." He discreetly touched her elbow, drawing her attention to him. The plea in his eyes had her nodding before she could consider the ramifications. She slipped past him and stepped out as fast as her heels would allow.

The stores at the mall were crowded and lines were long, but Candice still managed to get out of there to make it home by 4:30. She wanted to get something for dinner, but didn't want Jason to have to wait for her. Deciding to skip the grocery store was the right choice, because Jason was waiting on her porch when she arrived. He stood with red roses in one hand and dinner in the other. All she thought as she embraced him was, *he is wonderful.*

"Come on in and make yourself at home." Candice urged him forward, directing him to put the bags on the dining room table.

"These are for you." He passed her the vase, which immediately went to her nose for a whiff, and she nearly melted when his lips brushed across her cheek. "Congrats on knocking your proposal out the park."

75

She couldn't help the goofy grin that spread across her face. Her responding giggle made her feel like she was back in high school. Sight of the man in front of her quickly reminded her they were not in high school and he was in fact a beautiful chocolate temptation standing in her living room, looking unquestionably delicious. Her temperature shot up and she needed to do something about it before she exploded.

"If you don't mind, I'm going to grab a quick shower. Plates are in the top right cabinet and utensils are two drawers to the left of the sink."

He didn't hear any other words after shower and barely acknowledged she left the room. Glistening wet skin covered with sudsy scented soap permeated his mind and he stood there, practically comatose, from the lack of blood flowing to his brain. The sound of the shower nearly did him in, but with all the strength he had, he turned away from it and went in to the kitchen.

After opening several cabinets, he finally found plates. He set the table for them to eat, placed the cartons of Chinese food out, and poured some drinks. By the time she came out, he was sitting at the table waiting for her. She walked into the kitchen wearing a thin silk bathrobe that graced every curve. She hadn't dried off and he could tell she didn't have a stitch of clothes on underneath. Her wet body caused her perky breast to shine through the robe.

"Candice, come sit over here." He groaned out his frustration. "We need to talk."

That phrase always meant trouble, and Candice sat quietly waiting for the other shoe to drop in her perfect day.

"If you haven't noticed, I'm really trying to live for the Lord, but that is going to be next to impossible if you keep walking around half-naked. I wanted to lose myself inside you this morning."

"You did?" Fire pulsed through every inch of her body. He wanted her. That little admission spurred all kinds of thoughts, but most importantly, she recalled April's question. Do you want the man? She most certainly did, and she'd have him.

"I haven't had a woman in ten years. What man in my position wouldn't want you?"

76

Just as quickly as he'd ignited her, he doused her. She tried not to let her disappointment show. *Of course he doesn't want me for me.*

"It can't happen." His eyes caressed her as if trying to gauge whether she'd be worth the repercussions. Without question, he knew she would be.

She snickered off the awkwardness. "Guess I should put some clothes on then."

"Please." His groaned plea was granted.

She brought him his gift when she returned. "First off, I hope you know that I'd never drag you down. I just want to help you and be there when you need a friend." She slid the box across the table to him. "This is something I want to do for you, just a friend helping a friend."

He looked down at the offered box, not sure of how he should feel or react.

"I couldn't stand not being able to reach you today. I want you to have this. I got the bill covered. Please take it."

Hesitantly, Jason accepted the phone. He didn't want to offend her by not taking it, but didn't want her to think he needed her to take care of him. "Thank you. I really appreciate this, but—"

"No *buts*. Just consider it a welcome home gift. Besides, I don't have a land line. You'll need something to conduct business." She dug into her food as she waited for his response. He peeled the protective wrap off the box, and she internally celebrated the small victory.

"Is Ben okay with this—you buying me a phone and letting me move in?"

She nearly choked on her food as a laugh bubbled up out of her. "Ben isn't a factor. He never was. We went on one-and-a-half horrible dates. I don't think they could even be considered dates. So, his reaction to us sitting together was totally uncalled for."

"Dang, I'm really sorry. That makes my actions at the barbeque even worse."

"Well, I should've just explained, instead of getting all pissy."

"Please forgive me."

"There's nothing to forgive. Now finish your food before you make me feel like a pig for finishing before you."

Vince's face kept popping in her mind. Maybe she should clear the air about him. What would Jason think? Would he think she was a horrible person for using Vince?

"What's wrong? And don't say *nothing*. Your entire mood just shifted."

"Ben isn't a factor, but there is someone who is. Well, not really… At least not where it matters, in my heart."

"You really don't have to explain yourself to me."

"Yes, I do." He didn't know it yet, but they were going to be together. She didn't want the issue of Vince to pop up and ruin things. "Please don't think the worst of me. Now that I'm trying to formulate the words, it was a horrible thing to do."

"Like I said, you don't have to…"

"He's my boss." Those words hung in the sudden silence, dangling between them.

Jason's piercing eyes stung her and she fought not to tremble under their intensity.

Candice swallowed the lump in her throat and forced herself to continue. "He asked me out under the facade of a business meeting. He offered me an opportunity to present my ideas, and I couldn't just walk away. He didn't hide his attraction to me and I kind of just went with the flow."

"So, why are we here celebrating a victory you didn't rightfully earn? You are a woman of God. You don't have to manipulate the system or sleep your way to the top. Promotion comes from God."

"I wasn't trying to sleep my way to the top. I just seized an opportunity to make life better for my clients."

"I know you weren't and I'm sorry for choosing words that offended you. But, before making the decision to play someone's emotions, had you prayed and asked God to open a window of opportunity?"

Candice was up and stomping from the room, causing him to yell the last few words to her back. Jason braced for the slamming door, and she didn't disappoint.

He finished eating his food, hoping she'd calm down and see that he was right. He washed the few dishes and sat on the couch. He was just about to give up hope when he heard her bedroom door click open.

"You're still here."

"Where else would I go? I live here, right?" He didn't know how to interpret her shock at seeing him. He could practically see the wheels turning in her mind as she contemplated his question. He held his breath, hoping that his unfiltered mouth hadn't ruined things again.

"Yes."

Her mumbled response was music to his ears.

She stood there like she wanted to say more, but only watched him and then walked away.

Tim popped the last fry in his mouth and dusted the residual salt onto the napkin. "I saw Mom the other day."

"My mother?"

He nodded and Candice nearly fell out her chair. She loved that her brothers had taken to her mother like their own, but hearing the news actually hurt.

"She said you haven't been to visit in a while."

Candice's jaw nearly hit the floor. "Wow...that woman."

"What's going on? Y'all are always so tight."

"She didn't tell you she blocked me from visiting?"

"What?" Tim snickered at her terse nod and raised brow. "Why?"

She didn't want to give him all the details. To be honest, she was a little embarrassed. Was she pathetic to the point her mother had to issue an ultimatum to get her on the right track? "She thinks I'm spending too much time visiting her, wasting my life so to speak." She tried to hide the hurt, but when he reached across the table and grabbed her hand, she knew she'd failed. "It's okay. I'm glad someone is visiting. How is she?"

"She looks good. The doctor said there's an end in sight. Just a couple more weeks of steady blood sugar and then she could continue her rehab at home."

She couldn't stop the few tears trickling down her cheeks. She dabbed them with the napkin and lifted her eyes heavenward. How long had they been praying? *Thank you, Jesus.* She mouthed and shut her eyes to absorb the victory of Tim's statement. Her mom was making progress and possibly heading home.

"Thank you," she said, smiling, and Tim squeezed her hand.

"God works everything out in due time. We just have to learn to wait."

"Oh Lord, not the *W* word." She gagged in mock disgust and Tim laughed. How many times had he told her to wait on God to work it out? If she'd listened, she would've been spared months of stress. He laughed at her again and she tossed a napkin in his face. "I didn't invite you to lunch to be laughed at. I need to talk to you."

She adjusted her seat and scooted a little closer, as if the people at the next table even cared what she was about to say. "This is between me, you, and Paul. I know you guys will disapprove, but let me hear it, not Jason."

With a raised brow, Tim leaned forward.

"Well, I was really rude to Jason the other day."

"You think?"

She knocked the smirk off his face with a look she'd received millions of times from her mother. "I apologized, and we've actually become friends. He got to talking about his living situation and felt that moving out would be best for him."

"He still sees himself as a burden." Tim rested back against his chair, wondering how to make Jason see that he's not a problem. "Don't worry, I'll talk to him. Yvonne loves having—"

"He moved in with me." She saw the words stall in his mouth and in one—two—three seconds, the flaring of his nostrils. If the calm and collected brother was that incensed that it showed, then the hot-headed brother was going to be nuclear. "I just want to help him."

"Help him, but hurt your reputation in the process?"

"Well, it wasn't much to begin with."

"Candice…"

She halted his thought with a raised hand. "It's not like we will be sleeping together. I have the spare bedroom."

His responding chuckle lacked humor, and she started second-guessing her decision to tell him anything.

"Let's be real." His searing gaze captured her eyes.

She tried her best to sit still and stand her ground.

"You want to sleep with him." It was Tim's turn to silence her objection with a waved hand. "You do. Deny it to someone you have half a shot of convincing. You want to sleep with him and you are giving the devil room to make it happen."

"Well…" she cleared her throat and took a sip of water. What I want doesn't matter. He's not interested."

81

"He's a man, hasn't had sex in ten years, and you're a beautiful woman. He is interested."

His gaze was unwavering, and despite all her efforts, she shrank beneath it.

"I don't see this ending well."

"Thanks for having faith in me."

"Candy, it's not about having faith in you. It's about you setting yourself up for failure. When two people are attracted to each other and are trying to not have sex, living together is a mistake."

"He is not attracted to me like that and…" She rolled her eyes at Tim's chuckling. "I do have self-control. I'm not going to hop in his bed just because I find him attractive."

"Candy…"

"Like I said, this is between you, me, and Paul. You have something to say, say it to me, not Jason."

"This man is living with my sister and you expect me to not put the fear of God in him."

"I expect you to let me live my life. I expect you to not alienate Jason, the same thing you reamed me for doing." She paused while the waitress placed the check on the table. "Tell Paul to leave him alone or our brother-sister relationship will be nonexistent."

"And you don't see your willingness to sacrifice our relationship to be with him as a red flag?" He leaned back and grabbed the check, even though she was supposed to be treating him. "Fine, we'll stay out of it." He tossed a few bills on the table and stood to his feet. Candice followed and he pressed a kiss to the crown of her head. "But remember…" He stooped for better eye contact, gripping her arms when she refused to look at him. "A hard head makes for a soft bottom."

Jason sat on the porch, a box filled with his few possessions sitting at his side. He couldn't bare the hurt expression his mother kept tossing him, so he'd retreated to the steps outside her house. He didn't know what else to say to help her understand. All she kept saying was, "You'd rather stay with some strange woman than stay with your mother."

Yes, he did. Maybe he was crazy, but living with Candice made him feel less like a cancer that had been eating away at his mother's life for ten years. He wanted her to have a life outside of him. He refused to be the cause of her being single for ten more years. He tried to explain, but she couldn't see past what she wanted, so he got up to wait for Candice outside.

Candice's car pulled up along the curb. Jason hopped up and poked his head back into the house. "Bye, Mom. I love you." He waited for a response. There was nothing. His head dropped along with his heart. He hoped she wouldn't hold it against him for too long.

The door was just about shut when he heard, "Love you, too." He perked up bit, laughing at his mom pouting like a five-year-old, but was confident she'd see things his way in the long run.

The smile that greeted him when he finished loading his things in the trunk hit him in the gut. She was, without a doubt, the most stunning woman he'd ever seen. He pushed that thought aside and offered her a smile of his own.

Her smile faltered as she pulled away from the curb, and he couldn't help but ask, "What's wrong?"

She cut her eyes toward him and then quickly back to the road. The silence stretched as he waited for a reply. He figured she didn't want to talk until she sighed and nervously fluffed the mound of hair toppled about her head.

"I had lunch with Tim today."

His brow rose with interest, which she couldn't really see, but he remained silent for her to continue.

"I told him you moved in to my spare bedroom."

"Candice." Her name was a guttural groan on his lips. She was too busy imagining other scenarios where he'd say her name the exact same way to notice he was on the verge of telling her to turn the car around and calling everything off. "You should've let me tell them."

"I'm sorry, but with my brothers, it's best to get the truth out there early. They are easy to forgive if the truth is not clouded with lies and deception."

"That's the thing." He clenched his jaw, pausing to keep his irritation from turning to rudeness. "We aren't doing anything that needs

83

forgiveness. My not going to them myself makes it seem like I have an ulterior motive."

"I'm sorry." She reached across the center console and gripped his hand, holding it for longer than intended, but hoping he saw the sincerity of her apology. "But, it really is taken care of. There is no ill will. They won't even approach you about it."

Jason nodded, but remained silent for the rest of the ride to her apartment. Sensing that he was still a bit irritated with her, she led him to his room and went to hers to give him some space. She plopped on the bed and pulled out her cell to respond to the text from April she'd been ignoring all day.

*Call your dad.*

*I'll do it right now, pray for me please.*

She sat up and adjusted her clothes and hair like he would actually be able to see her. Just like when she was a little girl, she wanted to look perfect for him. She shook her head, nervously chuckling at the silliness of her actions.

His number was still saved in her contacts, but it had been a couple years since she'd used it. She tapped his name, partly hoping a stranger answered or the number was disconnected all together. The generic greeting did nothing to assuage her nerves.

"Dad—if this is still your number—it's Candice. I…um…was kind of hoping to get together. It's been a while since we've seen each other, even longer since you've seen Paul and Tim. I know you'd like to see them. Please meet with me. I promise they'll be there. I'll even pay for your plane ticket. I know you don't like to talk on the phone, but if you could at least text me back, I'll set everything up."

She hung up the phone, nearly in tears at how pathetic she sounded. She heard the sounds coming out of her mouth, but couldn't help it. He brought out the weak side of her. Now she'd gone and promised her brothers would be there, just so he would show up. Paul would absolutely kill her if he found out.

She tossed her phone aside, choosing not to worry about it. Her dad probably wouldn't respond anyway.

Candice bustled around the kitchen. Her pumps tapped a rhythm against the linoleum floor adding to the song in her heart. She had the Sunday morning feel goods. Her week had been productive, and she felt like she was really making a difference. For the first time, she was actually anxious to get to church.

Her joy bubbled up and she danced around the kitchen singing as she prepared breakfast. In no way was she a singer, but that didn't stop her. It got so good to her that she stopped flipping pancakes, turned the spatula over, and belted out the words like she was a lead singer with the church choir. She may have stumbled over a few words, but she was getting it. Mid-verse a male voice joined her. She paused, on the verge of dying from embarrassment until she saw Jason clapping and rocking like the sexiest backup singer she'd ever seen. She laughed and passed him a serving spoon. He didn't hesitate to flip the handle up and follow her lead. They gave Israel Houghton and Tye Tribbett a run for their money.

*Your love, Your love for me,*
*Is running wild and free.*
*Your goodness and mercy taking me over.*
*Your love, Your love won't change.*
*Your promises remain,*
*stronger than sin and shame.*
*I can't outrun Your grace.*

*Everywhere I go Your grace is right there.*
*Everywhere I turn Your grace is right there.*
*Even when I fall, Your grace is right there, right there.*
*Can't run, can't hide, from Your hand on my life.*
*Your love, Your grace, will never ever stop chasing me.*
*Can't run can't hid from Your hand on my life.*
*Your love, Your grace will never ever stop chasing, chasing.*
*Can't run, can't hide, from Your hand on my life.*
*Your love, Your grace, will never ever stop chasing me.*

*Can't run, can't hide, from Your hand on my life.*
*Your love, Your grace, will never ever stop chasing, chasing.*

*Will never ever stop chasing, chasing, will never stop chasing me,*
*Will never ever stop chasing, chasing, will never ever stop*
*chasing me,*
*Chasing, chasing.*
*Will never ever stop chasing me, will never ever stop, will never*
*stop, will never ever stop chasing me.*

They laughed and mumbled over words they didn't know, nearly burning breakfast. They were having such a good time.

"Girl, you're crazy."

"Look who's talking," she laughed. "Dancing around and singing by yourself is crazy, but to join in on someone's craziness is another level of insane."

"I couldn't help it. The choir killed that song last week, had the whole church rockin'."

"You ain't lying. I almost hopped out into the aisle and cut up with my sisters-in-law and the rest of the church"

"I know. I saw you. You were gripping the back of the pew so hard, I thought you were going to tear it in half." He threw his head back laughing.

"All right, keep making fun of me and I'm going to stop feeding you."

"What? You mean this good smelling meal is for me?"

"It was, but now I don't know." She couldn't contain the smile etching across her mouth. She enjoyed his company and already hated the day he'd move out and get his own place. His presence made her realize how dull and empty her life had been before.

"Well, you know the Bible says it's better to give than to receive…"

"Oh Lord, you done went to the scriptures on me."

"Hey, whatever it takes to get you to give up the goods." Jason laughed at her sassy little grin and corresponding hand on her hip. They'd been living together for a few weeks and if there was one thing he'd

86

learned, it was that she liked to flip the meaning of his words to embarrass him. He held his breath and waited for her response.

"So, you want my goods, Jason?"

"Those goods aren't free to give, so don't even go there." He wanted to high-five himself for that comeback. Her smile dropped, and he instantly regretted it.

"Touché." She shook her head and passed him a plate. Leave it to Jason to keep her in check.

"Hey." He reached out to touch her, but she backed away. "I'm sorry."

"No, don't apologize. You're right. I need to do something about my situation." She turned toward the stove and started piling food on her plate.

*Then could I be yours?* It was on the tip of her tongue to say, but she bit down on it, forcing her mind away from the fantasy.

"It had always been my intention to drop Vince once I got the approval for my programs, but..." She turned to Jason, pointing an accusing finger. "Ever since you made me feel guilty about my actions, I'm having a hard time following through." She waited for him to finish fixing his plate and then followed him to the table. "There is no fire, spark, or even a flicker when he touches me. I don't get butterflies when I see him. I want more, and he deserves a woman who feels all those things with him." Opening up to Jason was the easiest thing she'd ever done.

"Seems like you have your mind made up. So, why is it so hard to follow through?"

"Well..." She paused—worried he'd see how selfish she could be.

"Don't start holding back now. Give it to me straight."

"Two reasons." She ticked off on her fingers. "First, I don't want to be the woman you accused me of being. If I stay with him, then I'm not a corporate gold digger." She put up a hand halting his interjection. No matter how he said it, in essence, a corporate gold digger is what he'd called her. "Secondly, and I know this sounds bad, but hurting people hurt people. I drop him. He gets upset. I get fired." She shrugged her shoulders as if her logic was simple and she had no other choice.

"First off," he copied her, ticking off on his fingers just as she had. "Gold digger is harsher than anything I intended, and I'm sorry it came off like that." His eyes softened at his sincerity, but that was all the tenderness he would give her on that topic. "Secondly, staying with him doesn't make what you did any better. Just admit you screwed up and then you can fix it. Your logic is a bit flawed." He scooped the last spoonful of eggs and grits into his mouth. Candice grabbed his plate to get him another helping, hoping the sting of his words extinguished before she returned to the table.

"You know you don't have to cook for me, right?"

"I know, just like you don't have to fold my laundry when I leave it in the dryer."

"Touché." He accepted his plate and dug in again. "Like I was saying, it's flawed, but only because you don't have to accept a bad situation because you don't want to get fired." He pushed his plate aside to grip both her hands. He leaned forward, connecting their eyes to make sure he had her full attention. "I've been reading up on employment law and sexual harassment. Apparently, things like this happen all the time. It's a big deal."

"You're right, but I wouldn't feel comfortable filing a claim knowing that I willingly played on his interest in me to advance my career." She took advantage of their joined hands, rubbing her thumbs along his palm. He didn't seem to notice.

"Yeah, but he violated the law the moment he expressed that interest to you. He's your superior and he crossed the line." He dropped her hand to rest back in his chair, but changed his mind. "While I was locked up, I learned that to beat someone who's fighting dirty you have to fight dirty yourself." He tapped the table with the tip of his index finger to drive his point home. "Make your stand. If he wants to play dirty, give him a run for his money."

Candice was so caught up in her thoughts that Jason finished his second plate before she finished her first. Was her job even worth fighting for? Yeah, she'd made one change, but so what? In the end, Morning Side Senior Center didn't cater to the demographic she wanted to work with. But, wasn't it still about helping people?

"Come on, let's go praise the Lord." Jason grabbed their empty plates, rinsed them off, and placed them in the dish washer. "I want to see you let loose and give God some praise."

"Get the key off the table and you drive. I exhausted myself slaving over the stove for you and all I get is made fun of." She patted her eyes and contorted her voice as if overcome with emotion.

"And the academy award for best lead actress in a drama goes to…"

# 13

Pacing around the cramped quarters of his room, it seemed like the walls were closing in on him. Most nights were great, but some, not so much. It hadn't been this bad since moving in with Candice. He'd thought her presence had chased the demons away. He closed his eyes and the sounds of his imprisonment came back to haunt him—the anguished sobs bouncing off the cement walls, desperate pleas for mercy from the man being violated in the cell next to him, clanking of metal doors sealing him off from the world, and the judge announcing his sentence.

He marched around, scraping his palms over the crown of his head, trying to rid his mind of the horror of it all—the threats, the fights, the filth, showering around other men, not knowing who or when they'd try to attack you. The guards were a joke—females sleeping with prisoners and males turning a blind eye to injustice. By the grace of God, he'd survived.

Jason dropped to his knees to pray the turmoil away. That didn't work, so he laid out on the floor and tried to defeat his demons with physical activity. Up and down, he lifted and lowered his body until his arms cried for mercy. Then, he rolled onto his back giving his abs the same beating.

It wasn't enough. He wanted to forget. He needed to forget, to move on with his life and be free. He slipped into sweats and a tank top and tiptoed out of the apartment, careful to not wake Candice. The last thing he wanted was for her to see him like that. He needed air, the cool breeze, blowing on his skin in the middle of the night to remind him he was in fact free. He could come and go as he pleased. The bars, the sobs, pleas, the fear—they were no more. He was free.

He stepped outside and filled his lungs with the cool air. It was beautiful out and he took the time to enjoy the colors of the sky as the sun tried to chase away the night. He could see the lingering stars. Stars gave him hope…hope that there was something, someone out there bigger than his existence.

The trot down the stairs was nothing compared to the Olympic sprint he sped into once hitting the landing. His muscles celebrated the exertion, but it did nothing to ease his mind. He ran around the block and around again until the sun brightened the edges of the sky. When he couldn't run any more, he made his way back home.

He stepped into the living room, expecting the same quiet he left it in, but Candice was there to meet him. She turned to greet him and the smile she shined on him lit the dark places he'd been running to escape.

"Good morning." Her smile increased in wattage and he couldn't help but go to her. With the intensity of a soldier, he stepped forward and instantly her heart went on alert. "What's going on?"

"Nothing." He stroked a finger down her cheek, needing the human contact more than anything. "It's just nice to get a smile so early in the morning."

"What's wrong?" She placed her hand on his chest and his heart—still beating wildly from his run—thumped against her palm. Her eyes connected with his. She no longer needed him to tell her what was wrong. His pain crept inside of her and her eyes swelled with the emotion he was fighting to contain. "It's going to be all right." Her hand slid around to his back and her other arm followed. He leaned into her embrace and, of its own accord, her head rested against his chest.

Her whispered prayers clawed at the gloom trying to consume him. The cascading darkness surrendered to her light. It was her. She was all he needed.

"Why are you so nice to me?" He pulled back to look into her eyes, hoping she had the answer to why he felt so connected to her.

Candice peered up at him, trying to find the courage to reveal her secret. Tense seconds ticked by as she searched for the words to explain everything, but in the end, all she could come up with was, "When it comes to you, I don't know any other way to be."

Something was shifting between them. He couldn't explain it, but he definitely felt it. His eyes dropped to her lips. He knew that's where he'd find the joy, peace, and strength he required. It took all the power he had to release her and back away. He had to, or he'd forget she had unresolved issues and selfishly take what he needed.

"Why are you up so early on a Saturday?"

91

"Paul couldn't get ahold of you, so he woke me up looking for you." Candice watched his every move, her heart still bleeding for him. "I think he expected you to be in my bed or something."

"Yeah, that sounds like Paul," he laughed as he plopped down on the sofa. "What did he want?"

"The guys get together once a month and play basketball."

"They've been trying to get me to join them since I got out."

"Well, today they decided to move the game to the court at your youth center. I think you should go." Candice kneeled in front of him, rejecting his refusal before it left his lips. "It looks like you've already had enough exercise this morning, but the fellowship would be great. I don't have any plans for today. You can take my car and I'll have a nice breakfast waiting on you when you get back.

"You keep feeding me the way you do and I'm gonna need the extra workouts."

"Good." She patted his knee and hopped to her feet. "You go burn all those calories and I'll fill you back up." She walked away with her no-nonsense stride, picked her keys up off the mantle, and tossed them to Jason.

Jason pulled into the parking lot and hopped out of the car. If he sat there too long, he'd change his mind. Playing ball again wasn't the only thing making him nervous. He'd yet to get a phone call or text about his moving in with Candice. Paul and Tim had to have an opinion about it. What brothers wouldn't? Candice had assured him that she talked to them and explained everything, but a strong part of him felt he should've been the one to address it. At her pleading, he'd dropped it. He was getting ready to find out if they had as well. He made his way to the basketball court behind the building and crept closer to the group of men stretching and talking trash.

"Bro, how many years have we been playing, and your game hasn't gotten any better. Just stop while you're ahead." The group joined Tim in laughter and Paul didn't look pleased.

"All right, little brother, keep running your mouth."

"Do you two ever get along?" Jason stepped out of the shadows and on cue everyone shouted his name, surrounding him with back slaps and handshakes like they were excited to see him. He hadn't felt so accepted in a long time. He eyed Paul for any sign of that he was unpleased, but all he saw was the same brotherly camaraderie that was on everyone else's face.

"I got Jason on my team."

"I wouldn't be so quick to call that." Jason took the ball from Tim and smoothed his palm across the bumpy surface. "I haven't played in ten years." He palmed the ball in one hand and slapped his other hand against it.

"You didn't play at all while you were locked up?"

"I couldn't. Just looking at a court made me think of the scholarship, NBA, and the life I could've had." Jason eyed the ball, wondering if he even remembered how to play. The silence stretched on for minutes, and he hoped he hadn't spoiled their game.

"Well, in that case, you can be on Paul's team."

"It's like that?" Jason snorted, grateful for Tim lightening the mood.

"It's like that." Tim slapped a hand on Jason's shoulder. "You need to brush up on your skills. I was thinking we could host a three-on-three tournament to open the center with a bang."

Jason took a minute to toss the idea around in his head. He imagined the court filled with kids, bounce houses overflowing with children, lawn chairs spread out across the grass. The more he thought about it the better it sounded.

"What do you need me to do?"

"Just host the tournament and maybe make a speech."

"All right, man. Let me know if there's anything else."

"Are we ballin'? Who's the odd man out?" Pastor Hawkins stepped forward and looked around the group.

"Don't even worry about it. I didn't come to play. I just came for the brotherhood."

"Oh no, you're playing." Tim stopped him in his tracks. "You haven't balled in ten years. You are playing today. Old man Paul over

93

here needs fifty timeouts. You can just sub for him, so the game doesn't lose momentum."

All eyes were on Jason, and no one budged until he nodded his consent.

They hadn't played five minutes before Paul asked for his first time out. He walked past Jason barely perspiring, showing no outward sign of distress. Jason shook his head. Leave it up to that group of men to push him out of his comfort zone. *Game time.*

Jason took his time taking off his hoodie. Did he really want to get on the court and open a door to his past? Time seemed to stand still as he ran over the possibilities in his mind. He could get out there and still be great, or he could suck. Either way, would it matter? No. They were his boys, his brothers. They'd understand.

"Let's go, superstar. You're letting the old folks rest up." Tim passed him the ball. There was no mistaking the challenge in his voice.

Jason bounced the ball and the force of it springing back up to his palm awakened something in him. The skill, the instinct, the love for the game, all came surging back to him. It was game time.

"I guess I'm covering you then," Jason smirked at wise-cracking Tim and passed the ball to a teammate.

Cole dribbled down the court for the easy layup and missed. Tim ran around and leaped for the rebound, and Jason was right there waiting on him when he came down. His eyes honed in on the ball, ignoring Tim's fancy foot work and ball-handling skills. Tim was so busy showing off, he didn't realize Jason was measuring the time between the ball leaving his hand and it hitting the ground. With precision, Jason tapped the ball away from Tim, took it out, and arched up the prettiest three-point shot that was nothing but net.

"Ten years, yeah right." Tim walked away, shaking his head. "It's going to be a long game." He looked over at Paul all stretched out, resting against the gate, cheesing, and sipping on his Gatorade like he'd scored the basket himself.

Tim was about to tell him to get his butt up and get back into the game, but his thought was interrupted. Hand clapping echoed in the quiet morning and all heads turned to see where it was coming from.

94

Lamont walked on the court, his applause directed toward Jason. "Still the superstar."

Jason didn't dignify his stupidity with a response. He merely sneered down at Lamont, hoping his expression said it all. Without hesitation, his boys shuffled to his side.

"Tell them to stand down." Lamont lifted the hem of his shirt and rested it behind the butt of the gun in his waist band.

Jason raised his hands signaling for them to back up.

"Good, athletic, and smart—I see why you got the scholarship."

"I should've known you weren't a man of your word. Maybe I should beat you down again to remind you of our little agreement." He clenched his fists so tight, his knuckles popped.

Lamont's nostrils flared at the reference to their physical altercation.

"You really shouldn't roam the streets alone if you can't back up that mouth."

"Keep talking." The sound of car doors slamming brought out the evil gleam in Lamont's eyes. "You need to be reminded of how the hood works."

Jason's eyes cut to the group of men making their way toward him. His jaw clenched so tight, it hurt to talk. "What do you want?"

"Not so bad now, are you?"

"I could've said the same thing while you were laid out in my front lawn." In spite of the situation, Jason clucked, "I've made it pretty clear that I'm not rolling with you, so why are you here?"

"Just thought I'd come down here and check out this fine establishment I heard you were building." Having the top-dog persona, his insistence on making Jason bow strengthened as his boys stood behind him. Lamont turned around which and every way, hands raised in the air like he was king of the world.

"Well, take a good look, because this is the last time I want to see you down here."

"You still don't get it." The joviality left Lamont's face and he stepped even closer to Jason. He removed the gun from his waist and waved it around like an extension of his hand as he spoke. "This is my community, my neighborhood, I run this, and I…run…you."

95

"Correction." Jason didn't budge or show weakness. "This is my youth center, on my block, in my community. Do I have to issue another beat down to get that through your head?"

He stepped toe to toe with the Lamont and was met with cold metal against his temple. "I have enough bullets to plant one in your brain and every last one of your boys. We both know how easy it is for me to get away with it."

Jason froze. The cold metal sent a chill from his temple, down his spine, and to his toes. He knew one day it would come to this but always thought he'd be on the other end of the gun, barreling down on Lamont. Whatever the case, he wasn't going to punk out and allow fear to rule him.

"You're still a coward. After that beat down, who could blame you. I'd be afraid to step up like a man, too."

"Keep talking, homeboy. I got something for that—" Approaching sirens cut his words short. A sadistic smile spread across Lamont's face as he lowered the gun. "God must love you."

Jason didn't respond, simply watched Lamont back away and then turn to leave. As if remembering something very important, Lamont spun around. The look on his face made Jason's skin crawl. "How's your mom? It's not safe for a woman to live alone, especially an ex-addict. No telling what she could get into."

Blood drained from Jason's face. He watched Lamont walk away and pulled out his cell phone to check on his mother. The call went to voicemail and he had to tamp down the panic threatening to bubble over.

Lamont was gone before the police arrived. The flashing red and blue lights pulled up to the curb. Jason was torn between hanging around to give a statement and rushing off to see about his mom. A black man running to his car as the police pulled up wouldn't end well, so he restrained himself. They all gave a statement, Pastor Hawkins admitting he was the one who called. Jason's statement was short. What could he say? An unwanted guest was in the community expressing his second amendment right. The cops knew Lamont. They knew he was a thug, but on paper, he'd been a saint since his arrest as a juvenile.

# 14

Jason frantically dialed his mother's number, not letting her voicemail greeting finish before hanging up and dialing again. The call rolled over to voicemail for the third time. Without so much as a word to his friends, Jason jogged to his car. They called out to him, but he kept right on running. Even once behind the wheel, his incessant phone dialing continued, each time his pulse ramped up a bit more. He accelerated to eighty-five miles per hour without a care if cops were lurking about.

He pulled up to his mother's house, half expecting Lamont to be sitting on the porch waiting for him. He didn't understand why Lamont wouldn't just leave him alone. He'd already taken ten years of his life. What else could he want? That beat down didn't help things, but still, enough was enough.

The hair on Jason's neck stood up as he stepped out of the car. His mother's car was in the driveway. Knowing she was home and not answering the phone brought all kinds of images to his mind. He stood on the porch, regretting his haste to get to the basketball court that morning. He'd left his key to his mother's house in his room. He knocked on the door with a fierceness that left his knuckles raw. The responding silence heightened his anxiety.

Pacing around the porch, Jason tried to find his center and calm down. He needed that peace he felt when Candice smiled at him. He inhaled a deep breath, letting his mind wander over Candice. He didn't have time to analyze why thinking of her gave him clarity of mind. As soon as the thought came to him, he ran off the porch and scaled the fence to the backyard. If Lamont had done something to his mother, he didn't just walk through the front door. There had to be an open or shattered window somewhere.

Just as he thought, the window to his old bedroom was completely gone. He dusted a few glass fragments out of the way and wasted no time climbing in. Once inside, he paused, listening for the sound of intruders, but hoping he heard his mother moving about instead. There was nothing, not even the slightest sound.

97

Her empty room eliminated all hopes that she was just sleeping. He checked the bathrooms and other spare bedroom all with the same results. He stood in the hallway terrified to take another step, knowing he wouldn't like what he'd find in the front of the house. He inched into the living room and his heart calmed a bit. *Maybe a friend picked her up?* He turned toward the kitchen and his relief was short lived. His mother was slumped across the table. Even from where he stood, she didn't look good.

The shoestring tied around her arm and the needle in front of her said it all. How many times had he found her like that when he was a child? When he woke up for school, got up to go to the bathroom in the middle of the night, coming home from school, or even just coming in from playing with his friends. No matter when it was, it never ceased to steal the oxygen from his lungs. He moved toward her with the same thought that always lingered in the back of his mind. *Is this the time I find her dead?* His father's untimely death was the only thing that had prompted his mother to get clean. She wanted Jason to have a parent he could depend on. With his father gone, that left only her. Yvonne had dropped Jason off at his aunt's and disappeared for three months. When she reappeared, she was clean and had given her life to Christ. She had been the perfect mother ever since.

With his heart in his throat, Jason touched two fingers to his mother's neck. Feeling the slight thump of a pulse, he praised God. She was alive.

"Mom…Mom." He lifted her head and tapped her cheeks. "Yvonne, get up!" She listlessly swayed in his arms as he tried to make her sit up. What was it that she needed? He spun around trying to remember. *Water…or is it milk?* He grabbed two cups and decided to force her to drink both when the doorbell rang.

He marched to the door, wishing it was Lamont, but knowing he didn't have the time or the mental fortitude to ensure it would end well. He peered through the peephole. The way his heart thumped at seeing Candice standing on the porch forced him to admit what he'd been trying to deny. He wanted so much more than her friendship.

"What are you doing here?" He gripped the door in one hand and the frame in the other, forcing himself not to touch her.

98

"Tim called. I thought you could use a friend, so I had our neighbor drop me off."

*A friend...* His eyes roamed her face, lingering on her lips before connecting with her eyes.

"But you probably want to be left alone." She backed away, his silence stealing her nerve. "I should've called instead of assuming. Sorry."

"Stay." His one-word command halted her retreat.

She stepped toward him and placed her hand on his chest. "Is she okay?" His eyes dropped to her hand, relishing the fire burning there and retraced the path of her words honing in on their source. He needed her lips like he needed his next breath. She brought her hand to his cheek and he caught it mid-air. He pressed his lips to her palm and made that be enough. He couldn't, wouldn't take advantage of her kind heart. He laced their fingers, tugged her into the house, and showed her where his mother was.

"She's alive, but almost twenty years clean is now ruined by some psychopathic thug with a vendetta."

"Hey." Candice felt him getting riled up and that hand was back on his chest caressing circles and soothing him like only she could. "She still has her twenty years. This was not her fault."

His jaw clenched as he bit off the words he wanted to say.

Candice's free hand cupped his cheek, soothing the tension there. "I know you're upset, but going after Lamont won't make things better. Maybe we should call the cops, or take her to the hospital."

Malice was written all over his face. He dropped his head, touching his forehead to hers, soaking up the peace in her and the comfort of her caress.

"She hates hospitals and they'll just assume she did this to herself."

"What do you need me to do?" She watched her hands roaming and caressing the contours of his chest. She couldn't stop even if she wanted to.

"I just have to believe God is working it out. In the meantime, let's help her get more comfortable."

He looked heavenward and exhaled his stress. The vestiges of his control snapped. "What I don't understand is why does He continue to allow this stuff to happen? Haven't I suffered enough? Ten years, Candice!" His fists balled at his side and he growled through clenched teeth. "He allowed me to serve ten years in prison for something I didn't do, and this is the stuff I have to deal with when I get out. Why does Lamont keep winning?"

"Don't worry about Lamont. You didn't survive ten years in prison only to be defeated once you got out."

"Are you sure about that?" He stepped away—instantly regretting the broken connection—and looked down at his mom, still slumped across the table. "It sure looks like he's winning to me."

She walked up beside him and placed her hand on his shoulder. "I know it doesn't seem like it, but sometimes we have to go by what we know and not by what it looks like."

His tortured eyes broke Candice and she did what she'd wanted to do since walking into the house. She wrapped her arms around him, stepped as close as she possibly could, and laid her head on his chest. If she wasn't so concerned about him, she would've purred when his heavy hands landed on her back and slid around to embrace her.

She didn't have the words to comfort him and hoped her arms were enough. His face dropped into the crook of her neck and she held him a little tighter.

*God, please help him.* She wished her faith was stronger or she was better at praying. She hated that he was in need of something she couldn't provide.

Finally, he pulled away. Her soft smile melted him, and he knew it was time to back away. He caressed a finger down her cheek and the heat of his touch singed the smile off her face.

"Jason..." His whispered name on her lips nearly convinced him to take what he wanted.

"Hey." His hand dropped, and he backed away clearing his throat. "Help me move her to the bedroom." He focused his attention on Yvonne, but his heart was on the woman who had stolen it completely. He felt her eyes on him, heard her unspoken questions, but decided to ignore it. If he turned to her, spoke to her, looked in those eyes, or even acknowledged her, he'd give in to desires he had no business indulging. When she walked around to the other side of his mother and wrapped an arm around her waist, he was finally able to breathe freely.

With weak knees, Candice assisted Jason in steadying Yvonne on her feet. His touch had made her so light headed and off balance, she didn't know how much help she was. If he touched her again, he'd have to pick up more than just his mother.

Once they laid her on the bed, Candice stepped out of the room, giving him a moment to get her settled. She took the opportunity to make a phone call. She paced around the living room, waiting for Paul to answer. Instead of a *hello,* she got, "How is he?" He could piss her off to no end, but his loyalty and kindness always drew her back.

"He's been better. Just another crappy day heaped on to the hundreds he's had." She sighed and relayed everything that had happened. By the time she was done, Paul's indignation was seeping through the phone line. "We definitely need to get the window fixed. I'm also thinking security bars and an alarm system. How soon can you make it happen?"

"Today," was Paul's one-word reply before the line went silent.

"She's good for now."

Candice entered the room, turned toward Jason, and tossed her phone on the couch. His terse words were nothing compared to the fury etched on his face. He dropped to the sofa, weighed down by the day's events. Candice kneeled in front of him, timidly untying the laces on his shoes and removing them. She propped his feet up on the coffee table and then stepped behind the couch, guiding his head back to rest against the top of it.

She leaned forward, whispering in his ear. "Relax."

Her breath wisped along his neck. Relaxing was the last thing he wanted… He sank into the sofa, giving in to thoughts of Candice instead of the homicidal thoughts of Lamont. Her fingers slipped under the collar of his shirt, scratching, pulling, and kneading their way up to his temple and back again. *Repeat. Repeat. Repeat.* He teetered between relaxation and arousal. Her hand sank a little lower, caressing his pectoral. Her soft hand touching his bare chest tipped him over the edge. Relaxation flew out the window and every inch of him hardened. He shuddered, the current of electricity surging between them a little too strong. All too quickly, her hands retreated. She kissed his cheek and walked away. He watched the sway of her hips, wanting to chase after her. There was no way she hadn't felt that zap of electricity, so he let her run, allowing her a moment to regroup. That spark was wearing down his resistance. More and more, he was considering setting the nice guy aside and going after what he wanted.

Candice hadn't been gone for more than a minute when a high-pitched scream and glass shattering sent her running back. Jason was already up on his feet and racing into his mother's room. Candice followed behind him. Yvonne stood in the center of the room, bug-eyed and mumbling incoherently. The mate to the shattered lamp on the floor shook in her hand.

"Get them away from me!" She threw the lamp and Jason caught it before it hit the ground.

"Hey, hey," he tried to soothe her.

"No! No! Get them away from me."

"Come here, Ma. It's going to be all right." He wrapped his arms around her. Her arms flailed, fighting him off like he was a complete stranger. Jason tried to overpower her, but whatever was haunting her had her fighting like her life depended on it. Her swinging arm broke free and popped him in the mouth. He stumbled back—more out of shock than pain—and dabbed the corner of his lips. His distance calmed Yvonne a bit, but she still trembled with fear.

"Yvonne." Candice's voice alerted Jason to her presence and he instantly placed himself as a barrier between her and his mother. "Listen to me. There is no one here, but me and your son. Do you see your son?" Candice peeked around his bicep, offering Yvonne a reassuring smile. "I'm Candice, his friend. We are here to help you. No one wants to hurt you." She had no clue what she was doing. Talking someone out of a psychotic hallucination was one thing, but her training in drug abuse was minimal. She just went with what the books said. *Convince them that the hallucination isn't real.*

102

Whether the technique worked, or her soothing voice was the balm Yvonne needed, she seemed to calm. For Jason, it was definitely her voice. She eased out of the room, not wanting any sudden movement to ignite the situation and returned with a glass of cold water. Not giving Jason an opportunity to stop her, she inched toward Yvonne. She kept her voice soft and words measured until she reached Yvonne, who was now slumped in the corner opposite the door, drenched in sweat. Candice sat next to her and Yvonne flinched. Candice immediately put up her hand to halt Jason. She shook her head no, but kept her eyes trained on Yvonne.

"Take a sip of this water."

Yvonne resisted, but Candice urged her on. "It's good for you. It will make you feel better."

Sip by sip, she finished the entire glass.

Candice cradled Yvonne's head to her shoulder and stroked her hair.

As she held Yvonne, Candice thought of her own mother. She'd endured and sacrificed so much trying to be both mother and father. Here she was doing it all over again. It had been months since her mother blocked her from visiting. It was time to put a stop to it. She needed her mother, and her mother needed her.

Jason relaxed enough to sit beside her. He pulled Candice close, resting her head on his shoulder. That's where they stayed until morning, Yvonne resting on Candice, she on Jason, and him supporting the weight of them all.

# 15

After five days of sleeping in an unfamiliar place, Candice had reached her breaking point. Jason wasn't fairing much better. Setting aside her own grogginess, Candice crossed the kitchen to where he had plopped down at the table. She placed a steaming mug of coffee in front of him and commenced to massaging the stiffness that had accumulated in his neck from five nights of sleeping on the couch.

After sleeping on the floor the first night, he was shocked she'd returned the next day after work with an overnight bag. He told her to go home. She smiled at the lack of conviction in his command and squeezed past him into the house. He was so grateful for her presence that he didn't hesitate to give her his bed. She had objected, but he outright refused to let her sleep on the couch. She suggested they share the bed. Yvonne wasn't having it. With the lack of motherly filter Candice should've been used to, Yvonne reminded them of the hell fire that awaited fornicators. The heat that flared in Jason's eyes soothed her embarrassment. His eyes caressed the length of her and back up, never quite making it to her face. With the slightest smirk tilting the corners of his mouth, he licked his lips and did nothing to hide where his attention was centered.

"Jason!" Yvonne had gasped and swatted his shoulder as hard as her weakened body would allow.

Candice ran. She trembled at the sight of his hunger for her. It was exhilarating. He put his desire out there for her and his mother to see. She turned a deaf ear to the internal voice telling her that it was gratitude he was mistaking for desire and allowed herself a moment to hope.

"Do you want breakfast before I go get ready for work?" Candice increased the pressure on his neck and he groaned his response.

"If it means you stop, then no."

His hands dropped from the table, accidentally scrapping along her calf. Candice hoped he didn't notice the shudder his touch elicited, but he did. He touched her again. Purposefully, intently, and without shame, he caressed her calf. The contrast of his rough callused hands and her

104

smooth silky skin rendered her immobile. Too quickly, his touch was gone.

"I'm…I'm," she stuttered. Pausing, she took a deep breath, hoping her tongue would work if she got oxygen flowing properly. "I need to get dressed for work." She backed away and fled his hunger.

She turned and nearly jumped out of her skin at the sight of Yvonne standing in the doorway. Candice was too intent on escaping Jason to interpret the look on Yvonne's face. She nodded her good morning and left Yvonne to deal with her son.

Yvonne sat across from Jason, eying him with knowing eyes. She grabbed the mug that he'd yet to touch. Sipping in silence, she watched him.

"Ma, what?"

She smiled at the tone that would've gotten him knocked upside the head ten years ago and took a long gulp on the now lukewarm coffee.

"Are y'all dating?"

"No."

"But you want to."

"She has a situation."

"Then why keep touching her?"

"To remind her of what's waiting when she clears it up." Jason snickered at his response, but Yvonne was not entertained.

"Why not find a woman who's not in a situation?"

"Have you seen her?" He grinned, making the hour glass shape with his hands.

Yvonne shot him a glare, and he quickly clarified.

"Besides that, she takes care of me, prays for me, and treats me like her equal. What's better than that?"

Pensive, Yvonne let the conversation die.

Jason took advantage of her silence and fixed a bowl of cereal. He settled for his mom's tasteless bran flakes, wishing he would've taken Candice up on her offer of breakfast. He returned to the table, and Yvonne was still sitting there. He didn't know what part of his response had her thinking so hard, but he dreaded her comeback. His mom was sharp witted and could zing you before you finished your last word, but when given time to formulate a response, she could be downright deadly. Without a word, she left the table, leaving Jason to replay the entire conversation over and over in his head.

Candice walked back into the kitchen and gagged at the sight of his bran flakes. She grabbed the bowl and dumped it in the sink.

"I was eating that."

She stopped mid-stride to the refrigerator and cut him a look that shut him up, but didn't stop the amused grin spreading across his face. She grabbed the necessary ingredients and whipped up a quick bacon and egg sandwich. He could've kissed her, wanted to kiss her. She leaned forward, placing the plate on the table, offering him a smile with his meal. Her scent invaded his space, his lungs, and his mind. On their own accord, his eyes dropped to her ample cleavage, heating her as much as her presence was warming him. His eyes returned to her face, catching a brief glimpse of pink darting out to moisten her plush lips. Yvonne walked in and saved them, or ruined their chance, Jason couldn't decide which. Candice rushed off to work. Jason pinned her with a look, promising to resolve their unfinished business.

Jason had Candice off balance all day, making simple daily tasks long and taxing because she kept daydreaming. Come quitting time, she didn't hesitate to grab her purse and head toward the elevators. As she stepped in, Vince was stepping out, engrossed in conversation with one of the other social workers. He noticed her and shifted his entire focus. He smiled, revealing all he couldn't say with words. Candice almost felt bad that she couldn't return the emotion, but thought of Jason and how easily passionate she was for him. It should be that natural, not forced. She returned a polite wave and kept her eyes cast down until the elevator doors closed.

She rang the bell at Yvonne's house. Jason answered without so much as a smile, wave, or how was your day. Her heart—that had been hopeful eight hours ago—dropped into her stomach. Timidly, she stepped into the house. The scowl marring his face set off panic inside her, but she swallowed it back.

106

"Jason, is—"

His raised voice cut his mother off. "Ma, this is absolutely ridiculous."

"Watch your tone. You ain't too grown to catch this back hand." Her raised brow hinted at her irritation, but she sat motionless otherwise.

Jason, on the other hand, was pissed beyond containment.

"Hey." Candice placed both hands on his back, smoothing her palms along his tense muscles. They tightened further and then relaxed under her touch. "You all right?" she questioned, even though the answer was apparent.

"My mother is being stubborn."

Candice peeked around the expanse of his back and noticed the slight smirk on Yvonne's face. Whatever was going on, she was amused and trying to hide it. Jason lifted an arm, placing it behind Candice to guide her to his side. His arm draped around her shoulders, while one of hers wrapped around his waist and the other patted his chest.

"What's wrong?" Candice looked up at him, his touch removing all the worry she walked in with.

"Mom wants us to leave." His voice was much softer than it was moments ago. He dipped his eyes to hers and the same fire she ran from that morning kicked back up. He shook his head, releasing his mind from the spell she always seemed to place over him. "She didn't even want me to move in with you in the first place."

Candice tried not to let that sting and kept her attention focused on Jason.

"Now that she's in danger, she's gonna put me out."

"I'm not in danger." Yvonne released the laugh she'd been holding. "Thanks to Paranoid Paul, this place is safer thank Buckingham Palace."

"Mom," he groaned like a petulant child.

Candice ducked her head to hide her smile and chanced a glance at Yvonne.

"Jason, I'll be fine."

He grumbled something under his breath, kissed his mother goodbye, grabbed their already packed bags, and marched toward the door.

107

Candice froze as Yvonne walked toward her.

"Love him the way he deserves to be loved," she whispered before kissing Candice's cheek and walking away. Speechless, Candice followed Jason's path to the front door, where he stood waiting on her.

Candice sat in the passenger seat, grappling with the blow of Yvonne's words. She'd been greenlighted to go after Jason. Having his mother's approval gave her butterflies. Jason had made it more than obvious that he was interested. There was just one thing standing in her way: Vince. She pulled out her phone to end it right then and there. Her heart nearly stopped at the text notification waiting for her. She pressed her finger on the home button and held her breath waiting for the message to pop up.

*Send me the itinerary and I'll be there.*

Her dad had actually texted back. She dropped her phone in her lap as if it had bit her. Why had she let April talk her in to calling? Why had she lied and said Paul and Tim would be there. She groaned, knowing full well she'd have to lie to get them to show up. First, she needed to decide if she even wanted to be there.

# 16

By the time Friday arrived, Candice had never needed a weekend so bad in all her life. Making sure her new program was operating smoothly and helping Jason with his mother had risen her stress level to the hilt. As tired as she was, there was another issue she had to resolve. The thought of fighting with her mother wasn't pleasant. With the stubborn mother she had, an argument was highly probable, but it had to be done.

True to form, the freeway was at a standstill. She didn't have the patience for it. She exited and took the scenic route. Even then, it took an hour to get home. She was so frazzled that she put off calling her mother. If she didn't answer the phone or if she had some snappy reply, it would definitely set Candice off.

With one-track focus, she sought out the bottle of wine in her refrigerator. She could hear Jason's music and knew he was in his room sulking and irritated that Yvonne had sent them packing the night before.

She was a little irritated, too. She was also appalled her feelings had been so apparent that Yvonne had picked up on them and urged her to act on them. She was convinced Yvonne wanting them to leave had more to do with her and Jason getting some alone time than it did Yvonne wanting space. *Love him the way he deserves.*

Candice couldn't even deny it. She loved Jason. He was everything and had invaded her life so thoroughly that she wanted little else but him. Maybe a glass of wine or two would be the liquid courage she needed to tell him how she felt.

She settled on her couch—glassed poised for sipping—and her phone rang. She rolled her eyes at the name flashing on the display. Since her conversation with Jason, her interactions with Vince felt dirty. She'd played with Vince's emotions to get what she wanted. Her program was up and running with board approval. Technically, she didn't need Vince anymore, so why was she still stringing him along? Maybe the wine would give her the courage to drop him like she should've done a long time ago. She took a gulp and answered the phone.

"Hey."

"Hey to you, too. I know you've had a long week, so I thought I'd come by with dinner."

She could hear the smile in his voice and tried to match his enthusiasm. "Vince, that's nice, but you don't have to do that."

"It's too late. I'm already outside. Come open the door."

She stopped breathing or either her heart stopped. Whichever it was, everything within her cringed. She bit her lip to keep from shouting what popped into her mind.

"Hello…you there?" Vince asked in the ensuing silence.

Candice listened to the muffled music thumping through Jason's bedroom and her heart dropped into her stomach. She did not want Jason to meet Vince. She didn't want the evidence of how low she'd stooped to be paraded around her apartment.

The doorbell rang and for a split second she contemplated pretending like she wasn't home. He hadn't actually verified that she was in fact home. She could totally get away with it, but there'd always be another day. He'd would show back up or sequester her in his office again.

"Coming," she muttered into the phone before ending the call. She opened the door and tried to muster up a smile.

Without invitation, Vince stepped in to her apartment and closed in on her lips.

The few other times he'd kissed her, she couldn't deny he had skills, but in that moment, after the day and week she had partnered with him showing up uninvited, his lips were the last thing she wanted. She froze, wanting to shove against his chest, push him back down the stairs, and to his car. Instead, she searched his kiss for even tiniest bit of passion, fire, simmer, slow burn, heat, or insatiable need. Even with all his skill, there wasn't the tiniest bit of spark. Jason hadn't kissed her, but the thought of him doing so set her on fire more than all of Vince's efforts ever could.

It was as plain as day. She couldn't continue the farce of a relationship. Vince deserved more. She and Jason deserved a chance to explore whatever was simmering between them. Call her selfish, but she

110

deserved to have the man of her dreams. It was time to have the talk that could end her career.

She pulled back, searching Vince's eyes, but he was honed in to something over her shoulder.

"Who the hell are you?"

"You must be Vince."

Candice stood unmoving, heart hammering in her throat as Jason stepped forward with an extended hand. She was unconcerned about the fire flaring from Vince's nostrils or the accusations running through his mind. All she cared about was Jason and what he thought of her.

"Jason…Candice's roommate." That word sliced through her with its truth. They seemed like so much more. She wanted them to be so much more, but his walking in on that kiss made her desire seem as far removed from reality as unicorns and leprechauns.

"Roommate? I wasn't aware she had one, and a male one at that."

"That's our Candice, full of surprises. I'm gonna step out for a while and give you two some privacy. Nice meeting you, bruh."

She followed Jason out of the door, racking her brain for the words to say. How do you explain a kiss was unwanted when you let it linger for so long?

"You don't have to go."

"That kiss looked like there's a whole lot more going on than what you're willing to admit. I will not be the third wheel. Text me when he's gone."

"Jason." Candice wanted to wrap her arms around him, beg him to stay, let him know that he was the one she wanted, but all that came out was, "I'm sorry."

"You have no reason to be. I'm gonna check on my mom."

He walked away, and she stood there watching until Vince came up behind her and shut the door.

"Roommate?"

"Yup, roommate." She walked past him to the bags of food he'd set on the table. She didn't know how she'd eat with all the regret lodged in her throat. She gathered plates and utensils, mildly aware of Vince scrutinizing her every move.

"How long has he been living here?"

111

"Does it matter?" She paused, looking him in the eye for the first time.

"I guess not. What I should be asking is how long have you been sleeping with him?"

His question caught her so off guard, she nearly dropped the bottle of wine she was carrying. "Excuse me! How dare you insinuate something like that?"

"Well, something has you all frazzled, and I'm not one for beating around the bush."

"Have you ever thought that you're the one that has me frazzled, showing up here unannounced and kissing me like that?"

With the smile that spread across his face, it was obvious he'd misinterpreted what she meant. He stepped toward her once again, slipping his arm around her waist and pulling her toward him.

"So, I frazzle you?"

"That's not what I meant." She turned her head from his impeding kiss and successfully knocked the smirk off his face. "You can't show up here uninvited, kiss me like I gave you permission, and then expect me to be happy about it."

"Well, like I said, I wanted to surprise you with something nice and thoughtful to help you relax from your busy week. And I didn't think I needed *permission* to kiss *my* lady."

*His lady...* Candice nearly choked over the claim he'd tried to stake on her.

He moved toward the table to have a seat, but paused before planting himself on the wooden seat. "Or maybe I should go."

*Yes...you should.*

His inquisitive eyes bore into hers with such intensity she couldn't hold his gaze. "Of course not, please take a seat." After all, they did need to talk.

Silverware clanking on porcelain plates was the only sound in the house and it was grating on her nerves. Kicking Vince to the curb was supposed to be easy and it would've been if Jason hadn't made her feel guilty about using a man's feelings for her corporate advancement. The integrity of the man she wanted was hindering her from dropping the one

112

she didn't want. The irony of life should've been hilarious, but Candice couldn't even crack a smile.

Without a word, Vince finished his food, grabbed his glass of wine, and sat on the sofa. He was flipping through the channels before she grabbed her wine and joined him. He settled on some movie she'd already seen. The noise of the television was ten times better than the silence at dinner, so she wasn't about to complain. His leaving would've been an even better option. He slid his palm along hers, entangled their fingers, and tugged on her arm until she slid into the crook of his arm.

"I'm sorry about earlier. I know you're not that type of woman." He pecked her lips and turned his attention to the movie. Shock was the only thing to explain why she didn't pull away from him and put space between them.

Vince cradled her in the crook of his arm as it drooped lazily over her shoulders, his finger drawing idle circles on her shoulder. Her mind was so far gone into thoughts of Jason that she hadn't realized he was caressing her until his fingers trailed up the bare flesh of her neck. The act brought her back to reality, and suddenly she was on the defensive and ready to decline his advances. Her eyes flashed to the television. What she saw totally explained why he was touching her intimately. She was in no sense a prude, but the sensuality on the screen made her blush. Bare breast and backsides were on full display. There was no mistaking what was going. In spite of present company, Candice couldn't help but think it had been a while since a man touched her like that. She cleared her throat, clenched her thighs to ward off the heat starting to brew, and chided herself for enjoying the scene a little too much. The sight, the sounds, her imagination, it was all so intense the atmosphere hummed with possibilities.

Staying true to form, Vince went for it. He had her on her back, his lips pressed against hers before she had time to protest. The love scene was good, but not good enough to let Vince into her bed.

"What are you doing?" Candice squirmed beneath him, trying with all her strength to move.

"You are a grown woman. You know what's up." To drive his point home, he pressed himself between her legs. The feel of his hardened state sent her clamoring for a response.

113

"No! It's not going down." Her no-nonsense tone stopped him in his tracks. "I'm a Christian and the sex-before-marriage thing is not happening."

Vince clucked and continued his pursuit. "You almost had me for a minute. Quit playing; I've heard about how you get down."

"Vince, stop." She pushed against his chest and he pulled back to look in her eyes.

"You have got to be kidding me."

She shook her head and his head dropped to her shoulder.

"Come on, Candy." He growled in frustration. He restrained her hands above her head and pressed his self between her legs with such force the pain nearly took her breath away.

"Vince, get off of me!"

"Just calm down for a minute."

"No!" She bucked and squirmed beneath him, her resistance surging to panic. Her mind was consumed with thoughts of April and the violent attack she'd endured at the hands of some sex-crazed man. Was that her fate? No! It couldn't be. She wouldn't let it be her fate. She reared up and twisted, trying her best to get her leg between his. She fought like her life depended on it, until suddenly he was gone.

Candice hadn't realized what happened until the clatter of wine glasses shattering against each other and her coffee table being busted apart snapped her to reality. By the time she sat up, Jason had Vince pinned against the wall by his neck.

"Jason…Vince…Oh my God" She ran to Jason's side, faltering between elation that Vince was getting what he deserved and fear that Jason was going back to jail.

"Jason, let him go. He's not worth your freedom."

He'd left the apartment with the image of Vince kissing Candice burning a jealous rage through him. Walking in on Vince assaulting her lit an entirely different type of rage. Jason gripped Vince's neck a little tighter.

"Jason, baby, please. You don't want to go back to jail." The gentle caress of her hand down his cheek turned his head toward her. The tears in her eyes connected with his heart and that was all he needed to rescind the molten rage surging through his veins. He loosened his grip on

114

Vince, not caring that he crumpled to the floor, and gathered Candice in his arms. His lips caught the tears cresting the arch of her cheeks and before long they were on hers—or hers were on his—finally getting and giving what they'd dreamed of. Was she still alive? Was her heart still beating? Her body went numb and all sensation was in her mouth. The sparks that had been flying between them ignited into a full-on inferno, blazing so fiercely that it had drowned out Vince's gagging in the background.

"You son of a..." Vince spat out between labored breaths. "I ought to file assault charges."

"You do and I will, too." Candice tore her lips away from Jason to look Vince directly in his eyes. "Do not call me again."

"Yeah, I'll see you at work on Monday."

"You sure will and—"

"You lay a hand on her and assault charges will be the last thing you'll have to worry about." Jason moved forward, placing Candice behind him. Vince stumbled toward the front door so fast, Jason didn't have time to say anything else.

The rattle of the door slamming closed echoed throughout the apartment. The only sound remaining, Candice's shallow pants... *He kissed me.*

Vince's vitriol had interrupted, but her body still hummed with Jason's electric current.

"Jason." She rested her forehead on his back and tangled her hand in the t-shirt bunched at his waist. She stepped closer, laying her face flat against his muscled back and sliding her other arm around his waist. His muscles flexed against her cheek and she tightened her grip. "It's always been you." There, she'd finally let it out. Her desire for him—in not so many words—was laid out for his acceptance and reciprocity.

"Candice..." Her name rolled off his lips and hung in the air like worship.

"If I'd known we were possible, there would never have been a Vince."

115

"Am I a possibility for you?" He turned in her embrace, eyes cast down, hiding his feelings of inadequacy.

"You're the only possibility."

His eyes shot to hers and he was floored by the adoration he saw there. How had he not seen it before? Eyes glossed with tears sparkled back at him

"No one else makes sense. No one else makes my heart throb." Her heart—raw and unsheltered—climbed up her throat in anticipation of his response.

He pulled her closer and, with purpose, sought her lips. Their first kiss was uncontrolled impulse, but the second...every move was thought out. He inched closer, basking in the heat simmering between them, her breath brushed across his cheek and fire ignited in her eyes. His lips landed on her plush mouth and the softness pulled a groan from him that merely hinted at his hunger for her.

His hand slid up her spine, along the nape of her neck, and sunk into her lush mane that had been beckoning him to touch it since the first day they met. He brought her closer, eliminating all space between them. Her shocked gasp into his mouth lit him on fire and he took advantage of her already parted lips, plundering them like a buried treasure.

He was hot and shivering all at the same time. He knew he had to stop. With a control he didn't know he possessed, he broke their connection and set her away from him. He paced away, heart pounding, chest heaving like a caged animal.

"Jason." She stepped toward him, confusion lighting her face.

He put up a halting hand and her heart sank.

"I'm sorry... I—"

"No, don't." He moved toward her, but stopped. Within minutes, the dynamic of their relationship had changed, and if he touched her again, in that moment, they'd reach the point of no return. "I should apologize." He sucked in a deep breath to regain his composure and failed. "I need a cold shower." His admission knocked the confusion off Candice's face. "Let me go get my blood flowing in the right direction and then we can sort through what's happening between us."

"No sorting needed. It's simple. I'm yours." She smirked at his shocked expression and plopped down on the couch.

116

# 17

Working with Vince was hell. His intimidating looks, demands, and unyielding workload were more than Candice normally endured. Knowing Jason would be waiting for her when she got home was the only thing keeping her going. She highly doubted Jason's presence could soothe her from the day she was currently having though.

Already, Vince had called her three times to request reports she needed to prepare for the impromptu staff meeting he'd called. Something in her gut told her Vince was up to no good, so amidst gathering his information, she collected a bit of her own as well.

Walking down the corridor to the conference room felt like a death-row-inmate's stroll to the execution chamber. The calm confidence in her stride masked the anxiety surging through her.

Candice sat in the conference room silently praying as she waited for Vince and the rest of the staff arrive. She waved and spoke when spoken to. Her heart was so far into her throat, she couldn't manage much else. Sitting at the table, she ignored the sideways glances in her direction, tuned out their hushed conversations, and put on her game face. *Never let them see you sweat.*

Vince entered the room and all conversation died. Without even as much as a good morning, he started with his usual tirade of complaints. His eyes landed on Candice and she held her breath for the attack she knew was coming.

"Against my better judgement, I allowed Ms. Matthews to implement a program that promised to revive and rejuvenate our clients. The program has fallen short of its promises. I've decided to cut our losses while we can still save face."

"Fallen short? That's absolutely absurd!" Candice shouted her objection before her brain could filter her response. All eyes were on her. She didn't like being in the spotlight, but Vince was tripping, and she refused to let him get away with it without speaking her mind first. "How can you determine it's unsuccessful when we've barely had enough time to see it flourish? Have you talked to our clients to see how they feel about it?" Candice rushed on, not waiting for him to respond. "No, you haven't, but I have. All I've gotten are smiles and excitement. To me, that's success."

"Well, sometimes finances trump smiles and excitement."

"Let's put it to a vote."

His responding chuckle turned her stomach. "That's not how things work around here. Your program is cancelled. Now, sit back and don't interrupt my meeting again."

Candice didn't budge. She sat up straight, eyes searing and scrutinizing his every word. Once the meeting was over, she accepted the apologetic nods, ignored the smirks, and collected her belongings. She saw Heather lingering by the door and took longer than usual gathering and shuffling through her papers, hoping Heather would get tired and leave. Candice did not have the energy to deal with her. She was relentless and held her spot at the door until the only one left in the room was Vince. Candice chose the lesser of two evils, deciding to deal with Heather instead of facing Vince. Before she could make her escape, his whispered words stopped her.

"Typical black woman. A real man is trying to step up to the plate, but you're out there chasing some no-good Negro through the streets." Though his tone hushed, the venom in words stung all the same.

"Your assumption lets me know I made the right choice." She pivoted to leave, but his retort held her in place.

"Let's see if you feel that way in six months when he's locked back up, cheating on you, or knocking you upside the head. Don't come crawling back—"

"Vince." She bit her lip to check her tone. She'd had enough and wasn't about to keep listening to him degrade Jason. Heather was leaning against the door frame watching their every move, so Candice tried to remain even-tempered. With each word, it was harder and harder to do. "Give me a break. You're standing here acting like you're all in love and hurt. No, you manipulated the situation to get what you wanted and are mad because I manipulated you right back." She gripped the papers clutched against her chest a little tighter. "You cancelled my program like a weak, petty little boy lashing out because you didn't get the girl. A real

118

man would've accepted it and moved on. Don't punish the clients just because I don't want you."

Holding her head high, Candice turned away from him and walked the few short steps to the door. Just one more hour of holding it together and then she could go home and lose it. She graced Heather with a forced smile and stepped into the hall.

"Looks like someone's a lousy lay."

Everything in her told her to keep walking, but she was on a roll putting people in their place. Heather's head on the chopping block was long overdue. Without a stumble, misstep, or stutter, Candice rounded on her. The look on Candice's face gave no hint to the wrath burning for her palm to connect with Heather's face. It could only be described as controlled fury. If she hadn't been in her place of employment, she would have let it loose. Any sane woman would've seen the look on her face and backed down, but not Heather.

"How does it feel to be knocked off that pedestal?" Her lips had the nerve to turn up at the corner.

"I'd rather be at rock bottom with my dignity than on the mountain top knowing I sacrificed my self-respect to get there." She stepped back into the office and turned toward Vince. "Vince, have you met Heather? She seems to think she can give you everything you need. Then, maybe you can quit being petty." She didn't give him or Heather a chance for a comeback. She tightened her grip on her files and strutted back to her cubicle.

Candice spent the last hour of work meeting with the clients who'd had the opportunity to participate in the program. She wanted them to hear firsthand that things were changing. She almost told them she was handing in her two-week notice as well, but didn't want to make a rash decision out of such extreme emotion.

By the time she got off, she wanted nothing more than to head home and drown her sorrows in a hot bath, but she remembered it was Wednesday. Maybe being in church would change her perspective about her job, because she currently couldn't find a single reason to get up and clock in in the morning. She swooped by her apartment and picked up Jason. The moment he got in the car, she could feel his eyes on her. He had to be the most perceptive man she knew. She wasn't in the mood to talk and kept her eyes trained on the road.

The sanctuary was already filling up with people when they arrived. She and Jason grabbed their usual seats and waited as the praise team prepared to start service.

"You okay?

Candice looked up to see Jason watching her. The concern in his eyes made hers fill with tears.

"Just a rough day at work. Will you excuse me for a second?" She was up and practically running out the sanctuary before he could respond. Jason was on her heels and caught her before she could escape to the ladies' room.

"Baby, you don't have to hide from me. I know what we have is new, but I'm here for you." His arms circled around her and for the first time that day, her anxiety began to ebb.

"It's just Vince. He's making work…difficult."

"Oh really?"

"See? That look is exactly why I didn't want to tell you. I don't need you getting into trouble trying to defend me." He was holding her so firmly against him that she could barely get her arm loose. When she did, she touched her fingertips to the stubble of his beard, loving the rasp against her skin. "I'll be okay."

"Just friends. Yeah right."

*Oh God, I don't need this right now.* At the sound of Ben's voice, Candice's head dropped to Jason's chest.

"I knew that was a bunch of bull when you said it."

"Careful, son; watch that mouth in the house of the Lord." Jason let Candice go and guided her behind his back. "From what I hear, it's not even your place to be concerned about who she's friends with."

"I was in the process of making it my place."

"She wasn't interested, still isn't. Either you understand it, or I'll help you understand it."

"Careful, *son*; you shouldn't make threats in the house of the Lord."

Ben's mocking sneer glared at Candice over Jason's shoulder.

"It's not a threat. It's a prophecy of what's in your direct future should you approach her again. As a matter of fact, this isn't your church anymore. Find someplace else to go."

"Is that so?" Ben stepped a little closer and Candice gripped the back of Jason's shirt, silently pleading for him to let it go.

Jason didn't budge. It didn't even seem like his pulse accelerated. The vein on Ben's temple hammered away.

"You know what?" Ben chuckled, backing off. "She ain't even worth it."

"She's definitely worth it. You'll never have an opportunity to know how much."

She should've been ashamed at how those words excited her, but she was too thrilled that Ben was leaving to chastise herself.

"Now," Jason turned his attention back to her. "What did Vince do?"

*Yeah right, Vince...* "He cancelled my new program."

"Aww, baby, I'm sorry." He wrapped her tighter in his arms, bringing her cheek to rest on his chest. He kissed the crown of her head, hoping that he could soothe her.

"What's going on?"

Candice shook her head and stepped out of Jason's arms. This, she absolutely did not need. "Nothing."

"Doesn't look like nothing." Paul stepped a little closer, saw her red watery eyes and directed all his attention to Jason. "Why is she crying?"

Jason couldn't help but laugh.

"It's not him, it's the guy from work and I'm taking care of it."

"What did he do?" Paul's question was still directed toward Jason.

"I took care of it." Jason understood what Paul wasn't asking.

With a satisfied smile, Paul shook Jason's hand and walked into the sanctuary.

"You haven't told them we're together yet, have you?" He'd imagined their first interaction would be a lot more intense.

"Not yet." Her eyes dropped to the ground.

121

"What happened to honesty as quick as possible? I don't want to hide this." He motioned between them, but stopped when he realized what was really going on. "Unless you don't want anyone to know you're with me."

"No," she rushed to say, not wanting to give that thought time to settle in his mind. "I'm not ashamed of you, so don't even go there. I just want to enjoy this a little more. My brothers stayed silent about you moving in. They won't about this." She motioned between them like he had, giving Jason time to understand what she meant. "I'm not too worried about Tim, but Paul…" She looked around, hoping he hadn't come back out. "He gets mad at everything I do. I just want us to be solid before he starts in on me."

"I hear you, but I don't like secrets. Tell them soon or I will."

He walked back into the sanctuary and she followed behind him, dread clogging her throat. She was holding the biggest secret of all. Would he hate her once she told him?

Candice closed her eyes and tried to block out Vince, Heather, and all the day's events. She ignored her nagging secret and let the soloist's voice wash over her. She sucked in a deep breath, warding off the tears rushing to her eyes. Jason linked their fingers and she didn't care if Paul or anyone else saw.

"I got you, baby." He kissed her temple and Candice sighed. "It's going to be all right."

She opened her eyes, grateful for his presence, waiting for Pastor Hawkins to take the podium. He walked in with April following behind him. Candice sighed as she watched Pastor Hawkins carrying April's purse and Bible. He sat her, making sure she was comfortable before setting her things on the adjacent seat and kissing her forehead. On Sunday, they were all business, each with their own adjutants and armor bearers. On Wednesday, he gave her the affection and public attention that most first ladies never receive. Candice looked down at her fingers intertwined with Jason's and it hit her like a ton of bricks how bad she wanted that type of relationship. She cupped the back of his hand with her free one and said a silent prayer that they were well on their way to getting there.

April looked back over the seat at their joined hands. Her eyes slid up to Candice's and the biggest smile spread across her face. She turned back around nearly bouncing in her seat with excitement. Candice shook her head, knowing that as soon as bible class was over, her phone was going to be blowing up.

"God bless all of you who've pressed your way out tonight. If your week has been anything like mine, you came running for the mid-week boost."

Candice ignored the resounding *amen* from the congregation. Her week had been hell so far, but she certainly had not come running, more like dragging, limping, and darn near crawling.

"Turn with me to the book of Luke, chapter 5 and verse 6. Because you pressed your way, God has a special message for you tonight." He paused until pages stopped turning. "When you have it say amen. No need to stand. It's a short passage tonight, and I'll be done before you get to your feet." The resounding 'amen' was his cue to begin. "When they had done so, they caught such a large number of fish that their nets began to break." He smiled and Candice could see why her friend was so enamored, Pastor Hawkins was hot. "Tell your neighbor there is a blessing in doing it the Master's way."

With just the title, Candice was already on the verge of crying.

"I won't be up here long. God doesn't have a lot to say and neither do I. When I finish, don't go home. Come to the altar and have a talk with him."

"In this particular passage of scripture, Simon had just come in from a long night of fishing. He was standing at the shore, washing his nets. The word says he was out there all night and hadn't caught a thing. He decided to count his loses and call it a night. Jesus climbed into his boat." Pastor Hawkins chuckled. In spite of the emotions already churning in her, Candice smiled. His practical approach to the scriptures was sometimes comical. "Now, I'm a fisherman myself, and there is no way I'm staying in the boat all day if the fish aren't biting. I'm packing it up and stopping by the store to buy some fish on my way home. First lady can fry a mean piece of catfish."

The congregation laughed, Candice and Jason right along with them. She chanced a look at April and her friend's exasperated head shaking made her laugh a bit harder.

"Do you fry fish?" Jason's whispered words brushing across her cheek sent a shudder through her.

"I do." She smiled up at him, not caring what assumptions would be made at their hushed conversation. "Do you want me to cook it for you?"

His hesitant nod excited her. It was the first time he'd ever asked her for anything. She couldn't explain the delight she felt from being able to fulfill his request.

"Some of us approach life—spiritual and natural—with Simon's tenacity." Pastor Hawkins' voice drew her attention away from Jason and the meal her mind had already begun planning for him. "You work all day and are still living paycheck to paycheck. You cook and clean, but he still won't pay attention to you. You pay the bills and love the Lord, but she still complaining. You've fasted and prayed, but the doctors' still say there is nothing to be done." He paused, weeping the only sound breaking the silence. He'd gone from laughter to intense truth within seconds.

"Just like Simon, you've decided to call it a day. You've quit and are cleaning your nets to put them away. You stopped putting your best foot forward at work. You let the laundry pile up. You spend the bill money on something special for yourself. You put your Bible and prayer shawl away. What's the point of giving extra or being extra if it gets you nowhere?" He stepped away from the podium to kiss the crown of April's head and pass her a handkerchief. Her face was just as wet as Candice's.

"I can't fault you, because it is a natural reaction. It's been ingrained into us that it is idiocy—borderline lunacy—to continue doing the same thing day in and day out with no results. So, the logical thing to do is quit. But God defies logic. He works in mysterious ways."

Jason placed a wad of Kleenex in Candice's hand. "I know work has been tiring and I'm sorry for how I've contributed to that, but hang in there. God has a plan." She accepted the caress of his eyes, knowing he'd hold her if he could.

"Simon was tired and past the point of wanting to quit. He'd already given up until Jesus showed up. Without asking, Jesus hops in his

124

boat, making demands. 'Put out a little from the shore'. I wish someone would hop in my car talking about take me around the block." He laughed at himself. His humor never seemed to break the mood or detract from the power of the message. "Simon honored the request without complaint...until Jesus asked him to do the same thing he'd been doing unsuccessfully all night."

"He should've just done what he was told, but Simon got a little lippy. Those who have kids, I bet you recognize the tone of Simon's words. I can imagine the lip smack and eye roll that came with them. Verse five: 'Master, we've worked hard all night and haven't caught anything. But because you say so, I will let down the nets.' Ma, I did the dishes earlier. I already cleaned my room. I already looked for it in my room."

The congregation laughed, but Candice was bawling.

"It's okay to express your frustration to God. He understands it. Jesus Himself said, 'If it be possible take this cup from me.' He understands having to go through something that isn't pleasant. So, talk to Him, but let the last thing you say be, 'But because You say so'."

"That simple act of obedience garnered Simon a blessing he couldn't contain. His net started to break and he had to call over his partners to help him out. God filled two boats with the very thing he'd been toiling after for hours, just because he was obedient."

"Yes, Lord!"

"Say that, pastor."

One by one, the congregants rose to their feet in celebration and acceptance of the word.

"You could quit and ignore God's call," Pastor Hawkins continued amongst all the excitement, "And probably go on to live a happy, normal life, but you'd miss out on the possibilities that your obedience will create. Promotions are on the other side of your obedience. Love is on the other side. Peace, healing, financial security, answered prayers are all on the other side of your obedience. Do it the Master's way."

True to his word, Pastor Hawkins' message was short and sweet. Instead of heading downstairs as usual, he clasped hands with April and knelt with her at the altar. Others followed their lead. Jason and Candice

125

remained in their seats. His warm palm against hers was soothing all by itself. She sucked in a deep breath, letting the small touch comfort her. His mumbled voice caught her attention. The sight of him praying for her was the most affectionate thing she'd ever witnessed a man doing for her. She squeezed his fingers a little tighter and offered up a prayer for him as well.

# 18

Candice's stomach had been in knots all day. Receiving a text from her father saying he'd landed and checked into his hotel had nearly given her a heart attack. Although she'd bought the ticket and reserved the hotel herself, she never fully believed he'd show up. She sat in the restaurant sipping ginger ale, hoping her stomach calmed before her brothers arrived.

Punctual as usual, they arrived together. She couldn't help the tinge of jealousy she felt, but quickly reminded herself that she could have that closeness with them if she'd quit picking fights with Paul and pushing him away. She plastered a smile on her face and greeted them with much more joy than she felt.

"This is a nice surprise." Paul kissed the crown of her head just before Tim did the same.

"I hope you still think so later," she mumbled under her breath, but quickly recovered by passing out the soft drinks she'd ordered for them before they arrived. Right on cue, their father walked through the door. Her eyes shot toward him. Paul and Tim followed. Blood drained from their faces and the look they leveled on her could've frozen hell it was so cold. "Please don't leave. You want me to get over my daddy issues? This is how I need to do it, and I can't do it by myself. Besides that, you have daddy issues just as much as I do."

Her pleading softened them. Tim grabbed her hand and Paul simply nodded. As their father approached, tension rolled off of him, matching the tension already at the table.

"I'm here." He eased into his seat as if any sudden movement would set off the bomb that seemed to be sitting on the table

"Why?" Paul's unforgiving tone sliced through the air before Candice had a chance to respond.

"Candice asked."

"Really?" A muscle ticked in Paul's jaw and Candice held her breath, hoping that Paul didn't explode. "Last I checked, you weren't the type of man to do things because his kids ask. So, let me rephrase. What do you want? Because the last time you called me, you needed $5,000."

"You asked him for money?" Candice blurted out, causing people at neighboring tables to stare in their direction. She dropped her voice to a whisper and leaned a little closer. "What is wrong with you?"

"I'll pay that and then some if I never have to see you again."

Candice squeezed Tim's knee under the table. She couldn't say she disagreed. She was sure that if she'd actually endured some of the hell they'd endured at the hands of their father, she'd be writing a check herself.

"Amen to that."

"Look, I didn't come here for all this." Her father slid out of his seat and turned toward Candice. "This was a mistake."

"Sit down," Paul barked fiercely, making Candice jump and knock over her glass of soda.

She fumbled with the napkins, shakily wiping at the mess.

"You will sit down and give your daughter this one conversation." Paul's voice dropped to a low growl, just as lethal as his bark.

Her father tossed his hands up in surrender and plopped back in his seat. Candice moved her seat to be a buffer between him and Paul. She debated on whether to take the conversation outside. The restaurant manager was hovering nearby, and if Paul decided to leap, it wouldn't end well. However, taking the conversation outside allowed too much space and opportunity. She forged ahead, adopting the calmest voice she could, given the situation.

"Why couldn't you just be there?"

"Your mother and I didn't get along." He leaned forward, resting his forearms across the table, his mind seemingly retracing the last three decades. "And you were better off without me."

"You got that right." Paul took a swig of his Coke, eyeing it, wishing it were something stronger.

"How can you have a child—a daughter—and just abandon her?" She tried not to allow Paul's commentary to dissuade her. "You were supposed to be my first love, my hero, my protector, the one to show me how a man is supposed to treat a woman, but you weren't there."

His silence angered her.

"You know, in fifth grade, this group of boys used to taunt me and sing songs about how ugly I was. They chased me home and threw rocks at me. I used to hope they got tired before I made it home, because I knew momma was at work and there'd be no one home to protect me. You should've been there to chase them away." She leaned forward, jabbing a finger in his chest. Paul's firm and sure arms wrapped around her, containing the tornado threatening to spiral.

"I felt so ugly and unwanted. You should've been there to tell me I was beautiful, but guess what happened instead? I lost my virginity at twelve years old to some boy three years older than me just because he told me my hair looked nice. Life was long and rough and lonely. You are going to look me in the eye and tell me why. Why couldn't you be there?"

The entire restaurant was quiet. All eyes were on their table, some probably had cell phones out recording. She was unbothered. This conversation was long overdue. Candice watched her father, his attention more focused on the napkin he was ripping into tiny pieces than her.

"You ever stop to think that life was long, rough, and lonely for me, too?"

"It didn't have to be. You had us." She motioned between her and her brothers, still fighting the urge to lash out.

"Your mother," he finally made eye contact with Paul and Tim, "Was everything to me. Growing up, I was in and out of foster homes and group homes, and—"

"I heard about that, which makes it all the more confusing. You know the pain of living without parents, so why put your own kids through that?"

He continued as if she hadn't spoken. "I had nothing—no parents, no home, no other living relatives willing to take me in. I barely had clothes of my own. Your mother was the first thing I ever felt was just for me. She wanted to get married. Hell, I knew nothing about marriage or how to be a husband, but she wanted to, so I wanted to. She wanted to have kids, so I wanted to have kids. And then..." He paused, grabbing a random cup from the table to wash down the despair clogging his throat. He placed the cup down and his eyes landed on Tim. "You took her away from me."

129

Tim knew his mother died giving birth to him, and if it hadn't been for Paul, he'd hate himself for it. It was sad that his brother had been more of a father back then than the adult in his life.

Paul stiffened behind her and she hurried to respond before Paul lit into him. "You lost her, so we all lost you."

"There was nothing of me left to give. My heart and soul were buried right along with her."

"But she lived on through her children, and yet you beat them when you could've showered them with the love you had for her. She's probably turning in her grave at the life you've lived and the things you've done."

Tim was silent, and Candice wanted to go to him and embrace him until he couldn't breathe. If she moved, there was no doubt in her mind that Paul would punch their father. She caught his eye and asked with her heart if he was okay. His slight nod wasn't reassuring. She watched him, hating that her need for closure brought up the guilt he'd long since buried. Paul still hummed with fury behind her and she loathed that she was the cause. This conversation and what she thought she needed from her father was over. She had the protector she needed sitting behind her, her hero to her right, and her first love waiting for her at home. She no longer needed her father.

"Just so you know, my brothers are two amazing men who are so much more than the dollar signs in their bank account. They've been more to me these few short years than you have my entire life. You've missed out on knowing two wonderful people. And, not to toot my own horn, but I'm pretty amazing, too."

"Yeah, you are." Paul kissed her temple and like a light was flipped on, she finally understood all the hard lessons he'd been trying to teach her.

"I'm not one to shut you out, because you are still my father, but the ball is in your court. Be a deadbeat or be involved, the choice is yours. But, ask either one of them for money again and I'll hunt you down." She signaled the waiter, gave him a twenty for the three sodas, and then strutted out of the restaurant with her head held high.

Paul and Tim called out to her. She didn't allow the concern in their voice to hinder her stride. She just wanted to get in the car before her

130

façade of strength crumbled and she lost it in the parking lot. This would be the last she cried for him, but she would allow the tears because she deserved them. She deserved to scream, cry, and yell until the world felt the pain of the injustice of having a deadbeat father.

She'd just made it to the door when a hand shot out, preventing her from opening the door. Before she could turn around and unleash the fury circulating within her and intermingling with grief, two solid arms were around her.

"It's okay, baby girl." Paul kissed the crown of her head and, just this once, she didn't mind him being the father figure she needed. She leaned into his embrace and let the tears trickle down her cheeks. "You don't need him. You have us."

Yes, she did have them. They were more than enough. She also had someone else who was in her apartment at that very moment. She dried the last tears she'd ever cry for her father, thanked her brothers, and went to the man whose presence made her forget about the past and what she thought was missing from her life.

With one-track focus, Candice walked through the front door and beelined toward Jason. She didn't care that he was watching TV with a plate of food on his lap. She needed him. Almost too late, he realized her intent and moved his food before she straddled his lap. "Hey baby—"

She smashed her lips on his, cutting off whatever he was going to say. She trembled against him and, without words being uttered, he knew what she needed. He encircled his arms around her, infusing her with his strength. He kissed her as if he was apologizing for her father but promising to be more than enough to make up for his absence. She accepted his promise with a passion that simmered into a boil. She pressed down on the unmistakable bulge behind his zipper, causing her fingers to glide down the column of buttons straining to contain the swell of her heaving breast.

"Candice, what are you doing?" His hands gripped her waist, thumbs caressing the skin around her navel. Ten years without a woman—how he had the clarity of mind to speak must've been the power of God. "No sex before marriage, remember?" He spoke the words, but did nothing to move her from straddling his lap. Her heat seeped through his clothes, burning away the vestiges of his control. His hands slid up her back, gripping her shoulders, pressing her down as he pressed up.

The friction took her breath away, rendering her incapable of speaking. She shuddered, fisting his shirt. It was her only form of communication, letting him know he was going too far and not far enough at the same time.

Her soft lips against the sensitive skin of his neck pulled a groan from the depths of his loins. She desperately sought the buckle of his belt. The clanking of the metal brought reality crashing forward and he grabbed her wrists, stopping her from releasing him. His eyes locked to hers, a muscle in his jaw flexing for control. He held his breath and she slowly released hers. She moved her hands from his belt and he released her wrists, resting his forehead against hers.

Needing to do something besides focus on how she was still straddling his lap and how he didn't want to move her, Jason filled the silence. "Tell me what happened with your father."

"We could get married," Candice gasped, nearly choking on the tongue that seemed to have a mind of its own. Not wanting to talk about her father had her blurting out the private thoughts swirling through her head.

Jason's eyes bulged, and she was mortified. Any minute, he'd toss her on the floor and run so fast the carpet would catch fire. She slammed her lips against his to keep him from uttering the rejection she knew was on its way. She couldn't believe she'd said such a thing, but from the abundance of the heart the mouth speaks.

He accepted her kiss with as much vigor as she gave, but it didn't make him lose focus.

"You'd marry me just for sex?" He disengaged their lips and his eyes dropped to her proffered, black lace-covered breasts. Her hand on his cheek brought his eyes up to hers.

"I'd marry you because you're you."

"Shouldn't marriage be love, soulmates, and all that stuff in the movies? How can you be in love with a man you barely know?"

"Loving you is easy." Candice froze. She sat there, her throat seemingly closing up on her. Apparently, the synapses between her brain and tongue didn't connect when she was turned on. She lifted her eye to his, hoping he'd say something. She'd said it, meant it, and refused to back up off of it, but all she got was the same shocked expression that had to be on her face. "I'm sorry," she rasped out between labored breaths. She had to get away before the embarrassment of her unrequited confession consumed her.

She jumped from his lap and fled the room. Jason was on her and engulfing her in his arms before she could escape.

"Hey." He planted his lips in the crook of her neck and forced her arms around his waist. "I'm sorry. I've just never been loved before. I mean… I thought I had something with Chantel that would continue when I got out, but apparently, she realized I wasn't worth the trouble. I'm not worthy of your love, but I accept it. I'll treasure it and won't abuse it." He touched his fingers to her chin and lifted her eyes to his. "I don't have to run through a bunch of women to realize what I have in you. I will marry you. Grab your keys, let's go."

"What? We're doing it today?" Her excitement vaporized the tears that threatened to spill down her cheeks.

"Well, we can at least go file for a license and then go from there."

"Really?" She couldn't help the eagerness she felt.

A smile spread across her face and his heart thumped a little harder. He'd do what he could to see that smile every day.

Candice bounced around in the passenger seat with anxious anticipation like a kid on Christmas morning. How long had she been waiting for the love of her life to show up and whisk her away? *The love of my life?*

Yes, she had to face the facts. Jason was the love of her life. He had come from a place and a past she never would've considered. He had no money, couldn't buy her things, and didn't have a fancy car to drive her around. These all had previously been prerequisites of dating. But Jason… He had none of what she'd adamantly looked for in a man, and yet here she was rushing off to make him her husband. His heart, his inner strength, and the electric current they shared were far more crucial than his bank account.

133

*I'm going to be his wife.* Her smile brightened and she gazed out the window, letting her imagination take over.

Jason glanced over at her smile and it chased his apprehension away. Was he doing the right thing? Did he love her? Could he love her? Did he even know what love felt like? That smile erased the doubt. Yes, he was doing the right thing.

He turned the car into the parking stall and wasted no time further assuaging his doubt with her lips.

"Are you sure you want to do this?" She pulled back to search his eyes to see his true answer.

"I wouldn't be here if I didn't."

"Are you ready for what's coming next?"

His eyes dropped from her face down to her breast and the corners of his mouth tipped up. He licked his suddenly parched lips and, before he could utter a word, Candice slapped his arm.

"Not that," she giggled. "I'm more than ready for that. I meant my brothers. Are you ready to deal with the backlash? They are bound to be pissed."

"You let me worry about them." He stepped out of the car and walked around to open her door. Maybe everything was moving too fast. He'd been so caught up in finally having Candice that he'd never even considered a fallout. He opened her door and she rose to her feet in front of him. His heart thumped even harder at her nearness. Instantly he knew, being with her was worth whatever he had to endure.

Hand in hand, they walked into the county administration building. As they made it through security and grabbed their belongings from the scanning conveyor belt, Candice's excitement dimmed. The magnitude of what they were about to do overwhelmed her. Jason pulled a number and Candice sat nervously in the waiting area. Time moved in slow motion as she watched people come and go through the double doors she'd just walked through. Most looked happy and she wondered why they were there. Were they about to marry someone they didn't know that well, someone who didn't love them?

She could get up and run out that door, and only she and Jason would know what was going on. He'd understand that they were rushing and be more than happy to slow things down. She motioned toward the door, but before she fully built enough courage to flee, Jason stroked a finger down her cheek. Her eyes rose to his. The passion she saw there instantly calmed her racing pulse.

"I'm the happiest man in the world right now." He touched his lips to hers and though the contact brief, the power behind it nearly floored her.

*This is what you want. Since the day you met him, you've wanted him, and now he's yours.*

Their number was called and butterflies took flight in her stomach. She followed Jason to the counter, which she'd found herself doing a lot—following him, letting him lead her.

"We'd like to apply for a marriage license."

The clerk sighed and rolled her eyes. Any lingering giddiness Candice might've had quickly subsided and apprehension ramped up. "Is there a problem?"

"Marriage licenses and ceremonies are by appointment only. Here's a list of all our facilities and an application. Call and schedule an appointment. You can have the ceremony that day or you can schedule a future appointment. I suggest calling the offices in less populated areas, such as East County. You may get in sooner." She passed them the papers, her body language subtly dismissing them.

Candice stomped out of the office, disappointment turning to anger and she had to leave before she unjustly lashed out at the clerk.

Jason waited until they were in the hallway and called her back to him. The commanding tone of his voice should have infuriated her, but the strength it carried was exactly what she needed. Her steps halted and without hesitation she returned to him.

"I still want this." He pulled out his phone to schedule them an appointment. Once he put the phone to his ear, his eyes never left hers. Each word he spoke into the phone—no matter how minor—pebbled goose bumps across her flesh. When he hung up the phone and spoke directly to her, her entire body was covered with them. "In one week, you'll be my wife." The simple statement stole the oxygen from her lungs. Before she could recover, his lips were on hers, stealing her very soul.

"Jason." His name was a moan on her lips. She couldn't believe how hard she'd fallen for him. From the day she'd heard his story, she'd been fascinated. His strength and endurance were impressive. Then, she had a chance to meet him and, *oh God, he is everything*. Now she was holding him and kissing him. The reality of it overwhelmed her. She broke their kiss, pressing her head to his chest.

"Can I take you somewhere?" Her eyes met his, begging him to say yes, even though her request was vague.

"Of course." His response was immediate, signifying his absolute trust in her. He passed her the keys and guided her out to the car.

It had been months since she'd seen her mother. Walking beside her was the one thing that could put an end to their estrangement, her fiancé. She'd tried more than a few times to convince her mother that there'd be a time in every child's life that they would have to care for a parent, and taking care of her wasn't a burden. Her mother ignored text messages, voicemails, and even emails. Wondering how she'd respond to this surprise visit had Candice's stomach in knots.

"Candice!" Suzy's enthusiasm greeted her before she made it to the counter.

"Hey, Suzy! Long time no see." Candice tried to summon the easy cordiality she'd once shared with the woman. The quick change in Suzy's demeanor let her know she was failing.

"Candice, I'm so sorry for all this. Even right now, I have to apologize. I haven't received word that anything's changed."

"I know." She looked to Jason, standing at her side. He was the strength she never knew she needed. "Can you let her know there is someone I want her to meet and see what she says."

Suzy picked up the phone and Candice stood there nervously chewing her lip as she watched every word coming out of Suzy's mouth.

"You okay?" Jason guided her away from the counter and used his thumb to pull her lip from its grip. She nodded, but he wasn't satisfied. "Who are we here to see?"

"My mother." Shock morphed his face, and she wondered if she'd made a mistake bringing him there without letting him know what she was up to. "If you don't want—"

"No, no." He rushed to pull her into his arms. "I want to. I just assumed your mother had passed since you never talk about her."

"Nope, she is alive and well. She…" Candice shook her head and glanced away. Jason held her a little tighter. "Let's just say mother is my heart and everything she does is for my wellbeing, even if it stings at first. She blocked me from visiting."

"I'm sorry, baby." He squeezed her a little tighter.

"It's okay. It's funny, actually. She felt I wasting valuable time sitting around worrying about her when I should be out meeting men and making babies."

"What?" Jason couldn't help the chuckle that bubbled out.

"Yep, that's mom for you."

"Well…" He kissed the crown of her head. "You have the man."

"Yes, I do." She rested her cheek on his chest, but then snapped her eyes back to his. "But don't think that what I feel for you has anything to do with my mother."

"It never crossed my mind." He engulfed her, bringing her more securely against him. "Do you think she'll like me?"

Suzy interrupted before Candice could give her response. "She said to bring you back."

Candice was so excited, she jumped out of Jason's arms. He laughed and followed behind her.

"I'm sorry. I've just missed her so much."

"Don't worry about it. Trust me, I know how that feels." He waved away her sympathy, but she still smoothed her hand down his arm and squeezed his hand before continuing to her mother's room.

Candice paused, taking a deep breath before entering her mother's room, and was surprised at what she saw. Her cheeks were full of color and had lost the gray, sunk in, sickly appearance.

"Oh Mom, look at you." Candice rushed to her bed side, not even attempting to reign in her tears. "Guess all that praying Tim and Paul's been doing is paying off." Tim had said she was looking good, but that was an understatement.

137

"What do you mean Tim and Paul's praying? You ain't been praying for me?"

Candice kissed her mother's cheek and hugged her, probably harder than she should have. "Yes, I pray, but I'm not quite sure mine get to where they need to be."

"Child, please, a one-word prayer is just as good as any." She waved off Candice's statement as if it were the most ridiculous thing in the world. "I'm going home next week. Paul is helping me find a place."

"Mom, that is nonsense; you'll stay with me."

"No, I need my space." Her eyes cut to Jason. "It looks like you do, too."

"Oh, I'm sorry." She beckoned him over. "This is Jason he's my…" She raised a brow, searching for the right word. No one even knew they were a couple, and her mom couldn't hold water. The next person to visit would know all their business. Apparently, Jason didn't care. He answered for her.

"I'm her fiancé."

"Well!" Her shock turned to mischief. "I definitely need my own place."

"Mom," Candice gasped, but her mom shooed away her retort.

"Girl, please! A man like that can do things that I don't want to hear."

"Mother!" Candice wanted to die, shrivel up, shrink into the floor, and disappear. The only thing that saved her was Jason laughing next to her.

"Nice to meet you." Jason extended his hand and his future mother-in-law offered a hug instead. "We really don't mind you staying with us. And we promise to be quiet."

Candice wanted to punch him, but she fell in love a little deeper.

"Seriously, Mom, it will be easier for me to take care of you if you live with us."

"Candice, I don't need to be taken care of. Go live your life and make babies."

"You keep being stubborn and you won't get a grandbaby."

"You better watch your mouth."

Candice wanted to laugh at her mother's eye-bulging expression. Maybe if she'd used that line before, her mother would've removed her from the no admittance list without hesitation.

"Yep, think I'll get a consultation about having my tubes tied." Her mother gasped. Candice bit her lip to keep from laughing. Toying with her felt too good.

"Okay, calm down." Jason shook his head, smirking at Candice's behavior. "I have a solution that will ease everyone's mind, even mine. She can move in with my mother."

"What?" They shouted in unison.

Jason grinned. If they didn't like the idea, at least they'd stopped arguing and agreed on something.

"She can move in with my mom. She'll have plenty of space. She won't be alone and my mom won't be alone."

Candice didn't need long to think about it. Anything sounded better than her mother living alone. "It could work."

"There's just one problem, aside from you two discussing me like I'm not sitting here."

Candice's eyes snapped to her mother.

"I'm not moving in with some woman I don't know."

"Mom, you know Yvonne."

This was news to Jason.

"You met her. Paul and Tim had her over for dinner a few times. You were there."

"Yvonne, the one whose son is in…" Her eyes bulged as she put two and two together.

Her eyes slid over to Jason. His jaw clenched as he waited for the judgement, waited for her to say he wasn't good enough for her daughter, not good enough to be the father of the grandchildren she wanted so bad, and waited for her to call security to have him thrown out.

Her eyes walked up and down the length of him, lingering on his long, braided hair and toned biceps, the only things he had to show for ten years of incarceration. He felt so inadequate and almost walked out deeming himself unworthy, but then Candice smiled at him. There was no way he was giving that up. He firmly planted his feet, bracing for whatever her mother was going to throw at him.

139

"Okay," she mumbled, eyes still fixated on Jason. "If Yvonne's okay with it."

Jason sent his mother a quick text, still bracing for what she'd say next.

"I hate what they did to you."

His head popped up to compassionate eyes searching his. He'd seen many, but the ones staring at him were unexpected.

"You love him." She turned toward her daughter, "And make him forget everything he's been through."

"Yes ma'am."

Shell shocked was the only way to describe it. He had no response, and the look on his face, utter befuddlement. His phone buzzed and he glanced down at the screen.

"She said okay," was the only thing his brain could come up with.

# 19

Excitement flowed through Candice like there was a church full of friends and family waiting for her to walk down the aisle. It was her wedding day, and regardless of one witness or a hundred witnesses, she was overwhelmed with happiness.

Jason was everything. His past didn't turn her off. If anything, it enhanced her feelings for him. He'd been through hell and still hadn't given up. His perseverance enhanced everything she loved about him. Yes, she loved him. His smile, his body, his laugh, his straight forwardness, his compassion, and his drive—she loved it all.

She spun around in the full-length mirror hanging from the back of her bedroom door. It took hours of shopping to find the perfect outfit for becoming Mrs. Jason Stewart. Looking at her reflection, it had been well worth the hunt. It wasn't the long, flowing white gown she'd always envisioned. Funny how the right man could make all the details of a ceremony seem insignificant. As long as he was there saying *I do*, nothing else mattered.

"Candice, babe, you ready? We should head out soon."

She smiled at Jason's voice coming through the door. Of course she was ready. She'd been awake since the crack of dawn, styling and restyling her hair, applying and reapplying her makeup until she felt it was perfect. She took one last look in the mirror, inhaled a deep breath to calm her nerves, and opened the door. She was not prepared for what stood on the other side.

"Hey, beautiful."

She was speechless. Jason in jeans and a t-shirt was already pretty extraordinary. Jason in a single-breasted black suit nearly melted her on the spot. Without shame, she let her eyes roam the length of him and back up. It wasn't until he reached for her hand that she tore her eyes away and allowed him to lead her out to the car.

"I don't know if it's the dress, your hair, or the fact that you're about to be my wife, but you've never been more beautiful than you are right now." He pecked her lips, careful not to smudge her lipstick, and helped her into the car. They were nearly at the county building before her blush faded. She waved at the only two people they invited. They'd sworn their mothers to secrecy, but Jason with his *honesty works best* policy had already set a date to talk with her brothers.

They walked down unassuming halls, hyper-aware of each other. Her heart beat to his rhythm. His aura surged through her, syncing them, seemingly merging them to one before the vows were even exchanged. They went through the formality of paperwork, but he was already hers; she'd already surrendered to him. The words 'I do' left their mouths and the rush of a sudden wedding, the lack of grandeur of a traditional ceremony, faded to the background. They sealed their union with a kiss and it was done. They were husband and wife.

Candice turned to Yvonne and passed her the handkerchief she'd brought to dab the tears from her own eyes. With the grin spreading her face, she wouldn't need it anytime soon.

"You are everything he deserves." Yvonne grabbed the handkerchief and patted her eyes. "Please be patient with him. He's missed out on a lot and may need time to get up to speed. Relationships are new to him. Just love him and everything will work itself out."

Candice glanced over and saw her mother and Jason having their own private conversation. She had no idea what was being said to him, but she certainly didn't need anyone to tell her to just love him. It was already a forgone conclusion. She ran a reassuring hand down Yvonne's arm and went to snag her husband before her mother said something embarrassing.

The ride back to their apartment was thick with tension. Just the thought of the pleasures awaiting them made conversation seem foolish. He pulled the car into the parking stall and cut off the engine. He turned toward Candice and the look on his face put her on alert.

"What's wrong?" She didn't let him respond. Her anxiety had gotten the best of her. She gripped his cheeks between her palms and brought his lips to hers. "Please don't regret this."

"It's not that." He took a moment to enjoy her kiss before pulling away. "I used to be really good at this, but…"

Understanding lit Candice's face and she pulled him back to her.

He halted her pursuit. "I don't want to disappoint you."

142

She grabbed his hand and placed it on her chest. "You have absolutely no idea what you do to me." Do you feel that? With just a kiss you have my heart racing. You won't disappoint me. Regardless of what happens up there, you've already pleased me so much." She slid her hand to the back of his head and guided his lips back to hers.

Their apartment was quiet. Candice led Jason to the master bedroom and shut the door behind them.

"Make yourself comfortable. This is your room, too." She went into the walk-in closet to change in to something more suitable. She was grateful she'd treated herself to a mini-shopping spree. She pulled the black lace negligee from the rack and ran her fingers along the lace.

*I hope he likes it.*

She placed the empty hanger back on the rod and the shoebox on the top of her closet called to her. She tried to ignore its pull like she'd been doing all week, but it was next to impossible. It was time. She had to come clean, put all her cards on the table and maybe he'd forgive her. She grabbed the box—its contents feather-light, but the burden of it weighed a ton.

She walked back into her bedroom to find it empty and prayed to God that wasn't indicative of how she'd spend her wedding night after she told the truth.

"What's wrong?" Jason stepped out of the bathroom and her body language immediately put him on alert.

"I need to show you something." Fear strangled her voice. It was a wonder he even heard her. She cleared her throat, hoping for a little more strength in her tone. It was futile. "I probably should've shown you this before we got married, but better late than never, right?" She dared to look in his eyes, but they were cast down. His hands gripped his hips as if bracing for the force of what she was about to throw at him.

She pressed the box up against his chest and his eyes snapped up to hers. He hesitated. Did he even want to open it? He was finally happy, truly happy, not just faking it until he made it. He could let her have this one secret, but secrets always had a way of coming back to bite. He'd eventually lose the happiness anyway. He grabbed the box, walked over to the bed, and placed it on the bed next to him as he sat.

"Sit with me."

143

His soft-spoken command propelled her forward. She sat next to him, the offending box between them. Her lungs seized as he lifted the lid. His hand rifled through the stack of papers, and then finally settled on one sheet. He lifted it out and paused while his eyes briefly scanned the writing. He realized what he was reading and dug back into the box grabbing page after page, each one similar to the first.

"These are the letters I wrote Chantel."

"I know. I'm Chantel."

"What?"

"Candice Chantel Matthews."

"What?" His eyes jumped from the stack of papers in his hand to her face and back. "Why?" He hopped to his feet and she hopped up with him, rushing to explain.

"My brothers talked about you so much that I wanted to reach out to you, be another friend you could depend on."

"So, you create some alter ego and lie to me?" Jason tried to step around her and head out the door. Her hand on his chest stopped his movement.

His eyes dropped to her hand, the electrical current that burned through him every time she touched him held him there.

"But then you were wonderful and your letters began to mean so much more to me than friendship. I couldn't believe I'd fallen for someone I'd never met, but I had and I wasn't ashamed of it. I jumped at the opportunity to come to the barbeque the day you got out. I was going to put everything out there and hope we could be together. Then, I met you. You were more amazing than I could've ever imagined, but I saw the battle you had ahead of you. You had to focus on reclaiming your life and didn't need me cluttering up your space." She knew how he hated secrets, and his silence sealed the deal, she was losing her husband before they'd had a chance to enjoy each other.

Jason stepped around her and strode toward the door without speaking a word.

"I kept who I was a secret because I was trying to help you." She cried out in desperation, not wanting things to end that way.

"Help me? Really?" With that, he was out the door.

The soft click of the door closing was her undoing. She collapsed onto the bed and unleashed her anguish into the pillow.

Candice didn't know how long she'd lain there, but she finally forced herself to get up. She washed her face, took off her wedding dress, and put on tights and a button-down pajama top. She forged out into the rest of the apartment and, as she suspected, Jason hadn't just gone to his room, he'd left. Before she reduced to a sobbing heap again, she sought out the bottle of wine in her fridge and tried her best to drown her sorrows.

Jason barreled out the front door. As much as he wanted to run away, he couldn't. He took off his suit jacket, plopped down on the bottom step to their apartment, and laid the jacket across his lap. Though he was stationary, his mind was running a mile a minute.

*How could she do something like that?*

The longer he sat there, the more he understood that grown women weren't much different than the teenage girls who had tried to ride his coat tails to wealth. They were just as self-seeking and manipulative as he remembered. So many girls were throwing sex at him his senior year, he hardly ever had a free weekend. They brought condoms and had the nerve to act hurt when he insisted on using his own. He recognized their attempt to get child support from a baller. He wasn't having it. Starla was the only one who claimed to love him back then, but she was like all the rest. He should've known someone named Starla was looking for stardom. The weeks leading up to graduation, she threw sex at him twice as much as the others, claiming she was going to miss him while he was away at college. She even had the nerve to drop a few tears. Where was all that sadness and missing him while he was locked up? *Guess a convicted felon isn't worth missing.*

Then, there was Candice, writing him letters and forcing her way into his life. She made him believe there were good people in the world, telling him she loved him, knowing she was keeping secrets, and making him feel like he finally mattered to someone. *All that only to find out...*

He sucked in a deep breath and slowly released it, hoping the controlled breathing would settle his mind. He did it again and again until

145

his erratic thoughts calmed. When they did, he was stuck on one question. What was the big letdown to Candice being Chantel? Why had he stormed out the apartment? He thought it over and thought it over again. The only thing he came up with was that the woman he cared about is the same woman he'd always cared about, and she happens to love him.

Jason laughed out loud at himself. He had a wife who, since the day she introduced herself, sought out his wellbeing. Chantel, Candice, and his wife were all one. One mind that intrigued him, one heart that loved him, and one body he craved, which he could've been enjoying at that moment if he wasn't tripping. Without another delay, he marched up the steps and charged through the front door.

# 20

Candice tossed the empty wine bottle in the kitchen trashcan and headed back to the living room to continue her pity party. She made it to the living room and nearly had a heart attack from the commotion of Jason bursting through the front door. Her hand flew to her chest and she backed up against the wall, frantically looking for an escape.

It took a few seconds for her to realize it was Jason, and when she did, she could've done cartwheels she was so elated.

He stepped toward her, throwing his jacket onto the back of the couch. He moved so fast, she had no time to react. He pinned her against the wall and then his mouth was on hers. His kiss, frantic and desperate, was searching for something he couldn't find elsewhere. "You want to help me?"

"Yes, baby," she whispered against his lips, barely finding the air to speak.

"You are what I need. It's always been you. You've always been what I needed." He grabbed the waist of her pants and pulled them down. He did the same with her panties, sliding them over her hips and down her thighs. He stepped on the seam and lifted her out the rest of the way. He guided her legs around his waist and slammed her against the wall. His hands were on her, relentlessly groping, caressing, massaging, and stroking. His aggressive touch turned her on, but she refused to let their first time be like that. She'd planned seduction and had a negligée she wanted him to see.

"Jason, baby, wait."

He didn't respond. He just ripped the front of her pajama top open, sending buttons scattering across the living room. His lips on her gave new meaning to ecstasy.

*Oh, forget it.* Their first time was going to be like that, pinned against the wall, going at each other like animals in heat. He'd taken her too far, depleted her resistance. She couldn't stop him, didn't want to stop him. She returned his kiss with the same heat he dished out. She tugged at his shirt, and he momentarily placed her on her feet to take it off. His clothes disintegrated to the floor and her legs were back around his waist. He would've loved to take it slow and savor the moment, but he didn't have the strength to rein in his arousal. He surged into her with one long penetrating stroke and nearly buckled to his knees. Ten years without a woman was his undoing. He didn't—couldn't move. His eyes locked on to hers and she understood his plight.

"It's okay, baby. Get what you need."

He shook his head, not wanting her to hear the tension in his voice. He sought out her spot and, with very little effort, he brought her to where he was. It was the most glorious thing she'd ever felt. He rotated his hips and made a liar out of her. He did it again and she shattered around him. He lifted his head and let out a growl of a wounded animal. She placed her mouth on his and absorbed it all. She took his past pain into her heart and his seed into her womb.

His head dropped to her chest and she cradled him there. His warm breath traipsed across her skin in heaving gusts as he struggled to regain his composure. He planted a kiss between her breasts and helped her slide to her feet. He hovered over her, his magnificent chest at her eye level.

"Are you okay?" He caressed her cheek, bringing her attention to his face. "I shouldn't have—"

"Shh, no regrets. You can love me like that any time." She walked away with an extra sway to her hips. He didn't follow and she turned back to see what was keeping him. Just as she'd suspected, his eyes were glued to the swell of her backside. "You coming?" she crooked her finger, bidding him to her. "It's my turn to love you."

He followed without hesitation. He watched her turn on the shower, practically salivating over what was to come. "How is it that you spent all your adult life in prison, but know how to love me the way you did?" She bent over to test the water temperature.

"You keep bending over in front of me and you're going to get yourself into a whole world of trouble."

"I don't call that trouble. I call it fun." She wiggled her backside in front of him and nearly jumped into the tub when he smacked it.

She spun around, mouth gaped open. "Now, you have to answer my question. How do you know how to please me?"

148

"Let's just say I had a lot of practice before I got locked up and I guess it's like riding a bike."

Candice rolled her eyes and stepped into the shower. "That's right you were a star basketball player. You probably had all kinds of girls throwing their panties at you."

"Something like that." He stepped in behind her, instantly wrapping her in his arms.

"Well, I'm getting ready to put all those girls to shame."

He turned her to face him and whispered just above her lips. "You did that the day you wrote that first letter. So many of them claimed to love me, but all they saw were dollar signs and a way out of the hood. I got locked up and they disappeared. They didn't accept my calls and never wrote me."

"Oh baby, I'm so sorry you had to go through all that."

"Don't be sorry. Just love me."

He connected their lips and let her take the lead. Her kiss was slow and intoxicating. She sampled his lips like they were fine wine—not rushed, very thorough. Her hands roamed up and down his chest, pausing momentarily to grab a loofa and body wash. She lathered his upper body, never losing the connection with his mouth. She washed him from head to toe, paying close attention to a certain appendage. Her touch pulled a groan from deep in his chest and his head floated back, enjoying the sensation.

"Candice…"

"Yes, baby?"

"What am I going to do with you?"

"Wash me and I'll show you."

He grabbed the loofa and touched it to her body as if she were a priceless work of art. She moaned in enjoyment and he tossed the loofah aside. His coarse hands glided across her soap-slicked body. It was no longer about washing her. There wasn't a spot his hands hadn't visited. He studied her body's response. The rise and fall of her breast quickened to his touch. She moaned, squirmed, and lost all inhibitions. He committed it all to memory. By the time he'd finished his exploration, she was on the verge of exploding. Every erogenous zone was singing his praises. Her body trembled, crying out for release. He turned her into the

149

shower stream and the droplets of water beating across her bare breast nearly took her there.

"Not here." He reached around her to shut the water off. "This time we'll take it slow." He lifted her out of the shower and carried her to the bedroom.

"I thought I was supposed to love you this time?"

"We have a lifetime for that." He laid her on the bed and covered her body with his.

Every touch, every kiss, even the look in his eyes was an instrument in his symphonic prelude to what was to come. Her heart beat the tempo to their love song as moans melodically sang the lyrics. He joined their bodies and they sang in perfect harmony. Every stroke became a verse culminating in a resounding crescendo that left them panting in the stillness of the night.

He moved to roll off her, but she wrapped her legs and arms around him and held him to her.

"Baby, I don't want to hurt you."

"You're not hurting me. Nothing has ever felt this perfect."

He rested his head on her forehead and kissed her lips, but rolled them over anyway. "Now this is perfect."

For a moment, they lay in silence. Candice played with the sparse patch of hair on his chest and he traipsed his hands up and down her spine.

"Do you know how many times I wanted to curse God for what happened to me?"

Candice's ears perked up at the sudden conversation.

"I was a good kid. Lost my dad early. Mom was smoked out—I'd had my share of hardship. I didn't deserve what happened to me. That basketball scholarship felt like God was finally saying *good job* for hanging in there. Then, after I was arrested and convicted—it may sound silly—but it felt like God was picking on me. When the jury came back with that guilty verdict, I could have died right there on the spot. I wanted to take it all back. I wanted to snitch, accept the plea, or something. I never thought they'd find me guilty. My mom had begged me to snitch, said we were covered by the blood of Jesus, and whoever was threatening me would be taken care of. I couldn't risk it. I probably could've still snitched after they found me guilty, but when my mom got home that day, there was a slaughtered dog in her bed with a note that said *your boy still better keep his mouth shut*. She was so freaked out. All that *covered by the blood* talk flew out the window. For almost a year, I contemplated killing myself, but that would've meant the devil had finally won."

"Oh baby..." Candice was nearly in tears. How could the legal system fail so horribly? Didn't they know his character? Didn't they know he was being threatened? Why punish him for trying to keep his mom safe?

"If I had known that ten years in prison would bring me to you, I would have served each day with a smile on my face."

Tears trickled from her eyes and she was speechless.

"Candice, you being my wife is more than I ever hoped for."

She dropped her head to hide her tears, but he wasn't having it. With a finger to her chin, he lifted her head and met her lips with his. He took them slow and methodically, taking his time to once again enjoy his wife on their wedding night.

151

# 21

Jason sat at a table in Big E's, nervously waiting for Paul and Tim. The sports-themed restaurant boasted flat-screen televisions on each wall, each broadcasting some sporting event or another. Replicated jerseys of athletic legends, such as Michael Jordan, Larry Bird, Wayne Gretzky, Bo Jackson, and his personal favorite, Isaiah Thomas, were pinned to the wall. If that wasn't enough, each table was painted to resemble a football field, baseball diamond, basketball court, or a hockey rink. It was a sports fanatic's dream.

The restaurant specialized in enormous portions, burgers the size of his face, fries that looked like the chefs had cut a potato in fours and deep fried it, and hot wings stacked so high they'd give you indigestion for a month. At least he'd die with a full stomach if Paul and Tim decided to kill him.

Anxiously, he fidgeted and rearranged the condiments on the table. How do you tell a man you've been secretly seeing his sister and married her behind his back? Add to that the fact they weren't just random men, they were his friends and his relationship with them was vital to his wellbeing. If he pissed them off and they turned their backs on him, everything he'd been working hard for could be scrapped. He asked himself if he was willing to take the risk. Maybe he should've asked himself that before he married her, but he doubted it would've changed his answer. One hundred percent yes. Candice was worth it.

The waitress arrived with the appetizer. Potato skins covered with sour cream, cheese, bacon, and so huge they should've been called baked potatoes. Inhaling the aroma temporarily took his mind off the reason he was there, but when he looked up to thank the waitress, Paul and Tim appeared over her shoulder. It was time to man up. He hoped everything went smoothly, but if it didn't, he'd accept the consequences.

The plan was to soften them up with some good food and then casually bring it up as they enjoyed the football game. Tim stayed true to form, digging in to the appetizer as soon as he sat down. Paul elbowed him so hard he almost knocked over a glass of water.

"What?" Tim mumbled through a mouth full of potato skins.

"How are you going to just eat the man's food without asking?"

"Oh, my bad. I thought it was for everybody."

"It's all good. I ordered it to share, so help yourself." Jason laughed as Tim popped another piece in his mouth and Paul shook his head.

Tearing his eyes away from his greedy brother, Paul asked, "What's up? You said you wanted to talk."

Jason's laugh faded. Leave it up to Paul to get right down to business. Following Tim's lead, Jason joined him in devouring the appetizer. Unlike Tim, he took his time with each bite, as if Paul hadn't said anything. He paused briefly to give the waitress his order and then continued eating. Jason was so focused on his food and avoiding Paul that he missed the smirk Tim gave Paul.

The appetizer was gone and Jason took to his glass of soda. When that was done, he made an unnecessary trip to the bathroom. He took the time to weigh his options again. If Paul and Tim backed out, it would be hard finding another job as a convicted felon, but surely, he could find something. On the other hand, there was only one Candice. If he passed on her, for a job, he might not find another woman like her. With that thought, he marched out to his table.

His food had already been delivered. He pushed his plate to the side and blurted out, "Candice and I are in a relationship."

Paul nearly choked on his water and Tim yelled out. "I told you so. Pay up, big brother." Jason watched in shock as Paul pulled out his wallet and handed Tim a twenty.

"You should have known better than to bet me. I was there when they first met and I recognized that sappy look in their eyes."

"Yeah," Paul laughed. "It's the same look you had when you met Camilla and married her after only knowing her for a few weeks."

"Whoa!" Jason looked at Tim with astonishment.

"It's called love at first sight. Now close your mouth before something flies in there." Tim tossed his napkin at Jason and he swatted it down.

"For real though, you guys are cool with it?"

"We are if she is. So, what are you going to do about it?" Paul asked, trying to ignore Tim still gloating.

"What do you mean?"

"You need to find another place to live. Your living with her was cool when you were just a friend renting a room. Shacking up with my sister is a different story."

"Understood." Jason laughed nervously as he dug into his food. "That brings me to the second thing I needed to tell you."

"Jason, if you got my sister pregnant..." Paul clenched his fist around his fork, fighting the urge to knock Jason upside the head.

"Nah, you know me better than that. You know her better than that. Candice would never let that happen." His mind flashed to their wedding night. He'd wanted her so urgently that he hadn't considered protection. It wasn't until the next morning, when the blood had fully returned to his brain that he thought to ask about birth control. Thank God she was on it or this conversation would go in a totally different direction.

"Well, what has you over here sweating bullets?"

Jason dropped his fork on his plate and wiped his mouth with a napkin. It was time to man up. "I'm more like Tim than you thought." He sipped his soda, letting his words sink in. When they did, he saw all kinds of emotions play across his friends' faces.

"Do you love her?" Paul was on the verge of bursting.

"I have to—"

"Do you love her? It's a simple yes or no." Paul eased the death grip on his fork to pick up his drink. He needed something cool to douse the fire threaten to surge out of his mouth.

"It's not that simple. I can't honestly say I know the true meaning of love. I can say this, I think about her in the morning, at night, and all day in between. Just being around her gives me a sense of peace I never thought I'd have again. Even when I'm mad at her, I still need her. With her, I feel alive."

Contentment settled over Jason. It seemed as though he was finally receiving reparations for the unjust theft of ten years of his life. He was an innocent victim unknowingly looped into a crime by his friends, and everyone from the judge who sentenced him to the DA who prosecuted him to the detectives that arrested him knew it, but all because

154

he wouldn't snitch, they had taken ten years of his life away. That nightmare of the trial haunted him just about every day. He had contemplated revenge on the cops, attorneys, and most definitely his so-called friends, but time and the prison ministry had calmed that beast. Now, his life was lining up and it appeared as though God was restoring the years that had been stolen.

"For whatever reason, God allowed me to serve ten years in prison, and that's okay, because it all brought me to her."

"Sounds like love to me. Welcome to the family," Tim said.

"Just like that?" Paul was two seconds from punching something or someone. It was going to be Tim if he didn't get it together. "Welcome to the family? This man snuck behind your back and married your sister. You're just going to welcome him to the family?"

"I did the same thing. Unlike me, the brother faced us like a man and told the truth. I hid my marriage for months. I'm not getting ready to sit up here and be a hypocrite."

Paul stood, took two hundred dollars out of his wallet, dropped them on the table, and walked away, leaving Tim calling behind him.

"You should go. He's going to her house to chew her out. You want to be her husband, here's your chance. Just know that his anger is coming from a good place. I was almost thirty before Paul started acting like my brother and not my dad. He is protective, and Candice gets it ten times worse than I did because she didn't grow up with us. It's like he's trying to make up for lost time. Let Paul know his job as her protector is over."

"You staying here?" Jason rose to his feet, watching Tim still shoveling food in his mouth.

"You know me. Of course I'm staying. Call me and let me know how everything works out."

155

# 22

*YOU DID WHAT!!!!!*

Candice rolled her eyes at April's response. She didn't expect it to be pleasant, but all capitals and five exclamation points were excessive. At least she shouted in a text instead of calling and doing it.

*Why so surprised?*

*Umm...hello...YOU ARE MARRIED!*

*You of all people knew I loved him. Why so mad?*

*I don't care about that. Why wasn't I invited? I would've never gotten married without you.*

What could she say to that? Candice's fingers hovered over her phone. She could handle April being mad because of the marriage itself. She could defend her feelings for Jason. Explaining why she didn't invite her best friend was something totally different.

In spite of the situation, Candice chuckled. At least she wasn't being called desperate or foolish, which she was sure would be flying out Paul's mouth. She should've gone with Jason to be the buffer between him and her brothers, but he was adamant about handling it on his own. Whatever happened, she already had plans to relieve his stress in the most delicious of ways. Goose bumps pebbled across her skin just thinking about it. She was so caught up in the thought she missed three texts from April.

*Hello!*

*Hello...*

*Oh you will not ignore me. I'M COMING OVER!*

She rolled her eyes at the text, wanting to refuse the visit with an all capitals and five exclamation points of her own, but she and Jason had agreed to let everyone say what needed to be said, get all their anger out, and move past it. He felt it was the quickest way to their happily ever after. She felt it was the quickest way to writing folks and negativity out of her life.

In the end, she didn't reply to April. She tossed her phone on to the seat cushion beside her and rested her head back. She knew exactly why she hadn't invited April. April held so many of Candice's secrets and would keep them from everyone, except her husband. Pastor Richard Hawkins was friends with her brothers and Candice wasn't willing to chance them finding out and trying to stop her.

The sound of the front door opening drew her attention and she couldn't help but smile. "How did it go?"

Jason ignored speed limits and ran lights, praying he didn't get caught. Relief washed over him at seeing her sitting alone on the couch. He didn't think he could've contained himself if he'd walked in on Paul chewing her out.

He hesitated and the smile dropped from her face. "Tim's cool, but Paul…" He shook his head instead of finishing off his thought and then brushed his lips across hers. It wasn't enough. He deepened it, and she responded with a hunger he'd never get tired of.

"Sorry. I hope I haven't ruined things for you."

He touched a finger to her chin, stopping it from dropping to her chest. "You're all that matters. You haven't ruined anything. Paul will—" Pounding on the door stopped him mid-sentence. The little peace he'd garnered in her presence coiled into tension. "That's Paul."

"Are you sure? April's on her way over to give me a piece of her mind."

"Really?" His brow creased with confusion. "I thought she'd be happy for you."

"She is, but can't see the forest over the trees. She wasn't invited, and that's all she cares about right now."

His eyes widened in understanding.

The pounding at the door rattled the walls a little harder. Candice rolled her eyes; apparently, it was an eye-rolling type of day. It definitely had to be Paul. She moved to open the door and Jason stopped her. "I need you to go into the room and lock the door."

"You want me to hide from Paul? I'll just talk to him. It'll be okay."

"I want you to go to the room and let me take care of this." He stood and helped her to her feet. "Stay in there until I tell you to come out."

"He's my brother. He won't hurt me."

157

"I know, but he needs to learn real quick that you're my wife, this is my house, and he will not come over here stressing you out, making demands, and trying to control us."

Without another word, Candice left the room. She was without a doubt ready for Paul to stop controlling her life.

Jason answered the door with a smile on his face. "Didn't expect to see you again today." The shock on Paul's face was priceless.

"Where's my sister?" Paul stepped forward, trying to maneuver his way around Jason into the apartment.

"Hold on a second, brother." Jason stepped out in front of Paul and shut the door behind him. They stood eye to eye on the porch. Jason hated that he was about to lose a friend, but if he backed down, Paul would continue to run his house and his marriage. If there was one thing he'd learned from his father about marriage, it was to stand up and be the man. "First, you need to accept that she is my wife. Just like you won't let me come up in your house and get in your wife's face, I'm not about to let you do it to mine."

Paul stepped a little closer. "Your wife, that's funny. A few minutes ago, you didn't know if you loved her. Makes me wonder why you really married her."

The muscle in Jason's jaw flexed as he bit back his response. Was this the same man that had told him that God had a plan for his life and being in prison wouldn't stop him from fulfilling his purpose? "I'm gonna act like you didn't just say that. It sounds like you're diminishing your sister's value by assuming the only reason I'd want her is for sex."

"Can you honestly stand here and say sex didn't play a part?"

Jason thought back to how they'd gotten to the subject of marriage. Sex had definitely played a part.

"If she had given up the goods, would we even be having this conversation right now?"

Jason's silence was a loud enough response.

"Exactly, so don't stand there acting like I don't have a reason to be upset."

"Let me ask you this." Jason's mind finally jolted to life. "If your wife had been putting out, would you have married her so soon? Better yet, why hadn't you married the dozens of women who had put out?" He smirked at Paul's silence. "Because it's not about sex; it's about the woman."

He backed up and opened the door. "I'm going to let you in, but if you even insinuate that all I'm interested in is sex, I'll forget we're boys and lay you out."

Jason shook his head as he walked down the hall to get Candice. It looked like he'd definitely lost a friend. He couldn't help but wonder if all the lines Paul had fed him about being an ex-convict not defining him was a bunch of lies. It surely looked like it was defining him as a man Paul didn't find worthy of his sister.

He stepped into the room and closed the door behind him. Her miracle-working smile shined at him, lifting the load Paul had dropped. He didn't hesitate to wrap his arms around her, plant his lips on hers, and once again get the reassurance that she was all his.

Jason helped Candice get comfortable on the sofa and then sat next to her. She scooted closer and leaned into him, practically sitting on his lap. He kissed her cheek to hide the smile tugging at his lips. Again, she'd changed his mood without even trying.

As soon as Candice turned toward Paul, he started his interrogation. "Candice, what are you doing?"

"Loving and being loved in return. What are you doing?"

"He doesn't even know if he loves you."

She flinched. Paul might not have noticed, but Jason did. He hated himself for it. She deserved so much more than what he was giving her.

"Love is more than him saying the words." Her voice had lost the conviction she'd started with moments ago. "You, of all people, should know that love is being there when she needs you, seeking her wellbeing, desiring her, supporting, comforting, thinking of her day in and day out, treasuring her, and putting a smile on her face. Jason loves me, Paul." She spoke the words to Paul, but her head was turned, eyes locked with Jason's. In spite of Paul's presence, Jason guided her lips to his, further confirming the words he'd yet to speak.

"Why doesn't he know that?" Paul leaned forward pointing an accusing finger at Jason. He sure knew how to douse a fire.

"Because he doesn't recognize what love is."

159

"Do you think it's wise to start a marriage like that?"

"Paul…" She raised her hands in warning. She'd just about had enough. She knew Paul's anger was coming from love. He loved her and wanted to protect her, but it was time for him to dial it back a bit.

"What if he never figures it out?"

"He will. You know how I know? I'm going to love him. I'm going to love him hard until he recognizes the same feelings I have for him are the same ones he has for me."

"Do you even hear the words coming out of your mouth?"

Her phone vibrated next her. She took a moment to read it, hoping the pause would give her the strength to end the conversation with her brother.

*Richie told me to stay home and mind my business. But you owe me, Candy. Bridal shower, bachelorette party, shopping for wedding dress, honeymoon planning…you robbed me of my one chance of being a maid of honor.*

Candice laughed out loud. She'd prefer April's response than Paul's any day.

*How about a reception? You plan it, we will shop, and do all the fun stuff.*

April's response was three kissy emojis. That simple, all was forgiven. Candice turned her attention back to Paul and stood on her feet. "Go home."

Paul stood and Jason stood with him. "I don't want your heart to get broken."

"It won't." She placed her hand over Jason's heart, gave him the slightest smile, and then walked away. Having Jason there to deal with Paul was a huge relief. She couldn't count how many times she tried to end one of his lectures and he remained rooted to the sofa glaring at her like she'd lost her mind.

Jason turned to Paul and showed him to the door. "I hope we can remain friends."

"A friend wouldn't have played my little sister." Without another word, he walked out.

"A friend would know I'm not the type to play anybody." He spoke to Paul's back, hoping he hadn't turned away permanently. Jason

160

exhaled his frustration, glad things hadn't escalated as he'd anticipated, and shut the door.

The sound of running water reminded Jason of their wedding day. The thought of her wet and naked made the remnants of Paul evaporate. Without delay, he sought out his personal miracle worker and joined her in the bathroom. The sight of her stepping into a tub of water stole the words out of his mouth.

"Are you going to join me?"

He shook his head.

With a raised brow, she turned fully toward him.

His eyes flowed across the length of her, traipsing along the parts that made her a woman. His tongue stuck to the roof of his mouth. Never had a woman rendered him immobile.

"Are you just going to watch me?"

Her sultry tone tightened the bulge in jeans, but he shook his head again.

"Well, tell me, dear husband, what are you going to do?"

"Wash you."

His voice, rough with need, heightened the anticipation of his steps toward her. She'd planned to saucily resist, but the moment desire lit in his eyes, she'd already caved. He stepped to the edge of the tub and his close proximity made her moan. She should've been ashamed. He hadn't even touched her and she was on the verge of losing control. She was too far under his spell to care. When he did touch her, she nearly melted into the tub of water she was standing in.

# 23

Candice knocked on the front door, not fully comfortable using the key Yvonne had given her. The gesture had meant so much to her, she nearly cried. She admired Yvonne's strength, fighting drug addiction to give her son the life he deserved, standing through ten years of injustice, and then having the very substance she fought to overcome forced on her. She even further transcended Candice's expectation when she voluntarily signed herself up for a narcotics anonymous class, just in case the cravings started again. Impressed didn't even begin to express how Candice viewed Yvonne. The fact that she'd so freely accepted Candice as her daughter-in-law made Candice feel as though Yvonne saw something in her that she'd yet to recognize in herself.

Sylvia answered the door, and a smile spread across Candice's face. Her mom was looking good, out of the hospital, and moving around. Moments like these drew her closer to the Lord. She blinked back an errant tear, knowing her mom would have something to say about it. "You are looking good, Ma."

"You got that right. Now get in here before you let all the AC out."

Candice hugged and smooched her mom as she crossed over the threshold and laughed at her swatting away the affection. The smile on Sylvia's lips contradicted her actions. She loved it.

"We're almost ready. Yvonne's in there putting on all that make-up like you young folks. I got that natural beauty. It don't take all that." She patted the side of her curly afro, primping like America's next top model.

"Get it, Momma." Candice stood behind her, both strutting on an imaginary catwalk. "Work it, honey, work it. Show 'em that black don't crack."

"You got that right."

Laughter bubbled up out of them and Candice went ahead and let the tears of joy flow. Yvonne walked in the room and laughter infected her just at the sight of them sashaying and prancing around the living room.

"You two are a mess," Yvonne inhaled, trying to stop her giggles.

"It's good to have so many reasons to laugh." Candice patted her eyes dry. "You ready to head on out?"

Yvonne led the way to the door and punched in the code, arming the new alarm system. Candice's mind wandered back to the day that had made it all necessary. She shook off the thought as she stepped out into the warm San Diego weather and waited for Yvonne to finish locking up. "Did you ladies ever settle on a restaurant, or are we going to Pavoli's again?" She aimed those last words at her mother and knew the response before the words left her lips.

"Well, I haven't been since leaving the center."

"To be honest, I've never actually been."

Sylvia gasped at Yvonne's admission.

"I guess that settles it," Candice chuckled at Sylvia's shocked expression. "Pavoli's it is." It had been her mother's favorite restaurant since the day she found out she knew the cooks and could get a discount or, even better, a free meal. Marlon and Cole—being best friends with Paul and Tim—played right into it, fawning all over her just like her brothers.

Candice pulled out her phone to call ahead and make sure the chef's table was available, so they wouldn't have to wait in line. Her steps slowed and the words died on her lips as she approached the driver's side of the car. Her breath chilled as she met the ice-cold glare of Lamont watching them from across the street. Her hand slipped into her purse, two fingers immediately encircling the tiny metal can of pepper spray while the other three frantically search for her keys. They looped around the ring and she unlocked the door without pulling the keys out.

"Get in the car," she barked harsher than she'd ever spoken to her mother. Her tone left no room for objection. Lamont moved toward her and she didn't hesitate to follow her own command.

They were safely locked in before he reached the driver's side window. He rested his arms across the top of the car and leaned forward, almost resting his forehead on the window.

"If I wanted to get you, I'd already have you." He pressed his lips to the glass, growling as the mere thought of kissing her excited him. Even through the sun-heated glass, the gesture made ice trickle down her spine. His smile, as he backed away, spoke of malicious things and she tried to calm her shaking hand enough to start the car.

Her pulse didn't normalize until they were blocks down the road. She finally had the clarity of mind to call Jason. She opted for headphones instead of connecting to the car's Bluetooth system. She exhaled her pent-up energy and the fear that had threatened to choke her and strived for as normal a voice as possible. She failed.

Jason answered and with her one-word response of, "Hey." His hackles rose and he was on full alert.

"What's wrong?" At her hesitation, he pressed again. "Candice."

"Nothing baby, it's just—"

"Baby, you are killing me. What happened? Where are you?"

"I'm fine...*we* are fine. It's just that Lamont was outside your mom's house watching us as we got into the car."

"Come home." Only she would recognize the rage behind those two softly spoken words.

"Jason, we are fine." The small tremor in her hands said otherwise. "I promised our moms dinner, and I won't let him take that away. Besides, what if he's following us?" Yvonne and Sylvia spun around, checking through the back window for any signs of Lamont. Candice inwardly groaned for saying that out loud. Poor Yvonne must've been terrified seeing him again after all he'd done to her. "We don't want him to know where we live."

His responding growl of displeasure—although not directed at her—pebbled her skin. She'd come to appreciate that growl in other ways. Her mind quickly flashed to the nip of her lip or the added pressure on her hips that usually followed.

*My God!* She'd never craved a man as much as she craved him, never had one consumed her thoughts to the point where she flipped from being so scared she could pee her pants to being so overloaded with lust she had to bite her lip to keep from moaning in front of her mother.

"Come home, Candy." The soft-spoken command held so much dominance and heat that she succumbed without argument. "I'll drive you."

His words—innocently spoken—had her dirty mind thinking, "Yes, please *drive* me so I can *come* home."

"You coming?"

"What?"

"Are you coming home?"

"Oh, um… Yes, on my way." Candice ended the call and turned the AC on full blast. By the time she pulled up in front of her apartment, her fingertips felt like ice, but her core was still on fire. The sight of Jason casually lounging on the steps nearly made her combust. She was out the car and moving toward him before anyone had a chance to say anything. Her lips were on him, and she practically scaled his towering frame.

"Hello to you, too." He sat her down when she finally released his lips. "You all right?" He smirked at the heat in her eyes.

"You just…" She shook her head and looked away. How do you explain to someone that they turn you into a hormone enraged, self-control lacking, sex addict? She looked back at the car and inwardly cringed at the fact that her mother had just seen her behavior. "Um, you ready to go?" She linked their fingers and tried to pull him forward, but he wouldn't move.

Jason tugged her toward him and pinched her chin with his free hand, lifting it until their eyes met. "The feeling is mutual." He brushed his lips across hers. "You have no idea how much."

He understood the language of lust and if their parents weren't in the car, he'd haul her upstairs and show her how much. He escorted her to the car and helped her into the seat.

"So," Sylvia opened her mouth as soon as Jason started the car, and Candice held her breath, bracing for whatever would come out of her mother's unfiltered mouth. "When are we getting grandbabies?"

"Oh Lord." Candice turned around to give her mother a piece of her mind, but Jason's chuckling stopped her. *Maybe he doesn't want babies.*

The car was silent. Candice couldn't speak with her mind running rampant.

The parking lot at Pavoili's was packed, as usual. Sylvia pulled a handicap placard out of her purse, and Jason didn't hesitate to use it. They bypassed the line and were seated at the chef's table. Candice perused the menu as if she hadn't been there enough to have it memorized.

"Excuse me."

Jason looked up at the unexpected visitor standing next to their table. "You have got to be kidding me."

Jason's infuriated growl grabbed Candice's attention and she looked from him to the person who'd stepped up to their table.

"Wow, you have some nerve coming over here, Vince."

"If the rumor mill is correct, congratulations are in order."

"You know what, Vince? The work place is already getting a bit hostile. I'm partly to blame, so I haven't filed a complaint, but I will not put up with your nonsense out here in public."

"What do you mean hostile?" Sylvia questioned.

Candice ignored her mother's question.

"You're damn right you're to blame for it."

His tone made Jason rise from his seat

"You played me." Vince tried to stand his ground, but Jason hovering over him and pulsating with a wrath reserved solely for him took some of the steam out of his voice.

"And you assaulted her." Jason's commanding presence silenced the tables around them.

"Assaulted?" Vince's eyes widened as he raised placating hands. "I'm sorry. I shouldn't have put my hands on her, but assaulted? Hell no. She had some random dude living with her and—"

"And what? I must've been hitting it, so you might as well take what was she owed you?"

The look he flashed Candice said more than his mouth ever could.

"Wow…" Candice couldn't even respond with her firecracker of a mother sitting next to her.

"Oh, hell no." Sylvia struggled to get out of her seat. The chair scrapping across the tile floor and dishes clanking as she bumped the table garnered them even more attention.

"Mom, calm down. I don't want you back in the hospital." Candice passed Sylvia a glass of water, quietly admonishing her to take a sip and breathe. Candice rubbed a soothing hand along her mother's back while her eyes pleaded with Jason for him to sit and not allow Vince to rile him up.

"Vince, I wasn't playing you. You putting your hands on me is what made this happen." She gestured between her and Jason.

"And you're married already. Get out of here with that nonsense."

"You've got a huge set of balls." Jason stepped forward and Candice was out of her seat and standing between them before Vince even knew his life was in danger.

"You aren't smart enough to know when it's time for you to go. Let me make things clear for you. I'm not into you...never was. You knew that, so don't stand here looking all shocked. The only way I played you was using you to get my program started. Take that knowledge and do whatever you want with it, but if you don't get out of here, I'm going to let him loose on you." She turned her attention to Jason, easing him back until he plopped back into his seat.

Vince finally proved he had some common sense and was moving away before she had a chance to look back over her shoulder.

"You guys ready to order?" Yvonne waved a waiter over, ignoring the nosy eyes still trained on their table.

"Yeah, I already know what I want." Sylvia downed the rest of her water and turned to Candice.

"You just take it easy. All of this pasta and rich sauces can't be good for you." Candice placed her hand on Jason's knee under the table, rubbing slow circles into his rigid muscles. She was trying to move dinner along as if they hadn't been interrupted, but couldn't do it with a ticking time bomb sitting next to her.

Sylvia waved away Candice's concerns and proceeded to order a heaping pile of pasta in a creamy white wine sauce. Candice rolled her eyes, letting her get away with it this one time. Candice and Yvonne rattled off their orders and the waiter stood there, waiting on Jason. He was lost in thought.

"Baby, do you know what you want?" Candice tapped his leg and his eyes snapped to hers. "Do you know what you want?"

Jason pointed to some item on the menu, the waiter wrote it down, collected the menus, and walked away. Jason turned his eyes to

167

Candice and, with a voice that let her know it wasn't up for discussion, told her, "It's time to quit your job." He sipped his water and then started conversing with their mothers like he hadn't said anything. Candice blinked away the shock and joined in.

Dinner turned out to be a good time once Jason's tension let up. He charmed and regaled all three ladies with his wit and humor. When he'd finally laid Candice in bed that night, her heart had swelled even larger for him.

168

# 24

Dim light from Candice's desk lamp was the only thing illuminating the room. She wished her mind was shining as bright. She sat at the desk in her make-shift home office trying to rein her mind in. Her job was a lost cause as long as Vince was still in control; she could forget about ever having any influence. It was probably just a matter of time until he fired her. So, why was she having such a hard time writing her letter of resignation? Her livelihood, that's why. The thought of working alongside Jason at the youth center reignited the passion that had made her go in to social services. But, that was weeks away, and the only income they had was her job. She couldn't just quit. That thought alone was the reason she sat in front of the computer in the middle of the night, staring at an unfinished email to the center's director.

Normally, her home office, which was really just a desk and laptop in the far corner of her living room, was perfect, but that night, she was working with minimal light to keep from waking Jason, who'd fallen asleep on the couch. She considered waking him and helping him to bed, but his presence was comforting.

She adjusted her desk lamp, making sure the light wasn't hitting him. She'd read the same paragraph so many times that an alert mind would've memorized by now. She took a gulp of her coffee and tried to focus. The hot liquid warmed her from the chill that had settled over the room, but it did nothing to energize her. Jason's soft snoring—which she found totally adorable—was lulling her to sleep. She found herself listening to the rhythm of it and struggling to keep her eyes open. A few hours of sleep would do her some good. She set an alarm on her cell phone and went to join Jason on the couch.

She took a quick detour to the restroom, and when she returned, he was sitting on the edge of the sofa. His elbows rested on his thighs, his head hung low between his shoulders, and the pads of his fingers were on each side of his head, digging into his scalp.

"Hey, you okay?"

He didn't answer, but just kept burrowing his fingers into his scalp.

She walked over to him and kneeled in front of him. She caressed the side of his face attempting to get him to lift his head. "Is everything all right?" She tried to pry his hand from his head. "Jason you're—"

His other hand shot out and wrapped around her throat. She gagged from the collision of his palm against her windpipe. Strong thick fingers bore into her flesh. Her eyes bulged as she wrapped both hands around his wrist. She wanted to scream, but he'd cut of her oxygen supply. She dug her nails into his arm and scratched as hard as her weakened body would allow. His skin split and warm blood coated her finger tip.

"Oh God!" His head suddenly lifted and he released his hold on her neck. "Candice, baby…"

"Get away from me!" She gasped, the brisk intake of air sending her into a coughing fit. She crumpled to the floor, hand covering the sore marks on her neck as she crawled away from him.

"Baby, I'm sorry." Her trembling and gasping tore at his heart. He'd done that to her, put fear in her. He'd never forgive himself. "It's the nightmares. Sometimes it still feels like I'm locked up, still having to fight to keep those crazy sick perverts off of me." He'd woken many of mornings with his blankets and pillows strewn across the room, his lamp on the floor, and nightstand turned over like he'd been fighting in his sleep. It had been a while. He'd just assumed her presence in his bed had chased his demons away.

He crawled after her, pleading for her to forgive him. He needed to hold her, comfort her, and reassure her that he wasn't a monster. He reached for her and her trembling intensified.

"Candy, baby I'm—"

"Get out," she rasped, still trying to find a safe place away from him. She'd never even had a man raise his hand as if he were going to hit her. How had she managed to marry a man that would do such a thing? Tears poured from her eyes and her lungs still burned from lack of oxygen.

She was right, he needed to leave. His bare feet shuffling on the padded carpet seemed like the loudest sound in the world. He grabbed his

shoes sitting at the door and turned the knob. "I didn't mean to hurt you."
He knew he needed to leave, so that she was safe, felt safe, but it was the
hardest thing to do. He pushed off his heels and was out the door before
he could stop himself and come up with a reason to stay.

The cold night air slapped him across the face, nearly freezing the
lone tear he'd allowed to escape. Though his world was shattering right
before his eyes, he didn't deserve the release and cleansing that came with
tears.

The door clicked shut and Candice broke down. "Oh God!" The
physical pain of her neck had nothing on the gut-wrenching pain of her
heart breaking. She doubted even the power of God could heal the pain.
Her prayers were lost amongst her wails and she gave in to the sorrow
that engulfed her.

She'd waited a long time to find a man that made her feel the way
Jason did. He excited her and made her feel like she was the only woman
in the world. The one she thought was her perfect man, was a monster.
For once, she'd felt like she belonged, like someone got up in the morning
with her on his mind. How long had she felt like she was drifting in the
world, never taking root, or having someone miss her when she moved
on? Even with finding her brothers, it was hard to achieve that true sense
of family. She'd always assumed they'd taken her in out of obligation,
and sometimes wished they hadn't. She had her mother, but a mother's
love was supposed to be unconditional.

Everyone else whose place in her life was optional had chosen
another option, starting first and foremost with her father. What kind of
man loves his little girl until she turns five and then walks away without a
look back? She spent thousands of dollars to track him down, hoping to
reclaim the father she'd missed for fifteen years. What she got was an
introduction to the brothers she didn't know she had, along with a reality
check that the loving father she remembered hadn't raised his sons with
such fondness. He was abusive, and when she confronted him about it, he
drifted off into oblivion again. She anticipated that her brothers, April,
and the rest of the family she'd attached herself to would eventually do
just as her father had. With Jason, it felt different. He never said he loved
her, but she never assumed he'd leave. She'd found happiness, only to
have it stripped from her. How could she have been so wrong about him?

171

Her sobs turned violent and she clambered to her feet, rushing toward the bathroom before she heaved on the carpet. Her head hung in the toilet bowl as her stomach released its contents.

They'd had a great evening, cooked dinner together, laughed, talked, and then settled on the couch to watch a movie. The movie wound up being background noise to their lovemaking. The ending credits were rolling when her heart rate slowed and they drifted off to sleep. The discomfort of the couch woke her up and she couldn't help but wonder if she'd stayed put, would the night have played out differently.

She still smelled of him, of them. God help her. It didn't turn her stomach the way it should have. It made her yearn for his touch and to hear his voice, having it soothe her the way nothing else could. Nightmares or not, any man capable of harming a woman would have no place in her life. So instead of chasing after him, the way her traitorous fragmented heart begged, she clung to the toilet, emptying her stomach until it was depleted.

Once again, she forced herself to her feet and went in search of her cell phone. She dialed Tim's number and hung up before it started ringing. Calling him would pretty much number Jason's days on earth. She hated herself for even caring what happened to him. She dialed another number and waited for the only person she trusted to keep her secrets.

"April," she spoke over April's greeting. "Come over. I need you."

The sound of her voice put April on alert. Her response was immediate. "I'm on my way."

Candice ended the call and collapsed back on the couch, her mind still wondering how she could've been so wrong about Jason. She was so lost in thought that April was knocking on her door in no time.

"Oh, Candy." April hooked her arm around Candice's waist and guided her toward the sofa. "What happened?"

Candice opened her mouth to say something, but speaking it aloud made it all too real. She wanted to enjoy her delusion a bit longer. Where she could tell herself it hadn't really happened, that Jason had just run out to the store and would be back soon, that her happily ever after hadn't been ripped from her arms. It sounded much better than reality.

Candice plopped her head into April's lap and April attempted to fist her heap of hair away from her face. She pulled back the straggling strands plastered to the tears on Candice's cheeks and from somewhere materialized a hair tie.

April worked her first lady magic, as Candice affectionately called it, humming with that melodic voice of hers and stroking the tension from Candice's back. Her sobs settled, but the tears still trickled out the corners of her eyes.

"Where's Jason? Did you guys have a fight?"

Candice took a deep breath to ward off the wails April's questions were conjuring and shook her head. It was true. They hadn't fought. One second, all was perfect, and the next, all hell broke loose. She stood up and had to close her eyes until the dizziness her sudden movement caused had diminished. Her mind was in a whirlwind and she hadn't noticed she was pacing until April stood in her path.

"Settle your mind and talk to me." April led her back to the couch. "You didn't call me over here to figure this out on your own. Let me help you."

"Jason." The words clogged her throat and thickened with the memory.

Candice paused as she replayed it. All she saw was the look on his face when he realized his fingers were wrapped around her neck. His words looped through her head, *it's the nightmares, sometimes if feels like I'm still locked up.* Her heart dropped into her stomach and her eyes shut with regret. Why hadn't she realized what was going on before getting April involved. She could feel April's waiting eyes. Hopefully, she could fix everything. "He choked me, but—"

"What!" April shot to her feet, nearly knocking Candice to the floor. "Oh, hell no!" She had her phone out and was punching numbers into her cell before Candice could tell her to quit cussing. They'd all been repeating the phrase to her since the day she married the pastor that it was almost second nature. "Paul and Tim will handle him."

"No!" Candice jumped up and snatched the phone from her hand. "My brothers will kill him." She plopped down on the couch, glancing at the phone ensuring she'd hung it up. "April, I think there's something wrong with him."

"He choked you. Of course there is something wrong with him."

"Yeah, but I don't think he knew what he was doing."

"Come on, Candy; don't be that woman. I know you really like him, and he probably apologized, but men who hit women won't change."

"I know that, but I think this is different." She replayed the situation again and came up with the same conclusion. He absolutely was not conscious. "I think he might've been sleep. I was right in his face trying to get his attention and he wasn't responding. He was scaring me and I got a little forceful trying to get his attention. That's when he choked me. I think his mind was back in prison, and he thought I was attacking him."

April kneeled in front of Candice, examining the red marks on her neck. "Whatever the reason, he could've killed you."

"I know." That's ultimately what it boiled down to. He could've killed her.

"You have to stay away from him."

Candice dropped her head, studying her fidgeting fingers. "April, he's my husband. What happened to 'for better or worse'?"

"Candy…" April said her name in that sing-song way reserved for a mother warning her child they were stepping out of line.

Candice ignored April's censure. After the attack she'd endured, April would be the last person to tell a woman to honor her vow to an abusive husband or stay in an unsafe situation. But, Candice had to go with her gut.

"If we'd been arguing and he'd hit me, I'd agree with you, but I think he has PTSD. The more I think about it—as bad as I'm hurting right now—I shouldn't abandon him."

"While you're doing all that thinking, think about how you could be dead right now."

"He needs help, and I'll get it for him."

She'd studied a few cases of post-traumatic stress disorder. Jason's history fit the description of events that could cause the disorder. The humanitarian social worker in her wouldn't let him suffer alone.

"Candice, you're a grown woman, able to make your own decisions, but you're also my best friend. I don't want anything to happen to you. I wouldn't be able to live with myself if I just swept this under the rug and then he really hurt you."

Candice studied her fingers, toiling them in her lap. She hoped to God she was making the right decision. Her life could depend on it. "He won't hurt me. I'll keep my distance and make sure he gets counseling." Her shaky voice morphed into confident and controlled as a plan unfolded in her mind. "I won't abandon him." She looked up to let April know she wasn't changing her mind. The tears in April's eyes made hers come more rapidly.

"Candy, I can't ignore this. I'm sorry, but I'm going to tell Richard." She stood to leave, but Candice grabbed her arm.

"April, please." Richard wouldn't hesitate to call her brothers. The way he treated Candice like a little sister, he might be the one to show up at her door to beat Jason down. "How many times have I kept your secrets?"

"More times than I can count, but I've never asked you to watch some man hurt me." April dropped back down on the sofa and wrapped Candice in her arms. "Don't risk your life for him."

"You'd risk yours for Richard. Isn't that a part of marriage, *in good times and bad, in sickness or in health*? April, he's sick. Telling my brothers will isolate him and he won't get the help he needs."

"Yes, I'd risk my life for Richard, but you'd be there giving me hell about it every step of the way. That's what friends do." April kissed her cheek and walked to the front door. "Lock this door and don't let him back in here tonight."

Candice walked to the door, eyes pleading for April to reconsider, but the look on her face said it all. The conversation was over and April was snitching.

For the first time since his arrest, Jason drove down to the gas station where the crime he was convicted of had taken place. It wasn't where he'd intended to end up, but after fielding his mom's interrogation as to why she had to pick him up in the middle of the night, he needed some fresh air. Apparently, his subconscious mind wanted to visit the spot that had changed the course of his life.

Not much had changed in ten years; same game, just different players. A frail, thin man with sores on his face and a mouth that looked as if it hadn't seen water in years approached Jason's car, offering to wash his windows or pump his gas, no doubt trying to earn a few bucks to score his next hit. He was fidgeting and scratching so bad that desperation would soon set in and he'd make a foolish choice just to get high. That addictive rush of tranquility surging through your veins, the escape from the despair, heartache, and inadequacies of reality into a world where all things were possible could make a man do the unthinkable just for the experience. Jason eased out of his car, shaking his head to the man's offer and locking his door. He didn't want the man's desperation to wind up costing him.

Jason hesitated as he approached the spot where he'd parked his car that night. He had sat in that car listening to music like an idiot while his boys were inside robbing the place. They had driven around for hours in his broke down rusted Nissan Sentra that he'd worked hard and saved for. Lamont had just got out of juvenile hall and they hadn't hung out in a while. There wasn't a day since then he didn't wish he'd left it that way.

Two twelve packs and $150 were the price for Jason's freedom. Lamont had taken his freedom, his future, and now his wife. He wanted to run back home and beg Candice to forgive him, but how could he ever look her in the eye after what he'd done? He couldn't. Life without Candice would be worse than every single night in prison, but that's what he deserved.

In the morning, he was scheduled to meet with her brothers. Two men who selflessly sacrificed their time to visit him would soon become enemies, once they found out what he'd done. He and Paul still weren't back to being boys. Now, Tim's friendship would be lost as well. He could possibly be going back to jail. That terrified him, but not as much as hurting Candice again.

They were meeting with the contractors for a final walk through of the youth center. It should've been one of the happiest days of his life, but he'd yet to crack a smile.

He cut his little trip down memory lane short and hopped back into the car. He gripped the steering wheel and rested his head against it, sucking in a deep breath as he prayed for the strength to keep going. Maybe his prayer was all wrong. It wasn't the strength to keep going that he lacked. It was the desire to do it that he was missing. He started the engine and drove to his mother's, hoping sleep met him there, hoping sleep was the end.

He didn't know who would be harder to deal with, his mom or Candice's mom. The latter was sitting on the sofa, looking like she'd been waiting up for him. He tried to casually walk through the living room, not acknowledging her. It wasn't his lucky night. In the short time he'd known her, he should've known that wasn't going to work. He appreciated her frankness, but it might push him over the cliff tonight.

"You and that stubborn daughter of mine arguing?" She chuckled and patted the cushion next to her for Jason to join her. "I've been calling and texting her since Yvonne got back. I need to understand why her man is here and she is there."

"I'm sorry. I don't mean to be disrespectful, but I have a meeting in a few hours and would like to sleep a bit. Maybe we can talk later." He turned to leave, but her words stopped him.

"Don't give up on her or yourself. You've both been through a lot. You deserve this happiness."

"Yes ma'am," he answered without turning back.

She was wrong. He didn't deserve Candice. She deserved so much better than him. He wouldn't beg her to take him back. She needed to be free from the pollution that was his life.

Sleep fought him hard. It wasn't until it was almost time for his alarm to go off that he finally dozed off. His alarm buzzed. Immediately, he shut it off like his subconscious was wide awake and anticipating the

177

intrusion. His eyes burned like he had sand in them. The more he rubbed them, the worse they felt. Slowly, he lifted his heavy head and slid his legs off the side of the bed. He wanted to lie back and pull the covers over his head. If he did, a bottle of pills, a blade to his wrist, a bullet to his brain was imminent. He had to press on. His movements were sluggish, but he moved.

He was ten minutes late leaving the house, but couldn't bring himself to care. The youth center wasn't far. The drive to get there was a blur. He walked in the conference room and his steps slowed.

"What are you doing here?" His heart constricted at the sight of her. He'd never be able to control his body's intense reaction to her. He had no choice, but to try.

Candice turned in her chair to face him, trying to keep her game face intact. "Well, I was thinking since I'm the social worker that will be implementing programs, it would be best if I joined you guys today, so I could see the space I have to utilize." She hadn't officially asked for the position, but that was the answer she'd given Tim when he'd asked the same question, so she stuck with it.

She stood, smoothing her hands up his chest, along his neck, and up to his head. He couldn't believe she was there with the same love in her eyes. How could she forgive him? The goodness in her was the reason she deserved better than him. Her simple touch was everything to him, but he had to step away. He looked around, aware that all eyes were on them. He couldn't let her love deter him from what he needed to do for her.

"Candice…"

"Shh," she placed her finger on his lip.

Jason turned to Paul and Tim. The fact that they showed up and weren't trying to rip off his head was proof that Candice hadn't informed them of what he'd done. For that, he was grateful. He'd confess one day, but not today.

"For better, for worse…"

"I'm sorry." He whispered his apology against her ear as he wrapped her in his arms. He squeezed her, lingering because he knew it would be his last. "But I won't risk hurting you again. Please go home."

"No! I work here. I have a right to be here." If everyone wasn't watching before, they were after her outburst.

178

"You have a job. Don't make this more difficult than it already is."

"You told me to quit." Her chest heaved with the desperation she was holding in.

A muscle ticked in his jaw as his eye bore into her. His silence was suffocating.

"This is where I belong," she choked out. Her brow creased in confusion. Was he mad at her?

"What happened?" Paul jumped in, giving her a target for her frustration.

"None of your business," she snapped at Paul. His intrusion reminded her they weren't alone.

Jason cupped her cheek, wanting to take away her pain. He pulled her toward him, brushing his lips against hers, soothing himself just as much as he calmed her. No matter how right she felt in his arms, how alive she made him feel, he couldn't give in to his need for her.

"Go home." He moved her away, putting distance between them, so he wouldn't touch her again.

"It's not home without you!" She sucked in a deep breath to fight off the tears, lifted a defiant chin, and plopped back down in her chair.

"You left?" Paul was on his feet, moving toward Jason. "You have some ridiculous fight and you leave?"

"Mind your own business," Candice spat out, directing all her anger toward Paul. She waved away Paul's incredulous look and took a deep breath. "Now, about the youth center…"

She gave Paul a look that made him sit down. She inwardly smiled at the tremendous victory and turned that same look to Jason, daring him to tell her to go home again. The entire room was in a standoff with her, waiting for Jason to make the next move.

Jason's heart swelled. How could she love and fight for him after what he'd done? He had to do what he could to keep her safe, but she was not going to let him walk away. They needed to talk, but without an audience. He did the only thing he could. He sat down.

Candice expelled the breath she'd been holding while waiting for him to make a move. She wanted to break down and grovel at his feet when he pushed her away. She hadn't anticipated having to beg him when

179

she was the one who put him out. What was going on? She hadn't contacted him throughout the night to give her mind a chance to settle, but maybe she should have. Had the night apart made him realize she was more trouble than she was worth?

No, his heart broke as much as hers had. She saw it in his eyes as he walked out the door. This was something else. Whatever was going on, she wasn't going to let it happen. She sat up a little straighter, determination strengthening her spine. Jason was her husband, and she'd fight for him.

# 26

Candice dimmed the lights in her living room and lit a couple of candles. She grabbed a bottle from the wine rack on the kitchen counter and a glass out of the cabinet. Settling on the couch, she sipped her glass and let Jill Scot's soulful voice crooning through the speakers soothe her aching heart. Five songs and two glasses later, she was feeling a little better.

She took a long sip from her third glass of wine and went to answer her ringing doorbell. She hoped whoever it was didn't try to brighten up her mood. April had been trying all week and was on the verge of being cursed out. All the spontaneous visits trying to get Candice to go shopping, out to lunch, or on a girl's night out was grating Candice's nerves. April, Tim, or whoever was at the door better not kill her buzz.

Was it possible for the presence of a person to enhance your buzz? The sight of Jason standing on her porch sent her head spinning. She scanned him from his boot-clad feet, up his legs—remembering the power she felt in them—to the chest and arms she could never get enough of. She did nothing to conceal the moan rolling out of her mouth. She was so happy to see him that she didn't care he'd used the doorbell instead of his key.

Finally, her eyes landed on his face. It was dark out, but the light on the porch illuminated the distress on his face. Her heart broke for him. She tried to imagine what he must have endured in prison, but couldn't fathom the things he might've seen. Alone, afraid, and convicted of something you didn't do must've been torture. But he wasn't alone now, and he didn't have to suffer alone.

"You really want to help me?"

"Yes, baby. I do" She couldn't count how many text and phone calls she'd made that past week, begging him to let her do exactly that.

He lifted her and instinctively, her legs wrapped around his waist. He cradled her as he sat on the couch. He just needed to touch her. It was selfish. He knew that, but he was weak for her.

"Come home and it will be different. I didn't know what was going on last time. Now I do. If I catch you in that state, I know how to handle it. And besides," she reached for his belt buckle, "You seem to sleep pretty good after we..." Her lips caressed his neck and her hand slipped under the waistband of his briefs.

He couldn't argue with that. Being intimate with her always seemed to calm him, but he couldn't let thoughts of their love making deter him. He gripped her wrist and pulled it to his chest. The sudden movement brought her eyes to his. "I got a call from pastor."

"I'm sorry." She climbed off his lap, stuttering her explanation. "I was upset and hurting, so I called April. She was already here before I realized what was going on. You needed help. I told her what I thought happened, hoping she'd support me, but she told. I'm sorry."

"Don't be sorry. April did what every good friend should." Because he had to or he'd go crazy, he ran his fingers through her hair, letting them linger on her neck, down the column of her throat, and back again. "I just had my first counseling session with pastor. It was hard to talk, but I did because I want to get better for you."

Her eyes fluttered closed, his words flowing smoothly across her skin just like his hands. He was there in their home. She'd tossed and turned every night wondering if he'd ever come back.

"I love you."

Her eyes popped open and instantly filled with tears. His words changed the rhythm of her heart, slowing it almost to a stop. It beat out each letter, thumped each syllable, and pulsed over the words, savoring them like a long-awaited meal. They filled her up, his next words making her overflow.

"I always have. It took me a while to realize that my heart racing, how happy I am when you're around, and how empty I am when you're not was love, but it's been there since the beginning." He tried to wipe the tears streaming from her eyes. They came faster than he could clear them. "I'm going to get better, so I can come home and build a life with you."

"What? You don't have to stay away," she pleaded, climbing back into his lap to hold him in place. "Stay in the spare room if you need to. Just don't leave me." She sobbed into his chest, trembling with desperation.

182

He held her firmly to him, soothing her with the gentle caress of his hand up and down her back. He didn't know how long they sat there. Her sobbing tapered off. He continued to hold her. She was calm and he knew leaving would rile her up again, but he had to leave. It was getting late, and the peace he felt just being near her made all his restless sleepless nights close in on him. Any longer and he'd be asleep, and that couldn't happen.

"Baby," he shifted to move her off his lap and her legs clenched tighter at his side. He steeled himself not to give in to her tears. "I have to go."

"No!"

He moved her off him with more force than he wanted to use, but it was for her own good.

"Jason, please stay." She begged, not caring how needy or pathetic she sounded.

He didn't respond, couldn't respond, if he opened his mouth, he'd cave. With all the strength he had, he walked to the door.

Candice threw a sofa pillow at his retreating back. "Fine, leave then." She swiped at the tears streaming down her face, letting her anguish turn to anger.

The raw emotion in her voice stopped him in his tracks. He was hurting her, but there was no other way to keep her safe. He reached for the door knob and another pillow landed between his shoulders.

"Go ahead and walk out. I don't love you anyway."

Those words tore threw him and he couldn't stop himself. He stalked toward her, lifted her in his arms, and slammed his lips on hers. The thought of losing her love broke something in him. He stormed into their room, pressed her into the mattress, and tore through her clothes.

"Say you love me!" His pleading groan only hinted at his fear of losing her. In a short time, she had become his life. He never wanted to hear that she'd stopped loving him, even if it was out of anger.

Her sorrow mixed with their passion made a heady combination. She was speechless.

"Say you love me." His tone was commanding and lovemaking more demanding.

"Always," she managed through labored breaths.

"Say it." He rocked into her with such power and authority that she had no choice but to obey.

"I love you," she proclaimed in a scream as she shattered around him.

She pulled him over the edge with her and he growled the words back to her. Not even allowing his pulse to calm, he planted kisses all over her face, neck, and chest as he whispered his love for her. Within minutes, he'd cranked her back up and she panted his name in pleasure. He brought her to the pinnacle so thoroughly that she was falling asleep before her breathing returned to normal.

Jason watched her falling asleep and did all he could to help her. Her sleeping would allow him to slip out without making her cry. It wasn't what he wanted, but was just the way it had to be. Anything else would put her at risk. He tiptoed out of the room—his own heart dying a little bit—made sure all her candles were out, and left.

The sun peeked through the blinds and Candice opened her eyes with a smile. She hadn't slept that well since the day he'd left. She rolled over, reaching for him, and the smile slowly slipped from her face. She sat up, tossing the covers aside, and hopped out of bed. He couldn't have just left her like that, sneaking out in the middle of the night like she was some jump off.

She checked her bathroom, the guest room, and the guest bathroom. He was gone. Her heart dropped into her stomach. She was going to be sick. She shut her eyes, inhaling slowly, trying not to lose it. She blinked back the tears, trying to focus on his words. He loved her and was trying to get better for her. That thought wrapped around her fractured heart, holding the pieces together.

She made her way to the kitchen, trying to focus on his love and not his sneaking out. She walked through the archway of the kitchen and nearly crumbled to her knees. "You're still here." She choked out the words between her sobs.

"I shouldn't be." Jason leaned forward resting his arms across the table. "I tried to leave, but..."

"This is where you belong."

He nodded and blew out the deep breath he'd sucked in. "You sleep in the room with the door locked, and I'll take the guest room."

She nodded her consent, excitement drying up her well of tears.

"You have to promise me something first." He motioned for her to come closer to him, and she willingly climbed onto his lap. "If I ever get like that again, you call the police and do whatever it takes to be safe." She nodded. He gripped her chin and looked squarely in her eyes, making sure she understood what he meant. "Even if you have to hurt me."

Her smile dropped and she turned away from him.

"Promise me," he urged, "Or, I'll get up and walk out of here. I need to know that you won't allow your love for me to put you in danger."

"I promise." Her whispered response wasn't convincing, but he accepted it. She cleared her raspy throat and tried to change the subject. "Are you hungry?"

"What do you plan on cooking? I came in here to cook for you and the fridge is bare."

"Well, I guess I haven't had much of an appetite, so there was no need to buy groceries."

Jason shook his head, trying to ignore the pang of guilt. "Let's get dressed. I'll take you out for breakfast. I expect you to order the biggest thing on the menu and eat it all."

Candice giggled as he patted her backside to hurry her along. *He's home.* She sighed, her heart hopelessly in love. Things weren't perfect, probably never would be, but love would prevail.

Candice bounced around in her seat, humming and popping bites of pancake into her mouth. Jason was laughing at her, but she was starving and happy. It was the first time in months she'd been in a restaurant without drama popping off. Her husband was home, and he'd confessed his love. She had every right in the world to sing and dance.

Jason opted to sit next to her instead of across the booth, and she took advantage by tossing a leg on his thigh, locking him to her. He looked at her sideways, but didn't complain. In fact, the lazy circles he drew on her thigh let her know he very much liked her leg there.

A drop of syrup clung to her lower lip and he leaned over to sample the added sweetness. He groaned in frustration at her ringing cell phone interrupting them. It was a good thing, too. There were kids in the restaurant and Jason could get out of hand.

She pulled away and nearly cursed at the name glaring on her screen. She showed it to Jason and his brows nearly hit his hairline. He took the phone from her and answered, "How can I help you?"

"I was looking for my daughter, Candice."

"This is her husband. What can I do for you?"

"Husband?" The line went silent.

Jason checked the screen to see if he'd hung up.

"I'm sorry. I wasn't aware she had a husband."

"From what I hear, there's a lot of things you aren't aware of. What can I do for you?"

Jason smirked at the other man's stammering, and Candice leaned in to hear what was going on.

"Well, I... I know it's last minute, but I was wondering if Candice would like to meet for lunch and maybe bring Paul and Tim?"

Candice was shaking her head no, but Jason responded, "Sure, text the address." He hung up the phone before Candice could take it and rescind his acceptance.

"Jason, why would you do that?"

"You gave him the option to be in your life or not. Looks like he's choosing to be there; you have to give him a shot."

"What happens when he disappears again?"

"Then you've done your part, and I'll be here to help you pick up the pieces."

The address arrived via text almost instantly, and Jason forwarded it to Paul and Tim in a group text, telling them to meet him there in two hours. Paul's response was immediate.

*We do have jobs, baby girl.*

Candice grabbed her phone from Jason to type her reply.

*And you're both the boss, so take an extended lunch.*

Tim sent her the side-eye emoji, but neither of them told her no.

186

Jason paid the check and took Candice for a walk along the pier to calm her nerves. San Diego was a beautiful city. In some cases, the drop off to the water was right up to the edge of the sidewalk. Waves lapped against the rocks, sending an occasional splash onto the concrete. Candice peeked over the side, watching the shore crabs scurry between the rocks. She smiled at a man and his son collecting the crabs in a bucket. She tried to recall memories of similar times with her father, but came up with nothing. He was in her life for five years, but couldn't remember more than a five-minute visit. What she did remember was the day she let him break her heart.

*"Daddy!" Candice jumped off the sofa, her short legs stumbling to get to her father as fast as she could. "You came. I told mommy you'd come."*

*Derrick's eyes shot over to Sylvia's, the sneer on her face unmistakable.*

*"You're late for the party." Candice reached her little arms up, silently pleading for him to pick her up.*

*"What party?" He stepped around her and sat on the sofa.*

*"My birthday party." Her arms dropped and the tears filling her eyes broke her mother's heart. "You didn't tell him, Mom?"*

*"I told him." She was done covering for him. It was time her daughter understood what type of man her dad was. It would make times like these easier in the long run. She picked Candice up, embracing her tightly to make up for her father's snub.*

*"I knew nothing about it."*

*Sylvia sat next to him with Candice in her lap and shook her head at Derrick.*

*"Mommy doesn't lie, Daddy."*

*"Neither do I." He reached his hands out to her. "Come here."*

*Candice didn't move. She looked in his eyes, searched her mother's, and then back to his. "Yes, you do." She climbed out of her mother's lap and went to her room.*

*"Candice, get back here."*

*She ignored her father's command and shut the door.*

That was the last time she'd seen her father until she'd searched for him years later. Candice didn't know how long she stood there watching and not watching the shore crabs. The foreboding that history was going to repeat itself had her rooted to that spot. Why had she offered him the opportunity to pop up in her life whenever he got good and ready, knowing the pain she endured when he chose to be absent?

Jason tugged her hand, dragging her attention away.

"It's time to go."

She pressed her lips to his cheek and without a word led the way to the car. The address led them to a shabby apartment complex on the rough side of town. When they arrived, Paul and Tim were already there. They hopped out of the car as soon they spotted her. She kept moving, not giving Paul a chance to question her. Thank God the address was right off the street; she didn't want to be walking through the shady complex looking for it. He had to have been watching them from the window, because as soon as they stepped on the porch, he opened the door.

"You've got to be kidding me." Paul turned his head, biting his lip like he wanted to cuss her out. "You know what? I can't even say I'm surprised. The next time I meet you for lunch, it will be by my invite."

"Don't be mad at me. Jason answered the phone."

Jason chuckled at Candice throwing him under the bus as three sets of eyes leveled on him. He ignored them all. "So, can we come in?"

"Of course." Her father backed out of the way.

"I'm Jason, the husband." He crossed the threshold, extending a hand in greeting.

"Derrick." He shook Jason's hand.

"So, what's up?" Candice didn't wait for the front door to close good before she turned on her father.

"Well, I was kind of hoping we'd eat before we got to the heavy stuff, but I understand." Derrick sat on the couch, hoping everyone would follow his lead and relax a bit.

Jason did and pulled Candice down with him.

"I just wanted you to know that I heard you and I'm here. This isn't much, but it's my new place. You have the address and I'm here."

The room was silent.

Jason looked around waiting for one of them to respond, but he was the only one who had a voice. "For how long?"

188

Derrick cringed, but he knew he deserved far worse. "For good, I hope, but I'm human and still prone to mistakes. I've been running for so long, I may not know how to stay put."

"Well, please forgive me for not jumping at the opportunity to have you walk out on us again." Paul hedged a little closer, looming over his father. Candice hoped he didn't reach out with a punch, but the release might do him some good.

"That's fair, but all I'm asking for is a shot."

"You never gave us a shot. So, give me one good reason why I should give you one."

"Because you're a better man than me."

Paul was at a loss for words.

"Baby steps," Candice finally found the nerve to speak. "You can call, text, or maybe even meet up to help us work through our issues. You don't meet the kids or the spouses…well, except this one." She motioned toward Jason and he entwined his fingers with hers.

"You speaking for all of us?" Tim was so quiet she had almost forgotten he was there.

"Yes. It's time for us all to let go of this anger and hatred. Not many people get a chance to look their dead-beat father in the eye and say everything they've wanted to say."

"What happens when he can't take it and bolts?"

"Then, we can enter heaven with our hearts free and clear." She looked to Jason and his nod was all the encouragement she needed. "Can I send him your numbers?" Their barely perceptible nods were all she needed. She pulled Jason to his feet and followed her brothers out the door.

# 27

Jason was talking, saying something…something important. Candice couldn't get her mind out of the gutter long enough to understand a word coming out of his mouth. The room was full of people, notepads, and pens in hand, writing down instruction from their future boss, and there she was, not even listening to him. She sat there at the conference table between her brothers, no longer even trying to look like she was paying attention. The timbre of his voice sent chills down her spine and reminded her of the words he'd whispered as he made love to her that morning. His strong hands had roamed every inch of her, laying accelerant for his lips to ignite. Not once or even twice, but three times he'd pushed her over the precipice and then carried her into the shower, not once seeking his own gratification.

She caught a moan at the tip of her tongue and took a sip of water before she embarrassed herself. She had to find a way to reel in her thoughts. The center was set to open soon. If she didn't focus and finish setting up the programs, the opening might be delayed.

"Report cards have to be turned in every grading period," Jason was saying once Candice was able to tune into the conversation.

"I certainly understand your reasoning, but you don't want that to be a deterrent. Someone with low grades may be too embarrassed to turn theirs in. You don't want something like that to cause them to miss out on what the center has to offer." Paul continued to argue his point, but Jason wasn't budging.

"I don't want anyone to miss out, but I also don't want these kids to be in here every day on the internet, playing basketball, or watching movies and having F's. We would be doing them a disservice."

"I agree," Candice said.

"Of course, you do. What newlywed woman wouldn't agree with her husband?" Tim leaned a little closer and whispered for her ears only, "And you were too busy lusting to pay attention."

Candice punched Tim in the arm as her face heated.

Paul grunted at the comment and she wanted to die of embarrassment.

"I agree, because when your program is funded by grants, you have to be careful to adhere to the guidelines of the grant. You requested grant funds to facilitate a tutoring program for at-risk youth. How do you determine who's at risk if you do not have the report card?" Candice opened her mouth to continue putting her brother in his place, but was interrupted by a loud whistle coming from the hallway.

"Man, this is nice."

They all turned to the doorway as Lamont walked in, looking around like he was at an art museum. He lifted the hem of his shirt revealing the butt of his gun. The warning was heeded. Paul and Tim leaned back into their seats, their posture anything but relaxed. He walked around admiring the spacious conference room and then took a seat at the table. "Please continue. Don't let me interrupt."

"Lamont, what are you doing here?" Jason growled through clenched teeth.

"Any meetings about this community should include me. I'm offended that I wasn't invited."

"You are out of your mind." His presence made Candice sick to her stomach.

He took the gun out of his waistband and set it on the table. "Careful sweetheart, this has nothing to do with you." He smiled at her and the evil in his eyes made her throat clog with fear. "Stay in your place. When the men are through handling business, I'll show you exactly what concerns you."

"You touch her and I'll break your neck." Jason inched closer to Lamont.

"Damn, Jay, bros before hoes." He motioned toward Candice, looking her up and down. "I keep seeing her around. This has to be you."

A muscle ticked in Jason's jaw as he eyed Lamont's every move.

"Yeah, that's you. You always did like the ones who were sexy as hell but too uppity to give a brother the time of day. And she has a ring on her finger. You just got out of jail and have already wifed someone." He threw his head back and laughed. The sick cackle echoed throughout the

191

room. "If I had known that when I saw her at the house the other day, I would've definitely gotten me a taste."

"Watch your mouth." Jason clenched his fist. Candice knew he was seconds away from laying hands on Lamont

"Or what, Jay?" His eyes dropped to Jason's hands clenching and unclenching at his side.

"What do you want, Lamont?" He expelled a ragged breath. Candice sat up a little straighter, prepared to risk her own safety for Jason.

"Like I told you before, I run these streets. Did you think you were just going to open this establishment without my input?" Lamont smirked and shook a scolding finger at him. "I thought you knew me better than that. I've come by to see how we can make this situation profitable for the both of us."

"Profitable?" Candice chuckled. "Clearly you don't understand what a non-profit organization is."

"Clearly you didn't hear me when I told you to shut the hell up." He leaned forward and spun the barrel of the gun toward her, his eyes cutting her as he spoke. "You're trying to keep kids off the streets, which will interfere with my business."

"Lamont, I'm just trying to provide a place that we didn't have growing up. If we did, our lives would be completely different. I need you to back down and let me do this." Before he finished speaking, Jason knew it was pointless trying to reason with him. Even after ten years in prison, he'd never seen a heart as cold as Lamont's.

"The way I see it, you're costing me money, and we wouldn't want that, now would we?" Lamont leaned back in the chair, arms along the armrests.

Seeing an opportunity, one of Jason's employees leapt toward the gun. Lamont saw him coming and slammed his fist into the man's face. Blood gushed from his nose, but it wasn't in vain. He managed to tap the gun and it slid across the table right to Candice. The scuffle was brief, but the tables had turned.

Jason, as well as Tim and Paul, motioned for Candice to pass either of them the gun. Her gaze was honed in on Lamont, though. Just thinking about what he'd done to Jason made her hand shake with rage as she gripped the gun's handle.

"Careful, sweetheart," Lamont smirked. "You're not a killer. I am."

"I could kill you and not miss a minute of sleep." Her skin crawled with revulsion. She should shoot him and make him feel just a fraction of the pain he'd caused. She could kill him, but he was right. She wasn't like him. He wasn't worth her freedom. Having him caged like the animal he was sounded much better.

Lamont casually made his way toward the door, never turning his back on them. "We will continue this discussion later." He turned toward Candice and smiled. "I'll be seeing you around."

Paul slipped the gun out of her hand and followed Lamont. Tim ran around the table to check on the employee still sputtering on the ground. Jason went to Candice. She collapsed in his arms. Panic lodged in her throat making breathing a struggle. She clawed at Jason trying to get closer to him. She wanted to crawl inside him and hide in his strength. Her shallow hiccupping had her on the verge of passing out.

Jason pressed her head to his chest and cradled her in his arms. "Come on, baby; relax and breathe," he whispered against her cheek. "I got you." He inhaled a slow deep breath hoping she'd follow suit.

"Oh God," she cried out, finally pulling in enough oxygen to speak. "He isn't going to leave you alone, is he?"

"Doesn't look like it." He needed to handle Lamont once and for all. He heard the veiled threat toward Candice loud and clear. If it meant going to jail again, he'd keep her safe. He looked over Candice's head to Tim and his slight nod let him know Tim's mind was in the same place as his. It was obvious Lamont wasn't going to back down and his unmerited vendetta was going to get someone hurt.

Paul came back in the room and motioned for Jason and Tim to follow him. Candice took Tim's place in tending to the wounded employee while the three men walked out of ear shot.

"He had a mini-army waiting on him outside." Paul whispered, making sure Candice didn't over hear. "We need to call the cops."

"And what are they going to do? The same thing they did when he interrupted our basketball game: nothing." Tim did nothing to hide his irritation. "I highly doubt the restraining order they suggested is going to work on a person like Lamont."

193

"It might not keep him away, but it definitely covers us if we have to use lethal force to protect ourselves."

"I agree," Jason finally piped in. "Can you handle the paperwork for all three of our families?" He accepted Paul's nod and continued. "That's good and all, but we have to step to Lamont a little harder than having him served with papers."

"That's what I'm talking about. I'm not trying to sit around and wait for him to show back up." Tim clapped hands with Jason and patted him on the back. "Let's bring the fight to him."

"I'm with that, but…" Paul hesitated, not believing what he was getting ready to say, "What's the end game? To kill him? Have him arrested? If we step to him and leave him alive and freely roaming this earth, he will take us out one by one. Whatever we do must be well thought out and planned."

They nodded in consent and agreed to meet up to discuss everything. Jason grabbed his wife and opted to take his employee to the hospital to start a paper trail and basis for the restraining orders. He had a sinking feeling that something was going to go horribly wrong, but it was time. He felt he had no other choice. He had to stand up for himself and the people he loved, or they all would be under Lamont's rule.

# 28

Life with Jason was going so… There wasn't even a word for it. A smile was permanently etched on Candice's face. They were still sleeping in separate rooms, but everything else was so perfect, she overlooked it. He lay in bed with her each night until he could barely keep his eyes open. In the morning, she'd knock on his bedroom door with a cup of coffee. Occasionally, he'd wake up before her and would knock on her door. She wondered if those were the times he'd woken with nightmares. She'd open the door and he'd be all over her, not seeking sex, but trying to get as close to her as possible. Whatever was going on, she cradled him to her chest, squeezing her arms and legs around his, and held on like their lives depended on it.

Candice rolled out of bed and made her way to the bathroom. She brushed her teeth, washed her face—trying to ignore the silly grin on it—and headed out to make Jason's coffee. She stepped into the living room and fear froze her.

"Jason, what are you doing out here?"

He didn't respond, just kept pacing.

"Jason," she yelled a bit more forcefully, but got the same results. Her heart sank, making it a struggle to breathe. Memories of the night he choked her raced to her mind. If it happened again, it might not have a happy ending. She should've run and protected herself like she'd promised, but looking at him, she couldn't move.

"Jason!" she yelled repeatedly, pleading for him to respond. She needed to touch him, shake him, or something to draw his mind back to reality.

He paced to one side of the room and she hurried past him to grab the pillows off the sofa. It was easier for her to creep to the front door than it was to run back across his path to the bedroom. She opened the front door and stood there hoping for the best, but prepared to run outside if things turned bad.

With all the strength she had, she hurled the pillow at Jason. It sailed toward him, barely grazing his back before knocking picture frames

195

off the shelf. She waited, hoping the noise would do the trick, but Jason continued to pace. She had one more opportunity; missing wasn't an option. She waited until he was close enough to where she was guaranteed to make contact. She tossed the pillow. The power behind it hit him squarely in the face and knocked him off balance. He stumbled back, grabbing the arm of the couch for stability.

Candice held her breath and waited. His eyes shot up to hers and she took a step back out the front door.

"Candice."

Her mumbled name reached her ears and she finally exhaled, stepping back inside.

"Did I do that?" Confusion blanketed Jason as he asked. He pointed toward the pillows and the picture frame on the floor.

"No, I did, trying to wake you."

"Trying to wake me?" His brows shot up and he moved toward her. The look on his face wasn't menacing, but it certainly wasn't friendly. Candice didn't know what to do.

Jason nuzzled the side of her neck and whispered, "You shouldn't even be in here, let alone trying to wake me."

"Well, it worked." She closed her eyes to enjoy the scratch of his stubble against her skin.

"What if it hadn't worked? Did you forget the rule? Did you forget your promise?"

"Of course I didn't forget." She would've been offended if he hadn't been delightfully seducing her. "If it hadn't worked, I was prepared to run out the front door."

His lips left her skin. He sighed in frustration.

"Jason, baby, I'm fine."

He touched his forehead to hers, searching for the words to make her understand. "It's not a chance I'm willing to take. I'd rather live without you than hurt you again. Next time, in your room with the door locked or I'll leave and won't comeback." He pecked her lips and walked away.

She watched his retreating back and then went into the kitchen. She couldn't even be mad. He was right; she'd broken a promise. She brewed herself a cup of coffee and sat a mug out for him, hoping he'd join her eventually. She was on her second cup by the time he stepped into the kitchen. When he did, he was fully clothed with keys in his hand.

"I'll be back in a couple of hours." The panicked look on her face made him rush to say, "I have a meeting with pastor."

"I'm sorry." She bowed her head in shame.

"No, I'm sorry." He tucked her hair behind her ear and lifted her chin, so their eyes met. "I overreacted."

"No. I underreacted. I won't take it so lightly next time."

"Thank you." His parting kiss left her wanting more, but she let him go, vowing to get all she needed when he returned.

Jason tried to not let his body language show how much he didn't want to be there. It was too early in the morning to be crying over his past. After what had just happened, though, he knew he needed to be there.

Jason smiled at the receptionist, trying not to ruin her day with his sullen attitude. "Good mornin', I have an appointment with pastor."

She extended her hand in greeting. "Good Morning."

"Pastor left a note for you to meet him in the sanctuary. Do you know how to get up there or would you like me to escort you?"

"Thanks, but I know the way." He walked down the corridor, rounded the corner near pastor's office, and ran into April as she stepped out of her office. "Good morning, Lady April."

She lifted her head, smiling. That smile dropped as soon as she realized who he was. "Good morning."

He totally understood her reaction and tried not to let it hurt his feelings when she walked around him to continue on her way. It was kind of refreshing to have someone not handling him like he was fragile. Other than Paul, everyone else treated him like serving time was a feat that garnered special treatment. April was mad and wasn't about to be fake about it.

He turned, watching her as she walked away. Her steps halted and his mouth curved into smile. She was about to let him have it. April spun around. He knew what was coming before the words ever left her lips.

197

"You could've killed her." She marched the short distance back to him and got in his face. "She means the world to me and you could've killed her."

The words hurt, but he could relate to the anger she was feeling. "I tell myself that every day. She is my world and I could've killed her." His guilt was apparent, but April didn't care.

"If you know there's a possibility you could hurt her, then why are you back in that apartment with her?"

"Because leaving would kill her." He placed a hand on April's shoulder, hoping she understood. "If your husband—the love of your life—left, would you survive?"

The answer was written all over her face.

At her silence, he continued. "Rest assured that I'm doing everything I can to keep her safe. Just like you told pastor what was going on because you love her, I'm here because I love her. I'm here to ensure we can live a long, normal, happy life together. I'm not excusing what I did, but please know that had I been alert, I would've never put my hands on her."

"I'm trying to believe you, but moving back in with her is a big risk to take. If you hurt her, I will definitely have to hurt you."

"If there's anything left after I hurt myself." Just as he knew her threat wasn't empty, his wasn't either. He wouldn't be able to live with himself if he hurt Candice again.

She nodded and turned to leave. She'd drawn a line in the sand and dared him to cross it. She had absolutely nothing to worry about.

Jason continued down the corridor. His conversation with April had lit a fire under him, and he was more motivated for the counseling session than when he came in. He walked into the sanctuary. Music was playing softly. He couldn't say who it was or the name of the song, but the melody was nice.

Pastor sat all the way on the front row. Jason quickly padded his way down the aisle and lightly rested himself a seat down from the pastor. The usual boisterous brother-to-brother greeting didn't seem fit for the hallowed atmosphere, so he sat silent and motionless.

Finally, the song ended and pastor turned toward him. Jason expected to see the jovial face of a friend. The face that greeted him was one he'd only seen across the pulpit.

"The Lord had me praying for you, harder than I normally do. I tried to move on to the next person only to be brought back to you." He turned back toward the pulpit and the next song on the playlist engulfed the silence between them.

Jason faced forward again, trying to see what the pastor was seeing. Pastor was in a spiritual realm Jason had yet to touch. All he saw was the craftsmanship of the altar. The look on Pastor Hawkins face revealed a greater depth of sight.

"My wife likes to watch this reality show about people who are severely obese."

Jason's brows shot up at the sudden change in topic, but he didn't budge, didn't say a word.

"Morbid obesity is what they call it. Most of the people on the show have a tragic past that caused them to pick up unhealthy behaviors that led to the weight gain. What's more shocking than them weighing five hundred plus pounds is the fact that the weight didn't show up overnight. Every meal, they knew they were overeating. Every pound they packed on, they saw it, felt it, and knew what they needed to do to be healthy. But it was easier to simply be overweight. Sure, there was pain, swollen ankles, strain on the knee, back problems, not to mention all the internal problems and heart complications. It was easy to turn a blind eye to all of that and just carry the weight. What wasn't easy was doing the work to lose the weight.

Being obese restricted them to the point where they were simply existing and not living. Their minds had succumbed to the notion that there was no other way of life for them."

Jason knew exactly what show he was talking about. Candice liked it, too. He'd even watched a couple of episodes with her.

"Jason, you're existing, not living."

Jason's head snapped to the left and he nearly choked on his spit. Pastor Hawkins met his gaze without flinching.

"You are morbidly obese and on the verge of a massive heart attack if you don't put in the work to lose the weight."

199

"I don't understand." He understood enough, but that wall he'd built for protection popped up and refused to let him acknowledge the truth.

Pastor Hawkins didn't come to play and wasn't going to let Jason either. "From the moment you drove that car away from the gas station, you've been packing on the weight."

Jason sucked in a deep breath, fighting to get it past the lump in his throat.

"The lost scholarship, you put on pounds. The threats from Lamont, you put on pounds. The pressure to snitch, you put on pounds. The guilty verdict, the fear, the assaults, and with every day you spent in prison, you packed on pounds until you were spiritually morbidly obese."

Jason leaned forward, resting his arms across his thighs, shoulders drooping. He suddenly felt every last one of those burdens.

"Are you ready to do the work to drop the weight? Exercise will alleviate the ailments. The swelling will go down, the pain will subside, and you will lose the weight."

Tears dropped onto his clasped hands. He wiped his eyes on his shoulders, fighting off everything telling him to get up and walk out.

"You did all you could to exist in a horrible situation. It's time to give God your pain and live." He slapped a hand on Jason back. Jason's red-rimmed eyes shot up to his. "You don't have to be strong in front of us."

Jason dropped to his knees, burying his head between his arms and the floor. He held his breath, willing the back-shaking sobs to stay at bay. He lost his restraint and, breath by breath, anguish seeped out of his mouth. Pastor Hawkins dropped down next to him, laying a hand on his back, urging him to let go.

The most guttural animalistic sound roared out of Jason. The agony, heartache, and anger from ten long years of suffering surged to the surface. Memories of every time he was attacked tried to consume him. The deep-seated sorrow of missed opportunities filled his chest, the pain nearly crippling him, but he fought.

He lifted his arms—carrying the weight of his confinement—and cried out, "Jesus!"

"That's right, brother. Cast your burdens on the Lord."

200

Jason cried out again and again until his pain turned to praise. Yes, he'd praised God before, but not like that. His praise of the past was pretending the ten years in prison hadn't affected him. In that moment—on his knees, head bowed—he acknowledged his pain and praised God in spite of. Every *Thank you, Jesus* and *Hallelujah* singed pounds off his spirit.

Jason didn't know how long he'd been at the altar crying, praying, and praising. Every time he tried to calm down and get himself together so he could leave, he'd think of another facet of God's greatness and start worshipping all over again.

When God finally released him, he felt drained, but lighter than he had in years. He grabbed the tissues Pastor Hawkins offered and dabbed the sweat and tears off his face.

"You good, bro?" Pastor Hawkins grabbed his hand and brought him in for a shoulder hug.

"Never better." Jason sucked in a deep breath and closed his eyes to fully get his bearings. When he opened them back up, the love of his life was standing in front of him.

"You ready to go home? April picked me up. Pastor thought you might need someone to drive you."

He nodded and kissed the crown of her head. They linked hands and strolled out of the church.

# 29

Passing the bowl of popcorn to Jason, Candice sat next to him—glass of wine in hand—ready to enjoy whatever movie he'd picked out. She felt his eyes on her and turned to him, casually sipping her glass. His eyes tracked the glass, honing in on the swallow as it rolled down her throat.

"What's wrong?" As much as she wanted him to be staring at her because he wanted her, his facial expression said otherwise.

"You should really stop drinking."

"Why?" She sat the glass on their new coffee table, biting back her irritation. Paul had told her the same thing, many times. She refused to even engage in an argument with him about it. She wasn't going to tolerate the same judgement in her own home. "Even Jesus drank wine."

"No, he didn't," Jason chuckled and that beautiful smile of his rolled back her anger.

"You mean to tell me he was at a party where they were getting lit, turned water into wine to keep the party going, and didn't take a sip?"

Jason laughed so hard he spilled the popcorn. He picked up what he could and placed the bowl on the table.

"Come here." He guided Candice onto his lap. She straddled his hips and leveled her eyes on him. "Explain it to me. Why do you drink?" The slight peck of his lips against hers softened the blow of his question.

"Well, for one, I like the taste."

"I'm sure there's something out there that tastes better than wine."

"There is." Her eyes dropped to his mouth as he licked his lips. *Yes,* he *actually tastes better than wine.*

"Good...What else?"

"What? Um..." She stammered, trying to pull her mind far enough out of the gutter to remember what they were actually talking about. *Wine...right. Why do I like wine? Yeah...* "It relaxes me."

"Really?" He gripped her hips and with a smirk that could only be described as devious, pressed her core along his bulge. "I think I can find something more relaxing."

"Yes," she moaned, body becoming pudding in his hands.

"Good," he groaned, moving her pliant arms around his neck. "It's settled. No more drinking."

His teeth nipping at her earlobe diminished her response.

"You want something that tastes good? Something to help you relax? You come to me. I'll give you everything you need." He did exactly that. Their clothes disappeared in a rush of moans and whispered promises. That night, he gave her everything she needed.

The next morning, Jason slipped out of bed with a smile on his face. Waking up with that massive head of hair in his face and those curves wrapped around him just set the world right. He did what was necessary to get his mind right, so he could have that. Now it was time to set everything else in its place.

He checked the time and groaned. He'd overslept and would have to forego a much-needed shower, but wouldn't change a second about what caused him to oversleep. He couldn't even brush his teeth right he was smiling so hard. Because he was a glutton for punishment and the woman he left in bed, he pulled the covers back for one last look before he left for the day. His hands itched to be full of her ample backside, but if he touched her, the brothers who were no doubt already waiting for him outside would be pissed. He stifled a groan and let the comforter fall back in place.

Pulling the hood of his sweatshirt over his head, Jason stepped out the front door and strolled to the car idling by the curb. He slapped hands with Tim hanging out the front passenger window.

"What's up, little brother?"

Jason chuckled and hopped in the back seat. "Nothing much." He made eye contact with Paul in the rearview mirror and could tell he didn't appreciate Tim's comment. "I appreciate you being here."

Paul's eyes dropped to the windshield as he pulled the car away from the curb. "I'll do whatever needs to be done to keep my sister safe."

His eyes shot back up to the rear-view mirror. Jason was still watching him. "Besides, you're family. We ride together."

"Aww! I'm so proud of you." Tim dabbed his eyes like he was wiping away tears. Paul punched him as best he could without losing control of the car.

Tim was clowning around as usual, but Paul's words meant a lot to Jason.

Paul side-eyed Tim, shaking his head. "Seriously though, I had a problem with how quickly everything happened, but my sister couldn't have chosen a better man."

"Maybe we should've waited, but I'll do whatever I can to make her happy."

"And you don't recognize that as love...not even a little bit?" Tim twisted around in his seat, holding up two fingers pinched together as he squinted at Jason. Jason couldn't help the smile that spread across his face. "Oh shoot, that is the face of a man in love right there."

Jason leaned his head back, chuckling at the car full of brothers making fun of him. He'd expected the back seat to be empty, but should've known these brothers rode hard for and with each other. He was honored to be a part of the group. Jason made the seventh brother, he and Candice the seventh couple. It was God's number of completion; their family circle was whole.

"All right...all right," Jason fanned his hands in the air, calming the ruckus. "Yes, I love her. It's the most amazing and crippling revelation I've ever had."

"Yup, that's love. Your world is centered on her, and the fear of losing her is crippling." Pastor Hawkins was backed by a symphony of *amens*.

"Exactly! That's why I'm out here at the break of dawn." Jason sat up a little straighter. "I don't know what Lamont's problem is, but that little threat he tossed toward Candice got my attention. I'm not taking it lightly."

"So, where are we headed?"

"To do a little re-con and come up with a plan. Make a left at the light and head toward my mom's."

By the time they arrived, the sun had made its way into the sky. They pulled up to a park that Jason had avoided the latter part of his teens. He hadn't wanted to be a part of, or witness, the things that happened there.

"From what I hear, today is Lamont's birthday. And tonight, the homeboys are throwing a little get together in his honor."

"How thoughtful. Let's celebrate the sociopath." Tim shook his head as he surveyed the area. "So, what are you suggesting? That the seven of us roll up on a park full of gangsters and murderers? I'm not trying to die."

"I could call in some old friends for back up." Paul leaned forward pointing toward the scattered patches of trees. "Have them posted up in the trees with rifles, nothing like a few red dots on their foreheads to keep folks in line."

"That sounds like a plan." Jason had to hide his shock. Who had friends with those types of rifles just waiting around to back them up?

"Wait a minute." Pastor Hawkins spoke up from the back seat. "Do we really have to go to this extreme? I guarantee most of their mothers are members at my church. I should be able to reason with them."

"Sounds logical, but one thing I learned in prison, the gang mentality and their loyalty transcends all logic. They would sell their momma to the devil before they'd cross Lamont."

"Probably, but I'm just saying can we try passive first? Instead of walking in there, guns blazing, have some sort of signal to let the boys in the trees know we need back up. We step to them the wrong way and this one problem becomes an issue we deal with for the rest of our lives...our short lives."

They sat in silence watching the neighborhood wake up. They needed to leave before someone got suspicious of their car idling. All eyes were on Jason. They left the decision up to him and would follow whatever plan he set. He was humbled by the gesture. It helped him make a decision. They trusted him and he'd do what he could to keep them safe. "Pastor will take the lead and we need to have some sort of radio communication with your boys. They'll be able to see things we won't. A heads up would be nice."

205

"Done." Paul typed a message into his phone. "But like I said before, what's the end game?"

"I love you guys like family, but I'm not trying to catch a case." Marlon had been quiet up until then, but his concern was just as valid as all the rest.

"I'd never ask you to do that. If it boils down to getting physical, that's all on me." Jason patted his chest, making sure everyone understood.

"Are you ready to go back to jail, possibly for the rest of your life?" Jaleel asked.

"If it means Candice is safe, yes. I'll do what it takes."

The car fell silent.

"Jason." Paul shut the car off and turned all the way around. "There has to be a better way."

"Come on...we talked about this. Lamont is not going to back down, and I already proved that fighting him doesn't work."

"I've been thinking. If he wanted to hurt you or Candice, he would've done it by now. Maybe he's just talking a good game."

"Thanks for being concerned, but you and I both know what Lamont is capable of. If he takes Candice..." Jason looked away, shaking his head to rid it of the thought. "Besides, the moment I step to him, it's going to get physical. Last I checked, using deadly force to defend myself isn't a crime."

"Call me paranoid, but..." Cole cleared his throat and waited for Jason to face him. "You said you've been asking around the neighborhood about how you could get in touch with Lamont. How do you know it hasn't gotten back to him and he's not planning a little surprise of his own? He probably knows where every last one of us lives. I'm supposed to be out with you all night while my wife's at home by herself?"

He probably was being a bit paranoid, but considering his wife had been held against her will and shot, he had a good reason to be. Talking about Candice being taken probably sent Cole's mind spinning.

"Text your wives and tell them we're having a potluck tonight at my place." Paul started the car and pulled his Escalade away from the curb. "My community is gated with armed guards."

"You think we can all be in the same place and get up to leave at the same time without them objecting."

"Newlyweds." Tim laughed, shaking his head. "They don't question anything as long as we're all together."

"Why? Because pastor keeps you out of trouble?"

"No," Pastor Hawkins laughed. "It's because Tim is always snitching. I promise, Camilla must have a voodoo doll or some type of magic to get his mouth running."

Jason laughed along with everybody else.

"We skipped basketball a while back and drove up to Los Angeles for chicken and waffles. I hadn't even been home an hour when April comes in the room talking about 'Camilla said'."

"You ain't never lied." Paul, reached into the back for a fist pound from Richard and then looked over at Tim in the passenger seat. "As soon as Sheena says, 'Camilla said', I search my brain for what me and my little brother got into. What makes it even funnier; he doesn't do it on purpose. She puts that lovin' on him and he just gets to talking."

"You sound jealous, big brother."

"Of what? I get the lovin' and can keep my mouth shut."

"Please don't be like Tim. We don't need two snitches in the group," Richard pleaded.

"Hey, hey, hey," Paul growled from the driver's seat. "We will not talk about Jason getting any type of lovin'."

"Oh, you don't want to talk about it?" Marlon was amused. "You thought it was funny when Cole was hooking up with my sister. Now that the shoe is on the other foot, you want us to be quiet." He leaned forward laughing even harder. "So, Jason, is it snitch-worthy?"

Paul slammed on the brakes. "Get out!"

The back seat erupted with laughter. Paul was not amused. He eased off the brake, slowly accelerating until he was up to the speed limit. He was grateful when Jason changed the subject.

207

# 30

Jason came home to chaos in the kitchen. Candice scurried around from the stove to the pantry to the refrigerator and back again. He could only describe it as frazzled focus. She was so engrossed, she hadn't noticed him standing there watching. He took the opportunity to admire her beauty. Her massive mane was piled high on her head and held in place by a scarf. Her tights and tank were covered by a black apron, speckled with the same flour that was smudged across her cheek.

She stood at the sink doing God knows what. Unable to do otherwise, he floated to her. Like a moth to a flame, he was drawn to her. Instantly, his lips were on her neck and his arms around her waist. He smiled at the slight intake of breath his sudden appearance caused.

"Whatever you're cooking smells almost as good as you do." He inhaled a lung full and exhaled his appreciation on her skin.

The sensation was heavenly, but she had to stay focused. Jason had a way of making her forget she had plans. She had to keep her mind on the night's festivities.

"Don't distract me." She wiggled away—smiling at his petulant expression—and reigned her mind back in on the veggies she been washing at the sink. "This has to be perfect."

"Your food is always perfect."

"This is different."

"How so?"

"Well," the more she tried to put it into words it did seem a little silly, "Your text said it was a potluck. This is my first time cooking a dish for the family potlucks."

"You grill for them all the time."

"Yeah, but this is different." She glanced over her shoulder, too timid to explain. "Now I'm a wife, being asked along with all the other wives to bring a dish. I want it to be perfect."

"I did that." He turned her around and had his lips on hers before she could ask what he meant. "I made you a wife," was his easy explanation when he came up for air.

Candice threw her head back laughing. His proud expression made her laugh even harder. "Yes, you did." She tossed her arms around his neck, pecking his lips and all over his cheeks. "Now, let your wife finish before she burns something and has to start over."

"We wouldn't want that, now would we?"

"No, we wouldn't. I promise, afterwards, you'll have my undivided attention."

He stole a few more kisses and then left her to her kitchen craftiness. Candice watched him walk away. He was absolutely gorgeous, inside and out.

*How did I get so lucky?*

Without much effort, he'd come into the kitchen and stole her focus. His scent hovered around her and as excited as she was to bring a dish to the potluck, she couldn't bring herself to care anymore. Rushing to get to him, she nicked her knuckle twice with the vegetable peeler. She placed the prepped pan in the refrigerator—deciding to cook it just before they left—and jogged to their bedroom.

He was stretched out across their bed with the remote control in hand. She tossed her apron to the side and joined him. She snuggled in for whatever show he decided to watch. He chose a basketball game. Normally, she would've rolled her eyes and left the room. Him being able to watch the sport that he'd lost the opportunity to participate in showed so much growth and healing. She couldn't help but be proud of him. She wrapped her arms tighter around his waist, laid her head on his chest, and melded to the length of him. She held him the entire game, sneaking kisses during commercial breaks.

It never ceased to amaze her how perfectly they fit together, physically and spiritually. They had so much in common, it seemed as though they were made from the same mold. Where there were differences, it strengthened the other's weakness. When the game was over, he reminded her of another way they were perfect together.

Jason spent so much time thoroughly demonstrating how well they worked together, they were thirty minutes late for dinner. Even standing on Paul and Sheena's porch, Jason held their contribution to the potluck in one hand and the other hand was wrapped around Candice's waist while his lips were firmly on hers. He didn't even pause when the door opened.

"I'll take that. Feel free to join us in the dining room when you come up for air." Sheena took the dish and shut the door.

Jason didn't acknowledge Sheena's presence, choosing rather to use his newly freed hand to caress the nape of Candice's neck. His lips traveled along her jawline and down to her clavicle, soliciting a purr so foreign, Candice didn't recognize it as her own voice.

"Let's go home. They won't miss us." She pressed into him as close as she could, hoping to persuade him to take her home and continue what they'd started before they left.

"I can't." He backed away.

The look on his face made her heart drop in to her stomach. "What's wrong?" At his hesitation, she pressed again. "All day, I've been trying to ignore the fact that something was off, your early morning meeting, you coming home and making love to me like you'd never be able to do it again, this potluck, and how you've been standing here kissing me for ten minutes like the world is ending. What's wrong?"

"I don't want you to worry about it." He pecked her lips and tried to walk into the house. Her firm grip on his arm stopped him. "I have some business to take care of tonight and didn't want you to be alone."

She opened her mouth with more questions perched on her tongue.

He placed a silencing finger on her lips. "Trust me."

"You're scaring me."

"I'm sorry." He pulled her close, hoping his embrace comforted her, and then led her into the house before she could ask any more questions.

Candice walked into the dining room trying to act like everything was all right, like her heart wasn't pounding in her throat. Truth was, nothing was all right and her heart seemed to have permanently lodged itself in her esophagus.

Being that they were late, everyone was already crowded around the huge table in Paul and Sheena's dining room. The table was large enough to fit all the adults and the children were loud and rambunctious at the kitchen table. Jason led Candice to the two open seats, presumably left for them. She squeezed his hand as he seated her, hoping he heard her silent plea.

"So, it's definitely worth being late to dinner." Marlon chuckled, and Paul's responding groan had every other brother at the table laughing. Jason couldn't help, but join in.

Candice shot him an inquisitive glare and he shook his head. "You don't even want to know."

The intoxicating aromas of the dishes being passed around made Candice's stomach growl, reminding her she hadn't eaten all day. As hungry as she was and as tasty as the food looked, she'd barely placed any food on her plate. She was too busy noticing the silent conversations amongst the men in her life.

"Stop worrying and eat." Jason leaned in and brushed a kiss on her cheek.

She turned her lips to his and tried to appease her mind with his kiss. She pulled back to look at him and similar scenes were taking place around the table. They were usually an affectionate bunch, but it seemed more so than usual. Every other woman was smiles and giggles, but Candice's knotted stomach wouldn't allow her a smile.

"Hey." Jason's finger to her chin brought her attention back to him. "I love you."

That got a smile out of her.

"You make breathing and being so much easier."

"Aww!"

Jason rolled his eyes at Tim. He thought he'd spoken for Candice's ears only, but he didn't care who knew how much he loved her.

"Oh God." Candice nuzzled his neck, hiding her face in the crook. "This...you...us, seems so unreal I have to pinch myself. I mean really, did this happen?" She extended her hand wiggling the diamond sparkling back at her. The love she'd finally found was so surreal.

"It happened." He kissed the crown of her head resting against his shoulder.

"Aww, Candy, look at you."

Candice looked across the table at her sister-in-law, Sheena, and noticed every woman at the table had their eyes on her.

211

"I have to admit, I was a little skeptical about this." She motioned toward Candice and Jason. The other women nodded in agreement. "Especially how Paul was ranting and raving day in and day out."

Candice rolled her eyes at Paul.

"But look at you. He makes you glow."

"I agree." Candice shot straight up, eyes bugging out at Paul's words. "And he has that same 'surrendered to love' look the rest of us do. I couldn't be happier for you, baby girl."

There went the waterworks. She tried to act like his approval didn't matter, but it did.

"I've been hard on you because I didn't want you to miss out on this type of happiness, but in being hard, I didn't see that my prayers were being answered. I'm sorry."

"I'm sorry, too."

"You have nothing to be sorry for." He waved his hand, dismissing her apology. His tone became more serious. "I'm not saying I'll stop being hard or stop worrying about you, because I love you and that's just what I do, but I couldn't think of better person to step aside for." He nodded at Jason and raised his glass of soda to him.

Jason nodded in return.

Candice was too busy dabbing a napkin against her wet cheeks to notice the silent exchange of power. She finally got the leaky faucets—that most people called eyes—under control and Jason leaned over and kissed her cheek.

"It's time for me to go." He stood and every other brother followed suit.

Candice's mind was running a hundred miles a minute trying to figure out what Jason was up to. She looked around at the other men stand—mind racing over all the silent conversations and overt affections of the night—and she grew increasingly nervous. It all came to one conclusion.

She was out of her seat and dragging Jason to the bathroom before he noticed the change in her demeanor. He had to be after Lamont and she was not about to sit quietly while he risked getting himself locked up or worse.

"He's not worth your freedom or even worse, your life."

212

"But your life is."

His calm resolve to do whatever he could to keep her safe stole the words out of her mouth. He was risking his life for hers.

"Men like Lamont don't issue empty threats. He's going to come for you unless I get him first."

"So, what…you're going to kill him?"

"Once Lamont sees me, whatever I do to him will definitely be in self-defense."

The thought of Jason having to defend himself against that psychopath ignited her panic. She held onto him, trying to squeeze her will into him. Tears streamed down her face, unchecked and uninhibited.

He held her just as tight, angry for causing her pain. A knock sounded on the door and sobs racked her body even harder.

"Jason, let's go before we're late."

Jason peeled away from her and slipped out the door. Not looking back, he closed it behind him and set his mind to do what he had to do.

Candice didn't know how long she stayed in the bathroom trying to get it together. Maybe she should've run out and told the other wives. Surely, they would've been able to stop their husbands. No matter how distraught she was, the rational side of her knew Jason was right. Lamont wasn't going to stop. Going to the cops would only upset him more. What was the alternative, become a monster like him?

# 31

Jason shut his eyes and leaned back against the leather headrest, hoping the tears dried up before they rolled down his cheeks and embarrassed him in front of his boys. He couldn't help but feel like he'd just held the love of his life for the last time. He prayed to God he hadn't just brought the same fate upon his friends. He had already concluded that he would sacrifice himself if it came down to their safety. He owed them his life anyway. After all the visits, letters, and phone calls encouraging him to keep his head up, he owed them more than his life.

"You good?"

Jason looked up to see Paul eyeing him from the rear-view mirror. "As good as I can be."

"If it eases your mind at all, they are not alone. I have a couple guys stationed at the house. If they see anything suspicious, they know to move in quickly."

That eased his mind a bit, but he was still tense. Stillness fell back over the car. Jason swore everyone could hear his heart pounding. What were they doing? They weren't thugs, criminals, or cops. They were one ex-con, a pastor, and a car full of businessmen possibly driving to their death. "Pull the car over. I can't let you guys do this."

His outburst was met with silence. They were almost to the park when Pastor Hawkins spoke up. "It may seem crazy and we may seem eerily calm, but after everything we've been through, we've learned that we are stronger together. Together, we survived my wife being raped."

"The death of my daughter."

Wide-eyed, Jason's head spun toward Jaleel, but before he could say anything, Marlon and Cole chimed into the conversation.

"My wife being stalked."

"Mine being kidnapped and almost killed."

"We've overcome betrayal." Paul's eyes flashed to Jaleel in the back seat.

"And secrets," Tim chuckled, trying to lighten the mood in the car, but immediately sobered. "Through it all, we stuck together. Tonight, we'll stick together and believe that this is one more thing God will bring us through."

"Amen," echoed through the car as they pulled up to the park.

"Something's wrong. Where is everyone?" Jason looked around at the sparse gathering of neighborhood thugs, some old friends, and couldn't help but think something was up.

"Let's stick to the plan." Paul exited the vehicle and waited for everyone else to join him. "Pastor will take the lead and try to reason with them, but listen for my cue, in case my boys in the trees see something strange."

"You ready out there?" Paul spoke into a mic on his lapel that had gone unnoticed until he touched it.

At the responding, "Affirmative," Paul motioned for Richard to lead the way.

Jason couldn't help but feel like a walking dead man, like he was trekking toward his execution. An execution he didn't have to attend. They crossed the street and stepped onto the curb. Before they knew it, they were surrounded. The sparse group seemed to fill up with men who'd been scattered about. They swarmed so quickly, they had to be expecting Jason's group. His breathing grew labored, although outwardly, he appeared unfazed. He wished he was in the trees to see what they were really up against. He didn't know those men from Adam, but because he trusted Paul, he'd put his life in their hands. That was good enough for Jason. It had to be.

"What's up, fellas?" Richard randomly greeted people and introduced himself. Some easily accepted his handshake, others stared him down. "It's good to see a few familiar faces. For those whom I've never met, I am a local pastor—"

"A pastor? Man, please. You're in the wrong spot for that Jesus talk."

"For real, though."

Several others chimed in, but Richard didn't let it deter him.

"A little Jesus talk never hurt anybody. As much as I love the Lord and could talk about Him all day, it's not why I'm here. We're looking for Lamont."

215

"That's funny." The vilest chuckle climbed over the group as a man made his way from the back. His dark complexion and dark clothes had hidden him in the shadows. "You don't just walk up in here asking for him and expect him to just pop up." He took a long drag of his cigarette and focused his attention on Jason. "You, of all people, should know you rolled up on the wrong hood. I suggest you leave before things get difficult."

It took Jason a moment to place a name with the face, but when he did, the same hatred he carried for Lamont surged through him. "Well, since you want to be the spokesperson," Jason stepped to where they were eye to eye and did nothing to hide the hatred in his tone. "I served ten years for both of you. You could've spoken up at any time, but you punked out and hid behind Lamont."

The man took another drag on his cigarette and his eyes faltered. Jason saw his humanity and capitalized on it.

"Dane, let's talk, man to man, without the audience." He placed his hand on Dane's shoulder to guide him away from the crowd and the unmistakable sound of several guns being cocked froze him. "I just want to talk." Was his heart still beating? If it was, it certainly wasn't in his chest. "You owe me at least that."

"Hold your positions." He heard Paul say in the background. The reminder that he had back-up calmed Jason's nerves.

Dane used Paul's words to speak to his homeboys. He stretched out his arms and fanned back the crowd. He must've held some type of rank. One by one, guns were put away. "Let's go for a ride." Dane flicked his still burning cigarette at Jason and led him to a black Dodge Charger parked right in front of the park.

As fast as they could, Paul and the other brothers backed away from the crowd and jogged to their car to follow.

Jason checked the side mirror and prayed to God the headlights following were his boys and not Dane's. Riding solo was one of the most idiotic things he'd ever done, but what did he have to lose? He didn't have to ask if Dane was armed. With the artillery that had popped out at the park, he knew that was a resounding yes. The question was, where were they going?

216

A few blocks later, Dane pulled over in some random neighborhood and hopped out of the car. Jason sat there trying to hear the voice of the Lord. His mind told him not to trust Dane, but his heart said to do whatever he could to end this ridiculous feud. Before he could decide, Dane opened his door.

"Get out the car, homeboy. You walked into a park full of killers making demands. Now, you got me out here by myself and you want to act scared."

"Not scared; just trying to be wise."

"The wise thing would've been to give Lamont what he wants."

"And what is that exactly?" Paul and the other brothers walked up behind Jason. Paul saw the apprehension their presence caused Dane and tried to ease his mind by relaxing against the car.

"Control." Dane backed up and slipped his hand into his pocket, "Over everyone and everything. He'll do whatever it takes to get it."

"Is that why you serve him like he's God?"

Dane chuckled, attempting to hide his shame, but it was prevalent. "Trust and believe, after what happened in that liquor store, I wanted something different for my life, but Lamont can be persuasive. He's a psychopath, sociopath, or whatever the hell you want to call it. Anyone that goes against him either dies or eventually bows down. If it gets back to him that I'm out here talking to you…" He shook his head to ward off the thought of what could happen. "I'm only here because of what happened ten years ago and I have a debt to pay. I'm sorry, but…"

The pause made the hairs on the back of Jason's neck stand at attention. His entire body tensed, preparing for what Dane was going to throw at him.

"He knows where you live and he probably already has her."

"I didn't leave her there." Instantly, he knew who Dane was referring to.

"He knew you wouldn't and was at your place before you left. He followed you and probably already had her before you got to the park."

Without thought of consequences, Jason grabbed Dane by the collar and stuffed him into the passenger seat of the Charger. In two steps, he was at the driver side and hopping in. He grabbed the back of Dane's collar as he tried to exit the vehicle.

217

"Sit down, buckle up, and give me the keys."

"I could blow your brains out and your boys'."

"Do you think we showed up without a little back up of our own? Give me the keys." The control on Jason's fury was snapping. Dane must've sensed it and passed the keys without further argument.

Jason had to remind himself to breathe. He could feel his heart pounding in every pulse point on his body. Breathing was the only thing keeping him from maxing out the speedometer. Even still, he blared through stop signs, lights, and whatever else stood in his way.

218

# 32

Finally piecing herself back together, Candice joined the other women who'd made their way to the living room. She heard the thunder of little feet playing in the second-floor game room. Her niece and nephew were spoiled beyond reason. They had every toy imaginable. The children would be entertained for hours, if not days up there. She thought of joining them. It would help to keep her mind off Jason.

As soon as she walked into the living room, questioning glances greeted her.

"We thought you left." April said.

Candice tilted her head to the side, gazing at April. "When have I ever left without saying bye?"

"Um…well…" April chuckled, fidgeting with the phone in her lap. "Ignore those text messages I sent you." She smiled brightly, and Candice went in search of her purse.

She found it at the table, dangling on the back of her chair. Immediately, she grabbed her phone.

*Did you leave?*

*How rude!*

*And you're not answering me.*

*Get your butt back over here.*

She walked back into the living shaking her phone at April and laughing. "Four messages…really? I was in the bathroom." She plopped down on the sofa next to her friend. "Sometimes I wonder if you're my best friend or my woman."

"I'm both. Now, tell me why you were in the bathroom so long. And don't say you were using it. Something's wrong. I saw it all over your face when you first came in here."

*Intuitive April strikes again.*

Candice wanted to tell them the truth, so they could come up with a plan, but there was nothing they could do. She didn't want any of them to deal with the panic she was fighting. She looked around at everyone awaiting her response. She ignored their silent question until her eyes

219

rolled back to April. She wasn't the type of friend to be silent until you were ready to talk. Her eyes were already screaming *spit it out.*

"How do you deal with loving them so much?" Candice slumped onto the couch trying to let them know where her mind was without giving to much information. "Worrying that when they go out, they may never come back, dreading that phone call or knock on the door that tears your world apart? Or, even worse than that, what if he realizes that you don't deserve him and you have to live the rest of your life knowing that he's loving someone else?"

"First off," Meme kneeled in front of Candice, placing a hand Candice's cheeks, and looked her in the eye. "You have to know your worth. Before I met Cole, I allowed how a man treated me to turn me into a woman who destroyed her family just to feel love."

"I endured years of abuse because I didn't think I deserved more." Latrice sat next to Candice and grabbed her hand. "If he hadn't almost killed me, I'd probably still be there, suffering, because I didn't know my worth. Marlon, a good man, helped me discover my value. He showed me that the rubies and the dollars my ex dangled in my face to get me weren't nearly enough for my love."

"I know that's right." April high-fived Latrice over Candice's head. "Once you know your worth, the rest is left up to faith. There are at least ten women I could name right now who are after my husband. Being married to a pastor isn't easy. Women crave powerful men and want the seat next to him. I could let it drive me crazy, but I know my worth. I have faith in the Lord and faith in Richard's love. He could've had any woman he wanted, but he chose me. Just like Jason chose you."

"And if his eye does wander," Delisa sighed and plopped down on the sofa across from them, "That faith in the Lord will be the only thing to keep you sane. It's no secret that Jaleel was attracted to Sheena. When I acknowledged it, all hell broke loose! I knew what I deserved and could walk away, but I believed God was going to work it out. That faith kept me sane through the most trying time of my life. Now, I have the love I deserve and the companion I want."

"If all else fails." Her sister-in-law, Camilla, locked arms with her other sister-in-law, Sheena. "We know two men that would be more than happy to have a talk with Jason if he's not treating you right."

220

"Oh God," Candice rolled her eyes and the room erupted in laughter. "I want the man to live. Tell Tim and Paul anything and you're digging my husband's grave."

"I'm glad you ladies are having a wonderful time. I almost hate to interrupt."

All laughter stopped and everyone jumped at the sound of the foreign voice. His presence stole the words from Candice's mouth. Her eyes bulged in terror and it immobilized her. Lamont made his way into the room. Her eyes never left him

"Man, talk about the finer things in life." He spun, looking around, hands raised in wonder. "I've been aiming too small, need to step up my game."

Her brain said run for your life, but she couldn't get her feet to cooperate.

No one spoke as he walked across the room toward Candice. The limp in his gait might have been a turn on to some women, but that, combined with the smirk on his face, made her skin crawl.

"Hello, Mrs. Stewart."

He reached to caress her face and Candice swatted his hand down. A scowl replaced his smirk and his semi-jovial attitude disintegrated. He snatched a handful of Candice's hair and yanked her up off the couch. She trampled across Meme as he pulled her forward.

"Candy," April screamed, undoubtedly reliving her own trauma.

"Lamont," Candice managed to speak through the biting pain of hair being ripped from her scalp.

It took a moment for the name to register, but when it did, it was enough to send the ladies screaming and scrabbling. He pulled out his gun, threatening their lives if they didn't calm down. In all the commotion, no one noticed April had grabbed her purse. In the palm of her hand rested the most horrifying piece of metal she'd ever touched. Richard had given it to her—for her protection—but more so for his peace of mind.

April raised a shaky hand, hoping her time at the gun range had paid off, and demanded, "Let her go!"

221

Candice sucked in a calming deep breath, an inexplicable peace settled over her. The women settled down and she could feel their strength rising with hers.

Lamont's eyes snapped to April's. The pleasure that had settled on his face at seeing the gun was sickening. He molded Candice against him as his shield.

"Shoot him!" Candice commanded.

"I'll get you," April protested.

"No, you won't. I've seen you practice."

"Don't play a killer's game. You won't win." He put his gun to Candice's head. "Shoot me and the force will make me put a bullet in her brain."

"Oh God," April cried and her gumption faltered. Shakily, she lowered the gun and placed it on the table in front of her.

Candice closed her eyes. The sight of their only chance of survival crumbling was too much for her.

"Good girl." Lamont's free hand groped Candice's breast and she felt the unmistakable bulge against her backside. His sick twisted pleasure was revolting, but she kept calm.

"If I'd known there'd be this much honey up in here, I would've brought my boys with me." He scanned the other women in the room, a lascivious grin spreading across his face. "But I can handle it all by myself, starting with you."

"We are going to lean forward and you are going to pick up that gun...Understand?" He tapped the barrel of his gun against her temple, making sure she did nothing but comply.

Candice did as she was told.

He snatched the gun out of her hand and shoved her toward April. April caught her and embraced her like her life depended on it.

"Get on your knees, Mrs. Stewart." Lamont lowered the gun to unbuckle his belt.

"No!" The sight of two men adorned in black easing into the room bolstered her strength. She should've been terrified, but the fact that their guns were trained on Lamont calmed her.

"You want to do this the hard way?"

222

The buzz of his zipper sliding down cranked up her indignation. He was the second guy within a few months who had felt he could just take what he wanted from her.

"I like the hard way." He raised his gun toward Sheena. Candice sucked in a deep breath to scream. Before the sound rent the air, two shots rang out. Candice's heart stalled.

Jason pulled up to Paul's house and the blast of a gun firing nearly stopped his heart. He and the others barged through the front door, frantically calling out the names of their wives and children. Paul stopped short at the sight of Sheena crumpled in a ball on the floor. Her eyes lifted to his and relief was an understatement.

Jason pulled Candice into his arms.

"I thought…" He shut his eyes trying to ward off images of what he'd thought.

"He was going to shoot Sheena because I wouldn't…" She choked on a sob, and he squeezed her a little tighter.

"Shh, it's over now."

Jason turned his attention to Lamont, laid out on the floor, bleeding profusely, but still breathing. Dane hovered over Lamont—gun already drawn—whispering something for his ears only. Jason knew what was coming and should've been ashamed for allowing it. Two shots cracked through the muffled conversations scattered about the room. It erupted in a moment of chaos—women screaming, trying to claw their way into the safety of their husbands, men growling in fierce protection of what was theirs—and then there was silence, blanketing them like freshly fallen snow, shocking, but then refreshing.

Dane stood over Lamont, gun still drawn. All eyes were on him, anticipating his next move. "He's not the man you injure and leave to recover." Dane turned his back on Lamont and tucked his gun back into his waistband.

Jason nodded. Should he feel that relieved at someone's death? It was over. Lamont was over. They could live.

The room relaxed a bit, but the sound of hushed sobs and soft-spoken prayers permeated the atmosphere. It wasn't until police sirens entered the house did they realize the weight of what had happened.

"I'll be sure to talk to the detectives and the prosecutors to let them know you were defending us." Richard picked up April's gun off the floor and put the safety on before shoving it back into her purse.

"Don't worry about it. When word hits the streets, I'm as good as dead, in jail or out." He raised his hands, got on his knees, and waited for the cops to enter.

Paul went out front to meet the police.

Jason stood back and watched the day he'd dreamed of for ten years play out in front of him as Lamont and Dane finally got what they deserved. Cops filed in behind Paul. They tightened handcuffs around Dane's wrist and helped him to his feet.

"Let me get you a lawyer," Paul offered.

"Don't worry about it."

Jason wasn't as thrilled as he imagined he'd be. Dane looked tired, like ten years of running with Lamont had aged him more than the ten years in prison had aged Jason. Maybe it was the ten years of guilt added to it. Guilt was one beast Jason could live without.

"Can I have a minute before you take him away?" Irritated, the cop gave Jason a tight nod and backed away. "Don't talk until the lawyer gets there."

"Death is inevitable. Does it matter where?" Dane whispered, barely audible to Jason's ears.

"It doesn't have to be. We can spin our own truth."

"The only truth they'll see—the cops and the street—is that I did this. I knew where he was and what he was up to. Either way we spin it, my death is inevitable."

Dane walked away without the cops urging him on.

"Please get me out of here." The tremor in Candice's voice pulled Jason's attention away from Dane. He used his body to shield her from the sight of Lamont lying on the floor.

"We will probably have to go to the police station." Jason responded.

"That's fine. Just take me anywhere but here."

Candice barely acknowledged the other couples gathering their things and herding their children out the front door before they ran into the family room and saw the carnage there. She was an adult and it was a sight she wouldn't be forgetting any time soon. Their innocent little souls would be damaged for a lifetime.

They left the bustle of chaos in the house to an eerily quiet front yard. Red and blue lights flashed with no sound. There were no voices, even though she could see huddles of officers deep in conversation. The heel of her shoe sank into the grass as they made their way across the lawn to their car. She adjusted her stride to accommodate the soft terrain. The walk seemed to take forever. When Jason finally helped her into the passenger seat of their car, she could breathe freely.

# 33

Candice opened her eyes to the first streaks of the morning sun shining on her face. She smiled at the overwhelming body heat lying next to her. He looked so delicious peacefully sleeping next to her. She wanted to scale the mountain he was and have her way with him, like she did most mornings. That day was different. The months of planning, organizing, praying, and prepping were getting ready to pay off. It was opening day for the community center. It was the perfect time to grab as many young people as possible before another sociopath rose to power. The streets were quietly waiting, but they prayed the community center would be the next source of guidance, knowledge, and resources for a better future.

Jason's eyes blinked open and the good looks she'd been admiring multiplied in the depths of his brown eyes. When he shined them on her, she felt as giddy as the day they met. Her shy smile tipped the corners of her mouth and she ducked her head from his gaze. The simple gesture caused her tousled mane to tumble into her face. He ran his fingers through it to guide her face to his.

"Why do you watch me sleep?"

"Guess I'm still amazed by you." She lightly touched his lips with hers. "How did I get so lucky?"

"I should be asking that question." Before she could rebut, he'd flipped her over, devouring her mouth as he pressed her to the mattress. She tried to stress they didn't have time, but it just came out in a sequence of moans that further ignited the fire blazing through him.

*No need in breaking our morning routine.* Candice submitted to his wishes. So, they'd arrive a little later than the rest of the setup crew.

The community center was a mob of activity. Vendors were hustling about, setting up tables to display their products. The sound crew was setting up mics on the stage that had already been assembled. Racks of basketballs were being wheeled to the courts. The barbecue pit was smoking. A cleaning crew was dusting the inside, and Jason and Candice had just pulled up. They jumped out of the car, went their separate ways, and immediately got to work.

"There's only one thing to make a woman show up late to work glowing like that." Sheena and Camilla chuckled as they walked past.

Candice tried to ignore them, but it was hard to hide the smile creeping across her face. *Am I glowing?* She touched her finger tips to her cheeks. The heat that greeted her was her answer. Her cheeks, her face, and her entire body were flushed. She closed her eyes and sucked in a deep breath to calm down, but the moment her eyes shut all she could see was Jason.

Sheena came by giggling again. "Are you going to be all right?"

"Does it ever go away?"

"What…his spellbinding control over your body? Only if you let it."

"Good." She assumed it was a newlywed thing, but should've known by the examples in front of her. Their intense attraction could last a lifetime, if they let it.

"Now, snap out of whatever he put on you this morning and let's do a final walk through before guests start arriving."

"I don't want to. If I could I'd live in this euphoria all day…" Candice closed her eyes and raised her hands in reverence of the man she couldn't get enough of.

"I'm so glad you're happy. Your brother has relaxed and I have my man back," Sheena laughed.

"He could've relaxed from the beginning."

"Well, we all knew that wasn't going to happen."

They finished the walk through of the interior and headed outside. Everything was set and ready to go. They gravitated to the loud trash talking taking place on the basketball court and took a seat with the other ladies gathered there.

"These young bucks stay talking trash." Paul was saying as he checked his watch. "We have time before the festivities start. Let's end this once and for all. Big brother versus little brother let's go."

"I accept the challenge, big brother." Jason suddenly appeared and took his spot on the court.

227

"Yes! Let's go, baby." Tim pulled Jason in for a shoulder hug and laughed at Paul's smug expression dropping.

"I'm not dressed to ball. I'm out." Richard took a seat on the grass behind April and cradled her between his legs.

That left Paul, Jaleel, and Cole against Jason, Tim, and Marlon. Candice couldn't help the excitement bubbling in her. She felt it among the other women, too. In all the years they'd been connected, the wives had never seen them play. By the luck of the coin, the younger brothers received the ball first. Candice held her breath as it was passed in to Jason and he dribbled it down the court. She had no idea what he was doing or if he was doing it right. All she noticed was how the exertion affected his body. She wasn't the only one with her mouth hanging open from watching her man work. She looked around to see if anyone picked up on the thoughts running through her mind and saw the same awestruck expression on the other women. Every time Jason had the ball, it nearly stopped her heart. She didn't breathe properly until his team reached ten points. He and Tim ran and jumped into each other in celebration.

Paul plopped down next to Sheena, steadily complaining that ten points didn't even give them enough time to warm up.

"Just face it, bro...you're getting slow in your old age." Tim snorted.

A rebuttal was perched on the tip of Paul's tongue, but Sheena whispering in his ear interrupted his thought process. Whatever she said had him smiling and nuzzling the side of her neck.

Candice was speechless. Jason made his way toward her and she couldn't find the words to describe his performance. He lounged next to her and laid his head in her lap. She wiped the sheen of sweat from his brow and cradled his face between her hands. Still in awe, all she managed was, "You are amazing."

Their eyes locked and held for a moment before unwillingly breaking away. "We have to get up." Jason stood and helped her up as well. "People should be arriving soon."

As if on cue, cars were pulling up to unload their lawn chairs and canopies. Candice nearly tripped over her own feet when she noticed her father walking toward them, toting his lawn chair.

"What is he doing here?"

"I invited him."

Candice's eyes bulged at Paul.

"I didn't think he'd show up though." In utter shock, she and Tim followed behind Paul as he greeted their father.

In no time at all, the parking lot had filled up. Everyone was mingling, meeting new people, reacquainting with old friends, and having a good time.

The three-on-three basketball teams started to assemble by the courts and Candice made her way to the stage. Jason was expected to give a speech before the start of the tournament and he wanted her by his side. The initial hum of the microphone being turned on garnered the crowd's attention. Jason smiled at her and she found his nervousness adorable.

"My wife and I are amazed and honored that so many of you chose to spend your Saturday with us. Having a community center in our neighborhood, a place where our children can be safe, learn, and grow is an essential component to ensuring their success. I could've benefited from such a place when I was growing up. I had my struggles and family problems that led me to making connections with the wrong crowd, which eventually led to me serving ten years in prison for something they did. If this community center can keep one child from going where I've been, then I'll die a happy man." He signaled for the rest of the staff to join him on stage. "We are here for your children and I pray that, despite my past, you'll trust us to reinforce the ethical character you're endeavoring to instill. We hope you allow us to help them set goals for their future. And that you'll push with us as they endeavor to achieve those goals."

He took a moment to introduce the rest of the staff they'd hired. He wanted to give a shout out to Paul and Tim, but they'd instructed him that their involvement would remain undisclosed.

"Now it's time for what we've all been waiting for." The crowd went crazy, feeding off of the excitement Jason exuded. "You see them out there warming up, ballers from all over the neighborhood. So, here's how it's going to work. There are four courts with two refs, a scorekeeper, and timekeeper each. The sixteen teams will be divided into two rounds. They will play two fifteen-minute halves, and then winners will face off against winners all the way down to the last two teams. The last two teams will be competing for bragging rights and…" Jason paused for dramatic affect. "A three-hundred-dollar grand prize!"

The unexpected cash prize was enough to make the youth warming up on the courts pause and scream their gratitude.

"Now that's enough for a new video game, a pair of shoes, or something. So, without further delay, it's game time."

Parents scrambled, moving their chairs to whatever court their child was on. It was a moment of chaos, but by the time each game started, everyone was settled. Candice sat near the court with the only female player and cheered her on like it was her own daughter. When her team made it to the second round, Candice ran on to the court and gave the little girl a high-five. Candice introduced herself to the girl's mother and followed her to the next court.

The girl had skills, and Candice assumed her making it to the next round was a forgone conclusion, but the other team pulled ahead at the end. Candice made her way onto the court again. "Wow, you are amazing. You held your own with those boys."

"Thanks, Miss." The little girl brightened up and her mother mouthed 'thank you' to Candice.

"Make sure you come down here and see me this week." She passed her business card to the mother and gave the little girl another high five.

Candice spent the rest of the tournament introducing herself to the children and passing her card along to their parents. By the time the winner was announced, her mouth was dry, her feet were aching, and her body was exhausted. She tried to be a team player and help the cleanup crew, but Jason wasn't having it. He laid a blanket out on the grass and insisted she rest.

"I watched you interacting with the kids." He sat next to her, removed her shoes, and gently kneaded her feet. "You are going to be an amazing mother to our kids."

Candice snatched her feet away and sat up so fast she nearly knocked him on to his back. "You want babies?" She half-questioned, half-exclaimed.

"Of course I do. Lots of them. Don't you?"

"Yes, lots of them." She couldn't help the silly grin spreading across her face. "I didn't think you'd want to. You never said anything."

"Neither did you." He nuzzled her neck, finding her excitement endearing.

"That's different. I haven't been through the trauma you have."

"All of that is nothing now that I have you."

She was a goner. Without any resistance, she allowed him to pull her under his spell. Her mind swirled with thoughts of him, all the babies, and the fun they'd have creating them.

# Epilogue

Jason opened his eyes to the sound that never ceased to put a smile on his face. He hopped out of bed, careful to not wake Candice, and tiptoed toward the cooing figure in the bassinet. His daughter looked up at him, eyes bright, seemingly excited to see him. He thought falling in love and marrying Candice was the high point of his life. He never imagined the type of joy he felt when he held his little girl in his arms.

He picked little Chantel up. She stretched and grunted like she'd had the best sleep of her life. Jason chuckled, kissing her chubby cheeks as he lightly bounced her on his shoulder. "How's my favorite girl this morning?"

"Your favorite...seems like I've been replaced." Candice sidled up next to him, kissing him and then their daughter.

"You can never be replaced."

"That's good to know." Candice laughed and pressed her lips to his bare chest.

It was hard to believe that this was her life. It wasn't long ago that she'd been so focused on the materialistic things a man could offer. The way her life had been going, if someone had told her she'd be married and have a baby within two years, she would've laughed in their face. In that moment, she couldn't see her life any other kind of way. Married to the love of her life, who happened to be the hottest man she'd ever seen, and mommy to his child. Who could ask for anything more?

"Do you want to nurse her in the rocking chair or get back into the bed?"

"I was thinking, since she is not fussing, I could pump and make a bottle. You can feed her."

"I'd like that."

With the smile that spread across his face, Candice rushed to get her breast pump. She had no problem filling two small bottles. Jason was as antsy as a kid on Christmas morning as she showed him how to support their daughter while feeding her. The sight of him on the verge of tears, but smiling, melted her.

"She might not like the rubber nipple, but I'm hoping she'll be a good girl for Daddy." Their daughter latched on and sucked her little heart out. "Good girl. Now, Mommy is going to shower while Daddy feeds, bathes, and dresses you." She kissed Jason on the cheek, laughing at his horrified expression, and left them alone.

Jason lost himself in his little girl's presence. He laughed at her greedily sucking down the bottle and almost instantly falling asleep. He propped her up on his shoulder anyway, patting her back until an impressive burp rolled out of her. He was afraid to take her clothes off, thinking that his huge hands would break something. After a few seconds of fumbling, he'd mastered that as well.

He finally emerged from the room to find Candice sitting on the couch with Paul and Tim. He cringed, knowing why they were there. He couldn't believe he'd forgotten. He went to hand the baby to Candice, and Paul jumped in to grab her before Candice could.

"Just give me a couple of minutes to get ready." Jason laughed at the cooing noises coming from Paul and Tim. They all but ignored him. He couldn't help but chuckle at the sight. One little baby had turned two grown men into smiling, cooing, feet-tickling fools.

It took just a few minutes to get dressed and he wished it had taken longer. It was time to step out of daddy mode and enter a place where he'd sworn he'd never return. All the hoops he had to jump through being an ex-con and trying to visit an inmate made the final approval sweeter. Although he was apprehensive of being back in that place, it was something he had to do. At least this time, he was on the right side of the bars.

The doors shut behind them, locking them in, and Jason couldn't help but jump.

"You good, Bro?" Paul turned to him with raised brows. "You know you don't have to do this, right?"

"Yeah I do."

Jason ignored the worried glances and kept moving. He didn't breathe freely until he sat at that table, his brothers on each side. Despite the situation, he smiled at the man sitting across from them.

"Dane, what's good, Bro?"

233

"You'd know better than I would. So, what's up?" He nodded, acknowledging Paul and Tim, and then turned his attention back to Jason.

"We just wanted you to know that we are here for you, for as long as you want us to be."

Jason watched Dane try to keep his emotions from showing. His slight nod was all the encouragement he needed. It was the first of many visits he planned to make. When he was locked up, more days than not, he wished the tables had turned and that Dane and Lamont were incarcerated instead of him. Now he was out. He wouldn't wish that experience on his worst enemy. He'd come full circle, and the forgiveness and compassion he felt for Dane were proof of God's healing and deliverance.

Thank you for reading *It's Always Been You*.
I hope you enjoyed. Visit my website or any of my
social media pages and let me know your thoughts.
I love hearing from my readers.

**More books by**
**F. Y. Dawn**

Surrender to Love Series
Book 1: Serenity of Passion
Book 2: What Love Feels Like
Book 3: What the Heart Wants
Book 4: All I Ever Wanted
Book 5: It's Always Been You

www.fydawn.com
www.facebook.com/fydawn
Twitter and Instagram @fydawn

www.ingramcontent.com/pod-product-compliance
Lightning Source LLC
Chambersburg PA
CBHW072227170626
46813CB00003B/1117